## SLAVE ATTACK!

A hail of stones fell over Rheba, stunning her. Before she could recover, the slaves swarmed down on them. Most of the attackers chose to concentrate on Kirtn instead of on the woman whose hands had called forth fire. Even so, Rheba was swept off her feet in the rush, her head ringing from a glancing blow.

Kirtn was a deadly opponent despite being outnumbered, but even his huge strength could not withstand the onslaught of thirty enraged slaves. He vanished under a tumult of multicolored flesh.

Pulling herself up, Rheba lunged toward the melee. She screamed Kirtn's name, desperately grabbing energy from every source within her reach. Thin lines of fire sizzled over the slaves who covered the Bre'n. Kirtn clawed his way out of the pile with three men and their leader clinging to his shoulders. The leader's pale arm flashed upward as a club took lethal aim on Kirtn's skull . . .

## FIRE DANCER

# FIRE DANCER

by

*Ann Maxwell*

A SIGNET BOOK

**NEW AMERICAN LIBRARY**

TIMES MIRROR

SIGNET TRADEMARK REG. U.S. PAT. OFF. AND FOREIGN COUNTRIES
REGISTERED TRADEMARK—MARCA REGISTRADA
HECHO EN CHICAGO, U.S.A.

SIGNET, SIGNET CLASSICS, MENTOR, PLUME, MERIDIAN AND NAL
BOOKS *are published by The New American Library, Inc.,
1633 Broadway, New York, New York 10019*

FIRST PRINTING, DECEMBER, 1982

3   4   5   6   7   8   9

PRINTED IN THE UNITED STATES OF AMERICA

Onan was the most licentious planet in the Yhelle Equality. No activity was prohibited. As a result, the wealth of the Equality flowed down Onan's gravity well—and stuck. Nontondondo, the sprawling city-spaceport, was a three-dimensional maze with walls of colored lightning, streets paved with hope and potholed by despair, and a decibel level that knew no ceiling.

"Kirtn!" shouted Rheba to the huge Bre'n walking beside her. "Can you see the Black Whole yet?"

Kirtn's hands locked around Rheba's waist. In an instant her lips were level with his ear. She shouted again.

"Can you see the casino?"

"Just a few more buildings," he said against her ear.

Even Kirtn's bass rumble had trouble competing with the din. He pursed his lips and whistled a fluting answer to her question in the whistle language of the Bre'ns. The sound was like a gem scintillating in the aural mud of Nontondondo. People stopped for an instant, staring around, but could find no obvious source for the beautiful sound.

All they saw was a tall humanoid with very short, fine coppery plush covering his muscular body, giving it the appearance and texture of velvet. On his head, the fur became wavy copper hair. A mask of metallic gold hair surrounded his eyes, emphasizing their yellow clarity. His mask, like the coppery plush on his body, was the mark of a healthy Bre'n.

Although Rheba looked small held against the Bre'n, she was above humanoid average in height. Her hair was gold and her eyes were an unusual cinnamon color that seemed to gather and concentrate light. Other than on her head and the median line of her torso, she had neither hair nor fur to interrupt the smooth brown flow of her body. Almost invisible

1

beneath the skin of her hands were the whorls and intricate patterns of a young Senyas fire dancer.

Rheba slid down Kirtn's body until she was standing on her own feet again. As she regained her balance, a man stumbled out of the crowd and grabbed her. He rubbed up against her back, bathing her in unpleasant odors and intentions. The patterns on her hands flared as she reached toward a dazzling electric advertisement, wove its energy, and gave it to the rude stranger. He leaped back as though he had been burned. And he had.

"I don't think he'll play with a fire dancer again," said Kirtn in a satisfied voice.

Kirtn picked up the shaken man and lofted him onto a passing drunk cart. Then the Bre'n gathered up Rheba again and shouldered his way into the anteroom of the Black Whole. After the streets, the quiet was like a blessing. Kirtn smiled, showing slightly serrated teeth, bright and very hard.

Rheba scratched the back of her hands where the patterns had flared. Her hair shifted and moved, alive with the energy she had just called. Muttering the eighth discipline of Deva, she let both energy and anger drain out of her. She had come into this city willingly and so must abide by its customs, no matter how bizarre or insulting they might be to her.

"We should have taken out a license to murder," she said in a mild voice.

Kirtn laughed. "We didn't have enough money to buy a half-circle of silver, much less the whole circle of a licensed killer."

"Don't remind me. We could hardly afford to be licensed innocents." Rheba grimaced at the mere 30 degrees of silver arc stuck to her shoulder. "Come on, let's find the man we came for and get off this festering planet."

They had not taken three steps before a black-dressed casino employee approached them. His only decoration was a simple silver circle fastened on his shoulder. Kirtn and Rheba saw the man's license at the same instant. When the man spoke, he had their attention.

"No furries allowed."

Rheba blinked. "Furries?"

"That," said the man, hooking a thumb at Kirtn, "is a furry. You're a smoothie. Smoothies only at the Black Whole. If you don't want to separate, try the Mink Trap down the street. They like perverts."

Rheba's long yellow hair stirred, though there was no breeze inside the Black Whole's anteroom. Kirtn spoke a few rapid words in Senyas, native tongue of Senyasi and Bre'ns alike. "If we kill him, we'll never get a chance to talk to Trader Jal."

"I wasn't going to kill him," said Rheba in Senyas, smiling at the man with the silver circle who could not understand her words. "I was just going to singe his pride-and-joys."

Kirtn winced. "Never mind. I'll wait outside."

Rheba began to object, then shrugged. The last time they had bumped against local prejudices, she had been the one to wait outside. She could not remember whether sex, color, number of digits or lack of fur had been at issue.

"I'll make it as fast as I can," said Rheba, her hand on Kirtn's arm, stroking him. She took an uncomplicated pleasure from the softness of his fur. Kirtn's strength and textures were her oldest memories, and her best. Like most akhenets, she had been raised by her Bre'n mentor. "I can understand a prejudice against smoothies," she murmured, "but against furries? Impossible."

Kirtn touched a fingertip to Rheba's nose. "Don't find more trouble than you can set fire to, child."

She smiled and turned toward the licensed employee. She spoke once again in Universal, the language of space. "Does this cesspool have a game called Chaos?"

"Yeah," said the man. He flicked his narrow, thick fingernail against Rheba's license. "It's not a game for innocents."

Rheba's hair rippled. "Is that opinion or law?"

The man did not answer.

"Where's the game?" she asked again, her voice clipped.

"Across the main casino, on the left. You'll see a big blue spiral galaxy."

Rheba sidestepped around the man.

"I hope you lose your lower set of lips," he said in a nasty voice as she passed him.

She walked quickly across the anteroom of the Black Whole, not trusting herself to answer the man's crudity. As she passed through the casino's velvet force field, a babble of voices assaulted her. Throughout the immense, high-ceilinged room, bets were being made and paid in the Universal language—but gamblers exhorted personal gods in every tongue known to the Yhelle Equality.

Rheba knew only three languages—Bre'n, Senyas, and Universal—and Kirtn was the only other being who knew the first two. The multitongued room made her feel terribly alone. One Senyas, one Bre'n. Only known survivors of the

3

violent moment when Deva's sun had built a bridge of fire between itself and its fifth planet.

One Senyas, one Bre'n; one galaxy of strangers.

With an effort, she shut away the searing memory of extinction. She and Kirtn had survived. Surely others must also have survived. Somehow. Somewhere. She would find them, one by one, if it took all the centuries of her life.

Rheba dove into the gamblers congealed in masses around their games, blocking aisles and passageways with their singleminded focus on gain and loss. When courtesy, strength and flexibility were not enough, she gave discreet shocks to the people who barred her way. Soon she was beneath the glitter-blue pulsing galaxy that marked the game known as Chaos.

There were eight tables, six pits, three circles and a ziggurat gathered beneath the galaxy. At each station, humanoids won and lost at games whose rules were subject to change upon agreement of a majority of players or upon one player's payment of ten times the pot. There was only one inflexible rule: If a gambler could not pay he could not play. On Onan, penury was the only unforgivable sin.

Cheating was not only expected in Chaos, it was required merely to stay in the game. Inspired cheating was required to win. If a player was so inept as to be caught at it, however, that player had to match the pot in order to remain in the game. As the anteroom guard had mentioned, Chaos was not a game for innocents. But then, Rheba was an innocent only by default of funds.

She peered at the closer gambling stations, trying to find a man with blue hair, pale-blue skin, and a lightning-shaped scar on the back of his right hand. She saw various scars, as well as skin and hair of every hue, but none of the scars and skin tones made the correct combination. Impatiently, she turned and headed toward the third pit.

"Game?" asked a contralto voice at her elbow.

Rheba turned and saw a tiny, beautiful woman with satin-black skin, eyes and hair. She wore a metallic silver body sheath that covered enough for most planetary customs and not a millimeter more. A silver circle nestled between her perfect breasts.

"I'm innocent," said Rheba, smiling, "but I'm not stupid. No game, Silver Circle. No thanks."

The woman smiled and resumed playing with a pile of multicolored gems, arranging and rearranging them in com-

4

plex patterns, waiting for a player whose eyes would be blinded by the rainbow wealth of jewels.

As Rheba turned away, a blur of blue-on-blue caught her attention. She stood on tiptoe and stared toward the top of the crystal ziggurat. A man was climbing into the kingseat, the only seat on the seventh level of the ziggurat. His skin was blue, his hair a darker blue, almost black. As he settled his outer robe into place, she spotted the pale flash of a jagged scar from his wrist to his fingertips. Even more arresting to her than the scar was the superb ivory carving he wore around his neck. The carving's fluid, evocative lines were as Bre'n as Kirtn's gold mask.

"Trader Jal!" called Rheba.

The man looked down. His expression of disdain could have been caused by genes or temperament; either way, it was irritating.

"I loathe yellow-haired licensed innocents," said Trader Jal, dismissing Rheba. He sat back, taking care that his silver circle was revealed. The gesture carried both pride and warning.

"That's two things we have in common," said Rheba clearly.

"Two?" Jal leaned forward, surprised by the innocent who had disregarded his warning.

"Mutual loathing. An interest in Bre'n artifacts."

One side of Jal's mouth twitched, anger or amusement. "Bre'n artifacts . . . ?"

Rheba pushed back her mass of yellow hair, revealing a large carved earring. Like the pendant worn by Jal, Rheba's earring evoked a Bre'n face. Kirtn had never told her whose face it was. After the first time, she had not asked again.

"Recognize this?" she asked, lifting her chin to show the carving's fluid lines.

Jal smoothed his robes, a movement meant to disguise the sudden tension of interest in the muscles around his black eyes. "Where did you get it?"

"Three things in common," said Rheba. "That's the same question I would ask of you. Information is a commodity. Shall we trade?" As she spoke, her right hand closed around a packet of gems in her robe pocket. The stones were all the wealth she and Kirtn had. She hoped it would be enough to buy the answer to the question that consumed her: Bre'ns and Senyasi; did any others survive?

Before Jal could answer, a fifth-level player called out in a language Rheba had never heard. Jal answered, his voice like a whip. His purple nails danced across his game computer. Inside the crystal ziggurat, colors and shapes and sequences changed. Sighs and shouts welcomed the permutations. A new cycle of Chaos had begun.

Rheba called out to Jal. The trader ignored her. She did not need a computer to tell her that until this round had ended, Jal was lost to her. She looked at the man standing on her left, a dilettante's circlet whispering into his ear.

"How long did the last cycle take?" she asked.

The man looked at his thumbnail, where symbols glowed discreetly. "Seventeen hours."

Rheba groaned. Every minute their ship was in its berth at the spaceport, her Onan Value Account—OVA—was reduced by twenty three credits. She could not afford to wait until Jal won or lost or tired of gambling. She would have to find a way to end the cycle quickly.

Rheba wriggled into the dilettantes' circle, placed a circlet over her ear, and listened while the game computer's sibilant voice told her the rules of the present cycle of Chaos. Even as she listened, a rule changed, modifying the game like moonrise modifying night. She pressed the repeat segment and listened again.

At core, the present cycle was a simple progression based on complementary colors, prime numbers and computer-induced chance. On the first, or entry, level of the seven-level ziggurat, the money involved was modest. The bets doubled automatically as each step of the ziggurat was ascended. A bet of 100 credits on the entry level meant a bet of 200 credits on the second level, 400 on the third, and so on up to the kingseat, where the equivalent bet was 6,400 credits.

The base of the crystal ziggurat had no openings for new players in this cycle. Nor did the second level. There was one opening at the fourth level, but she could not afford the ante, much less the play. Jal, in the kingseat, collected one-half of every pot above the third level. He would not be leaving such a lucrative position soon. She would have to make an opening on the lowest level and dislodge him from the kingseat.

A walk around the ziggurat gave Rheba her quarry. The man was drugged-out and had less than fifty credits on his computer. She eased her way through the crowd until she was close to him. Her fingers wove discreetly, her hair stirred, and the man began to sweat like fat in a frying pan. After a few moments, he stood up abruptly and plunged into the crowd, headed for the cooler air of Nontondondo's frenzied streets.

Rheba slid into the hot seat before anyone else could. She

punched her code into the computer. Her OVA dropped by ten credits, ante for a single round.

She watched the center of the crystal ziggurat where colors, shapes and groupings shifted in response to energy pulses from each player's computer. She bet only enough to keep her seat while she sorted out the various energies permeating the ziggurat. The pulses were so minute that grasping them was difficult. She was accustomed to working with much stronger forces.

The game's markers—the colored shapes—were composed of energy, making telekinesis an unlikely, if not an impossible, form of cheating. The computer could probably be bribed, but it would take more time and credits than Rheba had to find out. Several of the players at various levels were in illegal collusion, setting up complex resonances that could only be defeated by chance or the end of the cycle. At least one player was an illusion. She could not determine which player was projecting the illusion, or why.

After several rounds of play, one of the many collusions was challenged and broken up. She began to feel more at ease with the tiny currents that created the colored markers. Slowly, discreetly, while credits flowed out of her OVA, she began to manipulate the game's markers, using a fire dancer's intuitive grasp of energy rather than her own computer.

It was a difficult way to cheat. Intense concentration made the swirling patterns on her hands burn and itch. Slowly, a red triangle changed to green, upsetting a fifth-level player's program and costing him 10,000 credits. The man swore at his bad luck and switched from building fives of green triangles matched with reds to building threes of yellow squares balanced on greens.

No one but the computer noticed that Rheba was several hundred credits richer for the man's misfortune. Rubbing the backs of her hands, she studied the shifting markers, placed her bet, programmed her computer, and went to work with her mind, shortening wavelengths of energy, shifting red to blue.

It was easier this time. Within minutes a red triangle blinked and was reborn as blue. The victim was a fourth-level woman. She stared around with harsh white eyes, as though she sensed that cheating rather than chance had unraveled her careful program.

Rheba was 300 credits richer. She used it as leverage against a third-level player who was barely able to hang onto his seat. His orange circles paled to yellow; he had no blues

7

to balance them and no credits to buy what he needed. His circlet chimed and informed him that his credit balance could not sustain a third or even a second-level ante.

In silence the man switched places with Rheba, who had bet against him. She had 1,200 credits now, enough for three rounds—if no one raised the ante or bet against her one-on-one.

Her progression from entry to third level attracted little attention. There were sixty players on the first three levels, and they changed rapidly. When she progressed to the fourth level, however, there was a stir of interest. Only twelve players were on that level, three seated on each side of the ziggurat, well above the heads of the crowd.

Twelve minutes and 46,000 credits later, Rheba settled into the fifth level, one of only eight players on that level. The players were seated two to each side of the ziggurat. Three of the players teamed illegally against her, but she did not have the skill to decipher their signals and thus prove how they cheated.

Credits drained precipitously from her OVA until she managed a desperate twist of energy that made a whole row of markers flash into incandescent silver. Though startling, the effect was not unprecedented; the computer of Chaos was known for its wry sense of the improbable. Nonetheless, there was a murmuring on the fifth level that was echoed by the crowd growing around the crystal ziggurat. Gradually, other games stopped. Gamblers and dilettantes flowed toward Chaos like a gigantic amoeba progressing from one viscous pseudopod to the next.

Rheba barely noticed the casino's slow transformation. The curling patterns of power on her hands were visible now, glowing softly, pale gold against the rich brown of her skin. She scratched the backs of her hands absently, totally absorbed in her strategy. For the sake of appearances she programmed her computer from time to time, but her success depended on other less obvious skills. Whistling quietly, she wove tiny increments of energy inside the transparent ziggurat.

Her circlet purred, signaling an end to programming. The players paid the ante. The instant that her credits were placed, Rheba's circlet chimed and whispered of changes: Jal and the other players had matched the pot in order to change the rules; player number 7 would now play nude or forfeit.

Rheba looked at the number 7 glowing on her computer and grimaced. She stood up and stripped quickly, knowing

8

that pragmatism rather than voyeurism motivated the others. They assumed that she had some electronic means of cheating concealed beneath her flaring, multicolored robe.

Naked and unconcerned, she cast aside both her outer robe and her brief crimson ship clothes. She sat and studied the markers while casino personnel studied her clothes. The searchers found a few personal weapons and the packet of expensive but otherwise ordinary gemstones. They did not find anything that could have been used to influence the Black Whole's sophisticated computer.

"The earring," said Jal coldly.

Rheba punched a query into her console. The answer flashed back. Smiling, she looked up to the kingseat. "Ear decorations are not considered clothing."

Without hesitating, Jal tapped his console and matched the pot ten times over, allowing him to change the rules without recourse to the rest of the players. The crowd quivered and cried out in pleasure, a single organism focused on the credits glittering inside the clear ziggurat. Rheba's circlet chimed and explained the new rule: All decorations must be removed by player number 7.

She reached up to the intricate fastenings of her Bre'n earring. It pierced her ear in seven places, both as decoration and as surety that she would not lose the carved Face depending from the lobe of her ear. The Face swayed, turning. No matter which angle of view, there was always someone in the carving, aloof and haunting and most of all sensually alive.

Before she turned over the earring to the casino employee, she punched another query into her computer. The OVA figure by her number plummeted as the game console spat a closed silver circle into her hand. She fastened the circle into her hair. Licensed to kill, she faced the casino employee once more. The earring dangled hypnotically between her fingers.

"I value this. Don't damage it."

The employee carefully took the earring, scanned it with exquisite machinery, and found only the molecular patterns associated with fossilized bone.

"Nothing, Trader Jal," said the employee.

"Satin?" snapped Jal to someone behind Rheba.

Rheba turned around and was startled to find the tiny black woman standing as close to Rheba's feet as she could get.

"Psi, almost certainly," said Satin with a graceful, dismiss-

9

ing gesture. "Yet none of the psi blocks have been bribed." She looked up. "Where do you come from, smooth child?"

"A planet called Luck."

Satin laughed, a sound as sleek and cold as polished steel. She turned back toward Jal and waited in amused silence. Jal stared hard at Rheba.

"It would have been cheaper to talk to me while I was still innocent," observed Rheba. "Forfeit, Trader Jal? I'll settle for what I came for—information, not money."

"Your tongue needs trimming, bitch."

"That's four things we have in common—yours does too. Do you accept my offer?"

"Forfeit?" Jal made a harsh sound. "No, smooth blond cheater. Never."

"A side bet, then," she said, curbing her temper.

Jal looked interested. "What are you wagering?"

"Answers."

"Too vague. Three weeks bonding."

Rheba blinked. If she won, Jal would be bonded to her for three weeks, virtually her slave. If he won, she would be bonded to him.

She would have to be very sure not to lose.

"Three days will be enough for my purposes," she said, not bothering to conceal her distaste for the man in the kingseat.

"But not enough for mine." He leaned down toward her, smiling unpleasantly. "Three weeks."

For an instant, she wanted to flee from those dark eyes boring into her. She desperately wished Kirtn were near, a solid strength at her back. Then she remembered why she had come to Onan. The need to find others of her kind had not changed. And Jal wore a Bre'n carving.

"Done," whispered Rheba.

Even as she spoke, the pot increased ten times over and the rules changed for a third time. Colors vanished from the markers. As the colors faded, so did Rheba's means of winning the game.

Rheba looked at her OVA reading. She had just enough to match the pot ten times over and thereby change the rules. Unfortunately, Jal had enough credits in his OVA to match even that pot ten times over and still buy drugs for everyone in the casino. Whatever rule she made, Jal could afford to unmake.

Credits drained suddenly from her OVA. Jal had programmed a matching series of threes and circles so quickly that no one had time to intervene. Before he could repeat the coup, a sixth-level player programmed counterinstructions. Jal's progression of shapes and numbers was irretrievably scrambled by the shrewd attack, but the damage to Rheba was done.

Silently, she dropped from fifth to fourth level. She ignored the cold wash of fear that made her skin prickle and concentrated on discovering a way to beat Jal's game. Making and holding black outlines was different—and more difficult— than merely changing the colors of existing shapes. She needed time to adjust, to learn.

Before she had done much more than measure the extent of her weakness, her circlet chimed and sweetly spoke of diminishing credits. She had to descend to the third level or leave the game.

"Forfeit?" inquired Jal in a bored voice.

Rheba stood between levels, staring into the ziggurat as though considering the offer. She frowned and scratched the back of her left hand, wondering why it was so difficult for her to make and hold outlines. She could do seven or eight at once, but it was difficult and dangerously slow work.

"Forfeit," urged Satin in her quiet voice. "Save what's left of your OVA. Jal isn't a pleasant master, but he's better than being broke in Nontondondo."

Rheba barely heard the advice. She contemplated Jal's markers, saw the pattern emerging in them, saw that one bet would complete his series. To defeat him she would have to create seven times seven markers with seven different shapes, and do it in less time than it took for Jal to instruct his computer on the winning sequence. Forty-nine shapes. Gods, it would be easier to suck out all the energy and leave a transparent void.

"Forfeit," murmured the crowd, echoing Satin.

Most people had bets on Trader Jal, a favorite among the habitués of the Black Whole. To them, she was a diversion, a lucky innocent whose luck had failed. Her hair stirred, strands sliding one over the other with a subtle susurration of power.

"No. I'm staying."

She slid into the the third-level seat and programmed a flurry of instructions into her console. The crowd murmured and shifted in surprise. Rheba had just swept the pot, betting every credit she had that for a period of fifteen seconds she could block each grouping of primes that any or all players tried to make. It was an impossible, suicidal wager.

Silence expanded out from the ziggurat. Circlets breathed instructions into players' ears. Behind privacy shields, fingers poised over computers. A chime announced the beginning of the game.

The markers vanished.

Frantically, futilely, players programmed their computers. The ziggurat remained empty of shapes. Players banged fists and consoles against the ziggurat's lucent surface, but no markers materialized. There was nothing in the center of the ziggurat except gold numerals counting off the seconds remaining in the bet. Four, three, two, one.

Zero.

The light permeating the ziggurat ebbed until all levels became orange, signifying the end of the game. The pot and Trader Jal belonged to Rheba. All she had to do was find her way past the bettors before anger replaced disbelief.

Quickly, Rheba pulled on her shipclothes, fastened her earring and gathered up her robe. The crowd watched soundlessly, still stunned by the sudden reversal of fortunes. Rheba glanced up at the kingseat. Jal smiled. She concealed a quiver of distaste beneath the colorful folds of her robe.

"We'll talk on my ship," she said in a low voice.

For a moment, Jal remained the still center of the room's silence. Then he came to his feet, and silence shattered into exclamations of anger and unbelief. Rheba looked out over the multicolored tide of upturned faces, sensed Jal climbing down from the kingseat behind her back and felt very vulnerable.

"Cheater," muttered a second-level player.

The sentiment was echoed on all but the kingseat level. Jal merely descended, smiling as though at a joke too good to share. Rheba began to wonder who had lost and who had won—and what precisely had been wagered. Insults and imprecations were called in many languages as Jal bowed condescendingly in front of her.

"Your three-week bondling suggests that you move your smooth, cheating ass out of here," he said very softly. "That disappearing act cost the crowd a lot of credits."

Unhappy voices swelled and broke around Rheba like angry surf. Deliberately, she looked only at Jal, ignoring the crowd edging in around her. "You first, Trader," she said, pointing to a nearby exit.

"And leave your back uncovered? Bad tactics, smoothie."

"Turning my back on you would be worse. Move."

Jal pushed through the crowd, breaking an uneasy trail for Rheba. The crowd surged and ebbed restively. Eight steps from the exit, a gray figure crowned with lime-green curls leaned out of the crowd. The woman yelled something in a language Rheba did not know. Obligingly, Jal translated the obscenities for Rheba. She ignored the incident until a gray hand poked out of the crowd. The gun grasped in the gray fingers needed no translation.

Rheba's foot lashed out, kicking aside the weapon. It went off, searing a hole through someone else's flesh and the black stone floor. The crowd erupted into a mob that had neither head nor mind, simply rage and weapons looking for excuses to be used.

She fought grimly, sucking energy from the casino's lights, weaving that energy into finger-length jolts of lightning. People close to her screamed and tried to push away, but the mob had become a beast that ate everything, even its own young. The people who went down were trampled. Those still standing did not seem to care about the bodies thrashing beneath their feet.

Rheba kicked and shocked a narrow trail to the exit, leaving a wake of tender flesh, until she stepped on something slippery and went down. She screamed, air clawing against her throat, calling Kirtn's name again and again. Her hands

13

and arms burst into incandescence as frantic flames leaped from her fingertips to score the legs of people trampling her.

A questing Bre'n whistle split the chaos. Rheba poured all her desperation into her answering whistle. She tried to get to her feet, knowing Kirtn could not find her at the bottom of the churning mob. A brutal heel raked her from forehead to chin, sending her down in waves of dizziness.

Abruptly, the mob parted. Kirtn appeared in the opening, shouting her name. Furiously he tore off pieces of the mob and fed it to itself until he created a space where he could lift her to safety. When he saw her bruised, bleeding body, his face became a mask of Bre'n rage.

"Burn it down," he snarled. *"Burn it!"*

Energy scorched through Rheba as the Bre'n's rage swept up her emotions. Overhead, high on the casino's arched ceiling, she drew a line of violent fire.

The Black Whole's "nonflammable" draperies, decorations and games had not been made to withstand the anger of a fire dancer goaded by a Bre'n. The ceiling became a white hell. Instantly casino force fields went down, allowing exits in all directions. The mob fragmented into frightened people seeking the safety of Nontondondo's cold autumn streets.

No one noticed a tall furry carrying a smoothie away from the fire. Rheba watched the flames with interest, her chin resting on Kirtn's hard shoulder. The ziggurat housing Chaos was a spectular staircase of flaming colors that reflected the progress of the fire. There was a great deal of fire. Too much. Once ignited, the casino's accouterments burned with an almost sentient fury.

She concentrated, trying to draw energy out of the fire before it could spread farther than the Black Whole. But the fire had grown beyond her, rooted in its own searing destiny. When she tried to gather up energy, she got too much, too soon. Fire leaped toward her, blistering her fingers in the instant before she gave up and released the monster she had birthed. She sucked on her burned fingers and tried again to quell the flames.

"Stop it!" growled Kirtn, shaking her. "You're too young to handle that much raw energy."

Rheba struggled against Kirtn's strength but could not free herself. "Just how else will I learn?" she asked in a strained voice. "There aren't any more fire dancers to teach me—remember?" Then, immediately, "I'm sorry, Kirtn," she whispered. "You lost as much as I did when Deva burned."

Kirtn's cheek touched the silky, crackling radiance of

Rheba's hair, silently forgiving her. "You've learned too much already. More than a young fire dancer should have to know. You should be doing no more than lighting candles and cooking food for akhenet children, not—"

"Cooking alien casinos?" finished Rheba wryly. "I seem to remember a certain Bre'n telling me to burn it to ash."

Kirtn looked startled. "Did I?"

"You did."

He frowned. "I must have lost my temper."

"You looked very fierce," said Rheba, only half teasing. "I've never seen you look like that, not even the day Deva burned."

He said nothing. Both of them knew that Bre'ns were subject to berserker rage, a state called *rez*. In *rez*, Bre'ns destroyed everything around them, most especially themselves and their Senyasi. *Rez*, while not exactly a tabu subject, was not a comfortable one.

Rheba shivered suddenly. She had lost her robe somewhere in the melee and would not be warm until she got to the ship. "We'll make better time to the spaceport if you put me down."

Kirtn measured the people surrounding them. No one seemed to be watching. He sat Rheba on her feet, saw her shiver, and gave her his cape. She accepted it with a murmur of thanks and no guilt; Kirtn's fine "fur" was as efficient as it was short.

Rheba walked as quickly as she could without attracting attention. Her left ankle complained of maltreatment. She ignored it. Time was all that stood between them and intense questioning by local police—or worse, the Yhelle Equality Rangers. She had not taken out an arson license, an omission that would cost her freedom if the Rangers caught up.

"You haven't asked me about Trader Jal," she said.

Kirtn made a noncommittal sound. His slanted eyes picked up every shade of gold as he searched the streets and byways for trouble.

"I won."

He glanced down at her without slowing his stride. His lips parted in a small smile, revealing the serrated edges of his teeth. "How did you manage that, little dancer?"

"I cheated. But I didn't have time to collect my winnings."

He chuckled. "Too bad. We could use the credits."

"The credits are registered to our OVA, if the locals don't block the account. But it was Jal I didn't collect. He's mine for three weeks." She smiled proudly up at her Bre'n.

15

He stopped and looked down at her, his face expressionless. "You're old enough to take a pleasure mate," he said evenly. "I'd hoped to have some say in the selection, but I suppose that custom died with Deva." He shrugged. "If Jal is what you want, I'll go back and get him for you."

Rheba's mouth opened and closed several times before she found her voice. *"Pleasure mate!"* she screeched. "I wouldn't use that cherf to wipe my feet! By the light of the Inmost Fire, are you in *rez?"*

Kirtn's expression remained bland, wholly unreadable. "The casino guard spent a lot of time explaining to me how virile Jal was," he said, turning away and walking toward the spaceport with long strides, "and how much chased—and caught—by local women."

She stared after him. "That guard has his head wedged so far up he can't see!" she shouted after the receding Bre'n. "Have a little faith in your akhenet's basic good taste!"

"My akhenet cheats," called Kirtn as he turned a corner and disappeared. The sound of his laughter floated back to her. "Hurry up, little cheater."

She cursed and hurried after him. When her foot slipped on a piece of rotten fruit, her weakened left ankle took the brunt of her fall. She smothered a sound of pain and exasperation as she pulled herself back to her feet. She rounded the corner at a fast hobble. Hands reached out of the darkness, grabbing her. In the instant before she screamed, she felt the familiar texture and strength of her Bre'n.

"I turn my back on you for a minute and you're in trouble again," he muttered against her hair. "And you say that you're old enough to have a pleasure mate. Gahhh!"

Rheba chose action over further argument. She ran her fingernails around the rim of Kirtn's sensitive ears, tickling him as she had done since she was four years old and had discovered how to get the better of her huge teacher.

"Rheba, if you don't stop that I'll—"

The rest of his threat was lost in an excited shout from a man down the street. "There she is! That blond with the big furry! She caused the riot at the Black Whole!"

Kirtn took a fast look down the street. One look was enough. The people staring toward him wore the red-and-silver uniforms of Yhelle Rangers. He would have preferred the local police. They were noted for taking bribes first and shooting only as a last, unprofitable resort. The Rangers were celebrated for shooting first, last and on the least excuse.

Bre'n muscles bunched hugely. Rheba grabbed Kirtn's

16

weapon harness in the instant before he leaped. He hit his full stride in a single powerful surge. Behind him a tight beam of lavender light smoked across the sidewalk. Her fingers frantically probed the pockets on his harness.

"Where's your gun?" she demanded.

"Ship," he said laconically, reserving his breath for running. "No license."

She whistled a Bre'n expletive between her teeth. Grimly, she hung on to him. Lavender lightning vaporized a puddle of water in front of them. He leaped aside with no loss of speed. Farther ahead, the spaceport's silver arch shimmered, separating spacers from downside spectators.

Kirtn was strong and fast, but so were two of the Rangers—and they were not carrying anything heavier than their guns. Rheba measured the distance separating pursuers from pursued, and pursued from safety.

The Rangers would win.

"There's an alley where those buildings meet," she said urgently. "Drop me there. I'll hide, then take the first ship out to Zeta Gata. You can pick me up there."

He neither commented nor paused. The alley whipped by, a slice of darkness wedged between two pale buildings.

"Kirtn, you can't outrun them carrying me!"

He lengthened his stride. She loosened her grip and tried to throw herself free, but the Bre'n had anticipated her. His arms tightened until she gasped. Struggling was not only futile, it ran the risk of unbalancing him.

Lavender beams split the darkness. Kirtn's breath rushed out in silver bursts, but his stride did not shorten. Rheba looked over his shoulder, cringing when the lethal beams came too close. One shot was so near it made her eyes water. She cursed her lack of a gun. Her aim would have been no better than that of the running Rangers, but return fire would at least have made them more cautious.

Light hissed across a building, leaving a head-high groove of incandescence. Desperately, she grabbed at the energy with the immaterial fingers of her will. She gathered what she could of the backwash of Ranger lightguns, shaped it and hurled it toward them.

Light burst over the Rangers, light so bright that it washed out the scarlet of their uniforms. Reflexively they shot again, spraying lavender lightning. Rheba grabbed what was possible, twisted it and gave it back to them with brilliant vengeance.

The result was blinding. Rangers stumbled and fell helplessly, but she did not see them go down. She had closed her own blinded eyes and buried her face against Kirtn's neck, expecting each instant to be cooked by Ranger fire that she could not even see coming. Kirtn ran on, knowing only that she had done something to stop the Rangers' fire. He did not know that she and their pursuers were temporarily blind.

As he raced under the spaceport's silver arch, a figure separated from the shadow of a nearby warehouse. The man's black robe lifted and fell as he sprinted after Kirtn. The Bre'n's back quivered in anticipation of another fusillade, but unless he let go of Rheba there was nothing he could do to defend himself.

"Rheba—" panted Kirtn. "Do whatever—you did to—the Rangers!"

She let go of his weapon harness long enough to rub her streaming eyes. Blinking frantically, she stared over his shoulder. The lone pursuer was less than a man's length behind.

Shaking with fear and fatigue, she began to gather harsh filaments of energy into herself. Her hair crackled with hidden life, but still it was not enough. She must wait for Kirtn to pass near one of the spaceport's powerful illuminators.

The man's hood fell back, revealing his features, blue on blue, grim.

"Jal!"

He did not answer. He simply held out his hands, proving his lack of weapons. Rheba sighed and let the energy she had collected bleed back into the night.

Kirtn pounded up the berth ramp to their ship's personnel lock. He slammed his hand down on the lock plate. The door whipped open. He leaped through, Jal right on his heels. Rheba's high, staccato whistle brought the ship's emergency systems to life.

Kirtn threw her into the pilot web and leaped for the standby couch. The ship's alarm lights blazed from silver to blue, signifying hits by small energy weapons. Either the Rangers had recovered their sight or reinforcements had caught up.

"Get flat," snapped Rheba, grabbing for the override controls. "This will be rough."

Jal dove for a second couch as the ship's downside engines blasted to fullmax/override. The *Devalon* leaped into Onan's cold sky, slamming Jal into the couch and crushing him until he moaned that nothing would be left of him but a thick stain. Then he lost even the air in his lungs, and consciousness.

18

Kirtn lay on his back, fighting to breathe. He did not complain. Rheba was doing what had to be done. The fact that Senyasi could pull more gravities than most spacefaring humanoids was a double-edged weapon that she rarely used. Grimly, he counted the red minutes until the ship would be far enough out of Onan's gravity well to safely initiate *replacement*.

The effort he had given to outrunning Rangers caught up with him. The ship's walls bleached to gray, them became shot through with impossible colors. He groaned very softly. He would have closed his eyes, but even that small comfort was denied to him; both sets of eyelids were peeled open by implacable fingers of gravity.

The minutes until *replacement* was possible stretched into eons.

Rheba felt the pilot web gouging into her body until skin parted and muscles pulled. She did not need to look at Kirtn to know that he was suffering. She wished he would just pass out as Jal undoubtedly had, but knew that the Bre'n would stay conscious. Bre'ns had a legendary ability to absorb pain without losing control. It was a necessary trait; otherwise, they and their dancers would never survive a dancer's adolescence.

An alarm light pulsed blue, then underlined the warning with a low sonic that crawled over her bones. She looked at the war grid. Three lights burned, Ranger patrol ships cutting tangents toward the green circle of the *Devalon*. The ship was being fired on. Worse, the pursuers would converge on her before she was far enough out of Onan's gravity well to slip safely into *replacement*.

Pain wracked her, leaving her weak and nauseated. The acceleration was too much even for her tough Senyas body. She could no longer breathe, and would soon pass out. She felt the contours of the override clenched in her hand and stared through a red haze at the grid. The *Devalon* was giving her all the speed it could, more than she could take. But it was not enough.

Her hand convulsed, closing contacts that hurled the ship into *replacement*. The *Devalon* vanished from Onan's gravity well between one instant and the next, but to her it lasted forever, a force wrenching her apart in all nine dimensions at once. She and the ship shrieked as one.

The ship came out of *replacement* eighty light-years distant from Onan. A short hop, but unexpected enough to keep the *Devalon* off Ranger patrol screens. The ship coasted with en-

19

gines off, circling the *replacement* point, waiting for new instructions.

None came. Inside the control cabin, Rheba hung slackly in the pilot's mesh, the override dangling from her nerveless fingers. Blood dripped from her lips onto the pale, resilient floor.

# III

Kirtn groaned softly as consciousness raked him with claws of pain. Gradually memory surfaced, galvanizing him to full wakefulness. Despite the white agony in his bone marrow, he forced himself to stand.

"Rheba . . . ?"

No answer.

"Rheba," whistled Kirtn raggedly, focusing on the figure hanging limply in the pilot web. "Rheba!"

He knelt by the mesh. With careful fingertips, he stroked her neck, seeking a pulse. A steady beat of life answered his search. She was bruised, bloody and welted, but still strong. A short time in *Devalon*'s womb would remove all but the memory of pain.

For several moments, Kirtn savored the warm rhythm of Rheba's pulse beneath his fingertips. The Rangers had been close. Much too close. He had not been so certain of dying since the instant he had realized that Deva's sun was finally beyond control of the akhenets. Fire dancers, storm dancers, earth dancers, atom dancers, mind dancers—even Bre'ns in *rez*—nothing had deflected that last outburst of plasma from Deva's volatile sun.

Rheba moaned as though in echo of his memories.

"It's all right, dancer," he murmured. Very gently he kissed her bruised lips. "We're safe. You snatched us out of the dragon's mouth again."

"I feel," she whispered hoarsely, "more like something the dragon ate and left behind." Her eyes opened, cinnamon and bloodshot. "Next time I'll let the Rangers win."

He smiled, tasting blood where his teeth had lacerated his lips. "Nothing can beat a fire dancer and a Bre'n."

"Except Deva's sun," she whispered.

21

His gold eyes darkened, but all he said was, "Can you sit up?"

She groaned and pulled herself upright. The sensitive pilot web flowed into a new shape, helping her. She cried out when her hands came into contact with the web.

"Let me see," said Kirtn.

Wordlessly, she held out her hands. Fingertips were blistered, palms were scorched, and akhenet lines of power had become dense signatures just beneath her skin. The lines stretched from burned fingertips to her elbows. A few thin traceries swept in long curves all the way to her shoulders.

Kirtn whistled a Bre'n word of surprise. He looked speculatively at her worn face. "What did you do to those Rangers?"

She frowned, remembering her desperation when she was certain the Rangers were going to kill her Bre'n. She stroked his velvet arm with the unburned back of her hand. "The beams were so close, even the backwash burned. I . . . I just grabbed what I could, trying to deflect it. That's what fire dancers were bred for, isn't it? Deflecting fire?"

He nodded. Absently, he traced her new lines of power with his fingertips.

"But I'm not very good at it," she continued ruefully, looking at her burned hands. "I drew the fire instead of deflecting it, I guess. I had to weave faster than I ever have, and then I threw all the fire away as quickly as I could. That, at least, worked well enough. The light blinded the Rangers so that you could outrun them."

She looked at the new lines curling across her skin. They itched. New lines always itched. She reached to scratch, then snatched back her hand when blistered fingertips came into contact with bruised flesh.

"You attempt too much," said Kirtn. His voice was soft, final, the voice of a Bre'n mentor. His words were a protest as old as Rheba's first awakening after Deva's death. She had vowed then to find more of her kind and his, to build a new world of Bre'ns and Senyasi out of the ashes of the old.

"I don't have any choice," she said.

"I know."

"Besides," she continued, holding out her arms, "what are these few skinny lines? Shanfara's lines covered her whole body. Dekan's skin burned gold when he worked. Jaslind and Meferri were like twin flames, and their children were born with lines of power curling over their cheeks."

Rheba dropped her arm abruptly. She dragged herself to

22

her feet, preferring physical pain to the immaterial talons of memories and might-have-been. Better to think only of now. "Is Jal alive?"

Kirtn glanced over at the second couch. He noted the blood tracked from beneath the pilot web, along the front of the controls, and then to Jal's couch. He concluded that the trader had recovered sooner than anyone else and wanted to keep that fact a secret. "He's awake. Don't trust him."

Rheba's cinnamon eyes narrowed. "I don't—though he wears a Bre'n Face."

Kirtn stiffened. "You're sure?" he demanded.

"He had it around his neck in the casino."

Kirtn came to his feet in a rush, pain forgotten. He crossed the cabin in two long strides, bent over Jal, and yanked the trader's robe apart. Hanging from a heavy gold chain around his neck was a Bre'n Face. Kirtn stared at the carving, his breath aching in his throat.

"A woman," whispered Kirtn at last. His hand closed tenderly around the Face. "A woman!" He turned toward Rheba. "Where did Jal get her Face?"

"We have three weeks to find out."

Kirtn's hand tugged at the chain, testing its strength. Jal "awakened" immediately, proving that he had been conscious all along. The trader looked from the huge hand wrapped around the carving to Kirtn's hot gold eyes. Deliberately, Jal ignored the Bre'n focusing instead on Rheba.

"My body is bonded to you for three Onan weeks," Jal said in Universal. "My possessions aren't."

"A Face belongs only to the . . ." She hesitated, seeking an analog in Universal for the Senyas word "akhenet." "It belongs to the Bre'n's scientist-protégé child."

Jal blinked. She had spoken in Universal, but the meaning eluded him.

"Where did you get this carving?" Kirtn asked in harsh Universal.

Both the question and the menace were clear.

"I won it," said Jal quickly.

"Where?"

"The Black Whole. The owner wagered it against a—"

Jal gagged as Kirtn's fist twisted the gold chain until it cut into the trader's throat.

"Don't lie to a Bre'n," said Kirtn. He loosened the chain, allowing Jal to breathe. "Where did you get the carving?"

"On Loo," gasped Jal. Then, seeing no comprehension on Kirtn's face, "You don't know about the planet Loo?"

23

Kirtn made an impatient gesture.

Jal managed not to smile as he turned his face toward Rheba. "Loo is part of the Equality. You do know about the Yhelle Equality, don't you?"

Rheba shrugged, concealing her interest in the subject. She and Kirtn knew almost nothing about the area of space called the Yhelle Equality; that was one of the reasons she had been disappointed to lose Jal in the melee at the Black Whole.

Trader Jal watched her closely, then smiled. He looked meaningfully around the ship. When he attempted to rise, a sound from Kirtn changed the trader's mind.

"You don't have to worry about me" said Jal, his voice mellow with overtones of trust and fellowship. "Even if I weren't bonded to your smoothie, I'm helpless in this ship." He looked at the pilot web and the enigmatic displays. "I've bought, sold and, um, borrowed every kind of ship built in the Yhelle Equality, but I've never seen one like this. I can speak, read and draw in the four major languages of the Equality, as well as Universal, and I can read spacer lingo in six more." He gestured around with one heavy-nailed hand. "But that doesn't do me any good here. None of my languages fits your ship's outputs."

Neither Rheba nor Kirtn responded. Jal looked at her closely, as though seeing her for the first time. "Your ship's different, yet there's nothing remarkable about you or your big furry. You clearly belong to the Fourth of the Five Peoples. Humanoid to the last cell."

She moved impatiently. "What did you expect—one of the Fifth People?"

Jal made a face. "You're not a Ghost. You proved that when you undressed in the casino. But at least you know about the Five Peoples?"

Rheba made an exasperated sound.

Trader Jal smiled slightly. "Can't blame me for checking. If your people didn't divide intelligent life into the Five Peoples, I'd know you came from another galaxy. But," he added, looking around the gleaming ship again, "this wasn't designed or built by any Equality race."

"No, it wasn't," she said. The tone of her voice did not encourage further questions from the trader. "Tell us more about the planet Loo. Particularly its coordinates.

Jal smiled. "Information is a commodity."

"So are you," she retorted. "Remember? It was your bet, Trader Jal. And your loss."

Jal smiled unpleasantly. "So it was. My compliments, by

24

the way. That was a novel form of cheating you used. How did you do it?"

"Mirrors."

Jal grimaced at the sarcasm.

"The coordinates," rapped Kirtn.

"Impatient beast, isn't it?" said Jal to Rheba.

Her eyes slitted. "A Bre'n woman is involved. Kirtn is Bre'n."

"Bre'n . . ." muttered the trader. He shrugged. The word was obviously as unfamiliar to him as the ship's controls. "Never heard of the beasties."

"Senyas?" said Rheba, hiding her disappointment that not even the name Bre'n was known to a man as widely traveled as Trader Jal. "Have you heard of a race called Senyas?"

"No," said Jal, replying honestly because he did not wish to be caught in a lie while the furry's big hand was wrapped around his throat.

"Then how did you get the Face?" she pursued, watching Jal with burnt-orange eyes.

"Loo imports lots of . . . ah . . . workers. The carving must have belonged to one of them." He shrugged. "Maybe the worker needed money and sold the jewelry to get it."

"No," she said, her expression as bleak as her eyes. "The Senyas man who wore that Face is dead, or the carving would be woven into his ear. But the Bre'n woman who made the Face for him might still be alive." Her voice hardened. "Loo, Trader Jal. The coordinates."

"Listen," said Jal in a reasonable tone. "You have something I want and I have something you want. Let's trade."

"Why?" said Kirtn lazily. "I can just wring the coordinates out of your greasy blue carcass."

"Ummm . . . yes," said Jal. "But Loo is a big planet. Their customs are . . . different. Yes. Quite different. I know the planet. I'll help you find the boychild."

"Boychild?" said Rheba sharply. "What are you talking about?"

Jal looked smug. "You don't think I believed that you'd go slapping about the galaxy looking for a common furry? I'm not stupid, smoothie. You're really looking for the little boy with hands like yours."

She looked at her hands where lines of power curled thickly beneath the skin. Hands like hers—*a child with hands like hers*. A boy. A boy who would become a man. A mate. If she could find him, the people called Senyasi would not be utterly extinct.

25

Carefully, she looked away from her burned, trembling fingers. If the boychild was very young, it would explain how the Face had left his possession short of his death. Theft. On Deva, such thievery would have been unthinkable.

The Equality, however, was not Deva.

"This boychild," she said, her voice empty of emotion. "Where did you see him last? Was he healthy? Was there a Bre'n with him?"

"Do we have a deal?" countered Jal. "My information about the boychild in return for your information about where this ship was built."

She turned toward Kirtn and spoke in rapid Senyas. "What do you think, Bre'n mentor? Do we trust him?"

"No, akhenet. We *use* him—if we can." He turned his slanted, yellow eyes on Jal. "Why did you come to the spaceport? You could have escaped paying the bet and no one would have known but us."

The trader smiled slightly. "I could give you some star gas about honor."

Kirtn laughed.

"Yes," said Jal, "I thought you would take it that way. Perhaps this will be more believable. If I'm found on Onan in the next three weeks, I'll be liable for all crimes committed by my bondmaster. I'm a rich man, but I've no desire to rebuild the Black Whole. Besides," he added, looking at his thick, blue-black fingernails, "there was always the chance that I'd learn something profitable from you."

"Like how to cheat at Chaos?" suggested Rheba.

Jal licked his lips with a startlingly blue tongue. "Among other things, yes." He looked around the ship with an avarice and curiosity he did not trouble to disguise. Obviously, he had not given up hope of striking a bargain. "Of the seventeen known Cycles," he said absently, "only a few have left behind working machines. The Mordynr is one, and the Flenta and Sporeen are others." He watched covertly, but the names elicited no visible reaction from Rheba or Kirtn. "And then there is the Zaarain Cycle. Ahhh, you know *that* name, at least."

"A myth," said Rheba.

"The Zaarain Cycle was real," said the trader quickly. 'It was the eleventh Cycle, the highest the Fourth People have ever known. The Yhelle Equality and its thirty one civilized planets are only a speck on the history of the smallest known Cycle. We aren't even an atom against the might of the Zaarain."

Rheba did not bother to conceal her skepticism and impatience.

Jal laughed at her. "Listen to me, you ignorant smoothie. The previous Cycle lasted two thousand years and held six hundred and seventy-three planets before it collapsed and the Seventeenth Darkness began. The Equality might or might not be the Eighteen Dawn. I'll be dead long before the issue is decided, so I don't care."

"Then, despite your knowledge, you aren't a scholar," said Kirtn dryly.

The trader laughed again. "I'm a merchant, furry. History tells me likely places to look for pre-Equality artifacts. Most things that I find I sell to the big universities or wealthy collectors. But some"—his glance darted to the pilot web—"some things I keep. Pre-Equality technology can be very useful to a trading man."

"You can't fly this ship," said Rheba curtly, "so you might as well forget about stealing it."

"Just give me the coordinates of the planet it came from," Jal said quickly.

A vision of hell leaped into Rheba's mind, Deva burning, streamers of fire wrapped around the planet in searing embrace. She looked at Kirtn and knew he was seeing the same thing, remembering the same glowing hell.

When she spoke, it was in Senyas, a language Trader Jal would have no way of understanding. "Do we deal?"

Kirtn's body moved in a muscular ripple that jerked on Jal's gold chain. "I'd sooner pat a hungry cherf." His lips quivered in a suppressed snarl. "We could probably find Loo without his help, but we'd be a long time finding anything as small as a child. The boy probably wouldn't survive until we found him. Loo doesn't sound like another name for Paradise."

"Then we'll give Jal Deva's coordinates. Maybe he'll burn his greedy hands on her ashes." She flexed her own hands gingerly, remembering fire. "If there's even the smallest chance that the boychild is still alive, we have to move quickly. Jal, damn his greasy blue tongue, is our best hope."

"Use him. Don't trust him."

She laughed shortly. "Oh, but I do. I trust him to skewer us the first chance he gets. We just won't give him that chance."

Kirtn's lips lifted, revealing sharp teeth. It was not a beguiling gesture. Jal moved uncomfortably, tethered by the heavy gold necklace that Kirtn still held.

"We have a bargain to offer," said Rheba in Universal. "You'll take us to Loo and act as our guide until we've found the Senyas boychild and the female Bre'n, and have taken them off planet. Then we'll give you the coordinates of the planet where we got this ship. We aren't," she added deliberately, "ever planning to go back there again."

"Outlaws," said Jal. "I know it!"

Rheba simply smiled. And waited.

Jal made a distinctive clicking sound, tongue against teeth. "Agreed." He looked at the hand still wrapped around the bone carving hanging from his necklace. "After you leash your furry, I'll give you Loo's coordinates."

"The Face isn't yours, Trader Jal. It never was."

"But it's my good-luck piece. I have to have it!"

"No," she said curtly. "That's not negotiable. Either you agree or we take the Face off your dead body."

Jal sputtered, then agreed. The concession was graceless and after the fact; Kirtn had snapped the heavy chain quite casually as Rheba spoke. Gently, he freed the carving from the chain's thick golden grip. He touched the Face's curves with a caressing fingertip. The Face turned beneath his touch, revealing profiles both provocative and gentle, intelligent and demure, changing and changeless as the sea.

Rheba looked away, feeling she was intruding on his inmost fire. He held in his hand hope for a new race of Bre'n, and his eyes were deep with longing. A tide of weariness washed over her, making the cabin waver like an image seen through moving water. She reached out to catch herself, only to find that she had not fallen. Instantly Kirtn was at her side, lifting her from the pilot web.

"Into the womb with you," he said in Senyas. "I'll handle the first *replacement*."

She started to protest, then realized that he was right. Her fingers were too blistered to program a *replacement*, and her mind was much too blurry to interface with the ship's computer.

Kirtn sensed her agreement in the sudden slackness of her body. He unsealed one of the ship's three wombs, tucked her inside, and resealed it. Jal watched with interest, but could see no obvious means by which the Bre'n operated the ship's mechanisms.

"Is that a doctor machine?" asked Jal as the panels closed seamlessly over Rheba.

It took Kirtn a moment to translate the concept of "doctor machine" into the reality of the *Devalon*'s womb. The Bre'n

28

shrugged. "It's a specialized bunk," he said finally. "It helps the body to heal. Nothing miraculous," he added as he saw Jal's expression. "If you go in dead, you come out dead."

Jal's tongue flicked, touching the edges of his lips. "Where did you get it?"

"It came with the ship." Kirtn stared at the trader. "The coordinates," he demanded, lowering himself into the pilot web. He sensed Jal looking longingly at his broad Bre'n back, particularly at the base of the neck where a sharp knife could sever the spinal cord. But as Kirtn had known, Jal was too shrewd to kill the only available pilot.

"Quadrant thirty-one, sector six, twenty one degrees ESW of GA316's prime meridian," said Jal, sighing. He watched closely as Kirtn addressed the ship's console, but could make no sense out of the changing displays. Kirtn whistled rapidly, intricately, as he worked. The combination of light and sound made Jal wince and rub his temples. "Loo is just over two *replacements*," grated Jal. "The coordinates for the first *replacement* are—"

The words were forced back down Jal's throat as the *Devalon* leaped from standby to maxnorm speed. When the pressure finally lifted, Jal yelled, "Listen, you furry whelp of a diseased slit, we'll be lost in Keringa's own black asshole if you don't follow my instructions!"

"Save your breath," Kirtn said. "We tell the *Devalon* where, the ship decides how. Unless we use the override, of course."

Jal's expression went from fury to disbelief. "That can't be true! Only seven of the known Cycles had computers that could—" He stopped abruptly as the implication of his own words coalesced into a single name. "Zaarain! Is this ship Zaarain? Did the eleventh Cycle's technology survive on your home planet?"

Kirtn laughed. "There's more to the galaxy than the Yhelle Equality. This ship was built by Devan . . . scientists/dancers . . ." He whistled an expletive and stopped trying to find a Universal word to describe akhenets. "We built this ship, Bre'ns and Senyasi dancing together."

"Dancing? A bizarre way to describe it."

"Universal is a bizarre language," retorted Kirtn.

Jal settled back, watching the pilot console with consuming eyes. "Valuable," he muttered, "very valuable. But so ignorant."

"What?" said Kirtn, only half listening, watching the console.

29

"You're ignorant. On Loo, that could cost you your life and me my chance at a new technology. Unless you'd like to give me the coordinates to your planet now . . . ?"

Kirtn made a sound of disgust. "Not likely, trader."

"Then listen to me, furry. Loo is a difficult place. Every life form known to the Equality is represented on Loo. Its people . . . collect . . . odd things. That makes Loo unique and very, very dangerous."

Kirtn concentrated for an instant, sending pulses through the pilot web. The outputs in front of him flashed and rippled and sang. He whistled a note of satisfaction that locked in the programming.

"Are you listening, furry?"

"Yes," he said, swinging around to face the trader. "You're saying that Loo is a dangerous place." He shrugged. "So are most planets with intelligent life."

"It's the animals, not the people, that are dangerous. Have you heard of a Mangarian slitwort?"

Kirtn blinked with both sets of eyelids and settled more comfortably into the pilot web. "No, but you're going to take care of that, aren't you?" He yawned and stretched.

Jal ignored Kirtn's lack of attention. As the *Devalon* leaped toward the instant of *replacement*, the trader launched into descriptions of the most dangerous life forms of the thirty one planets of the Equality. Despite his initial reaction, Kirtn began to listen with real interest. The more he heard, the more interested he became. By the time Rheba emerged from the womb, Kirtn was wholly enthralled. After a few moments, she was too.

Jal was hoarse by the time the ship emerged from *replacement*. After a three-note warning, the *Devalon* reversed thrust, pinning the occupants against couches or pilot web. Dumping velocity as quickly as possible, the ship cut an ellipse through Loo's gravity well. Even before the ship achieved a far orbit, telltales began pulsing across the board. The *Devalon* was under attack.

"*Keringa's shortest hairs!*" shrieked Jal. "Open the hydrogen wavelength for me!"

"Open," snapped Rheba instantly.

Jal spewed out a series of foreign words, all liquid vowels and disturbing glottal stops. As his voice was transmitted beyond the ship's hull, the telltales slowly subsided. Jal moaned in relief and mopped his chin with the edge of his robe. "Stupid," he whispered. "Tell them about the wildlife and then forget the vorkers. Stupid, stupid, stupid!"

Neither Kirtn nor Rheba disagreed.

"What happened?" asked Kirtn, his voice controlled, his lips drawn thin.

"The vorkers—the satellites. Loo has pre-Equality defense installations through the system. If incoming ships don't have the code, they're vaporized."

Another light appeared on the board as the ship inserted itself into median orbit. The light pulsed in subtle tones of lime and silver.

"Do we want voice communications?" asked Rheba.

"Yes," said Jal quickly. "Let me handle it. The Loo are a bit . . . xenophobic. Yes. Xenophobic. They'll respond better to me. They know me."

The light changed to emerald and white.

"Talk," said Rheba.

Instantly, Jal began speaking the odd, gliding/lurching language he had used on the vorkers. There was a pause, laughter on both ends, and then a brief reply from downside. Still smiling, he turned to Rheba. "There's a tight beam at fifteen degrees to the night side of the terminator, on the equator."

She frowned and drew her finger across one of the console screens. Her hair trembled. "Got it."

"Ride it down. My berth is waiting for us."

The ship rode the beam down, docked, and opened the ship's doors. The instant the last door unlocked, Jal took a pressurized capsule from his robe and broke the seal. Immediately the cabin was filled with a potent soporific mist. As he never went without protective nasal filters, he would not be affected by the drug unless he was careless enough to breathe through his mouth.

Rheba slumped in her mesh, totally unconscious. Kirtn caught a tinge of the sweet drug odor, held his breath and lunged. Jal pulled out a gambler's stunner and held down the button. The gun was small, disguised as a calculator, and carried only a ten-second charge. It was enough. After nine seconds Kirtn collapsed in an ungainly pile of copper limbs.

# IV

The Imperial Loo-chim's receiving room was a white geodesic dome with billowing draperies that resembled thin waterfalls. A narrow stream ran the length of the huge room, curling around ruby boulders. Crystalline ferns shimmered along the banks of the stream. Immortal, sentient, the ferns were one of the many lithic races collectively known as the First People. They trembled in a remembered breeze, chiming plaintively of their long slavery on the planet Loo. The ruby boulders sighed in mournful harmonics.

Rheba shivered. The First People's melancholy was like a cold wind over her nakedness. She tugged discreetly, futilely, at the woven plastic binding her elbows behind her back. A similar plastic binding shortened her stride by half. The slip-chain around her neck glowed softly but had razor teeth. Blood trickled between her breasts, testifying to the chain's sharpness.

Behind Rheba walked Kirtn, as naked as she. His woven bindings were far harsher than hers. Each bit of outward pressure he exerted on them was answered by an equal and automatic tightening of his bonds. Struggle was not only futile, it was deadly; the edges of his bonds were tipped with the same razor teeth that lined Rheba's neck chain. Kirtn's arms and chest wore a thin cloak of blood.

Jal looked around the room, saw that the glass-enclosed Imperial bubble was still unoccupied, and turned quickly to his captives. "The Imperial Loo-chim understands Universal, but it's customary for it to ignore the yappings of unAdjusted slaves. I wouldn't bet my life on its tolerance, though. Understand me?"

She looked through Jal and said nothing. He deftly twitched her slip-chain. A new trickle of blood joined the old on her neck.

"Listen, smoothie bitch. I'm doing you a favor."

Rheba said something in her native tongue.

"Same to you, no doubt," Jal retorted. "But I could have taken you to the common slave pens—the Pit—where only one in ten survive Adjustment. But if you tickle the Loo-chim's interest, you'll be taken in to the Loo-chim Fold for your period of Adjustment. More than half survive there."

"What about Kirtn?"

"He's going to the Fold. The female polarity of the Imperial Loo-chim wants to breed new furries with gold masks. Yes, smoothie. There's another furry here like yours. The female polarity will pay a high price for your beastie. People with obsessions always do."

The Loo-chim bubble seemed to quiver. It opaqued, then resolved again into transparency. The bubble was no longer empty. The ferns shook and began producing an eerie threnody that was echoed by the boulders in the stream.

"The Imperial Loo-chim!" hissed Jal. "On your bellies, slaves!"

When neither Rheba nor Kirtn responded, Jal kicked Kirtn's feet out from under him. Rheba tried to evade the trader, but her razor leash could not be escaped. Bruised and bleeding, Kirtn and Rheba stretched out face down on the floor. Neither stayed down for more than a few seconds.

Trader Jal hissed his anger in Universal, but did not require further obeisance of his captives. They were, after all, unAdjusted; the Loo-chim expected little more than bad manners from such slaves.

Jal dropped both leashes and performed a brief, graceful obeisance to the Loo-chim. Neither Rheba nor Kirtn moved while Jal's attention was off them. They had learned that when he was not holding the leashes, the least movement caused them to tighten, slicing into flesh.

The Loo-chim gestured for Jal to speak. He picked up the training leashes and launched into a speech in Loo's odd tongue. Rheba and Kirtn listened intently, understanding nothing except their bondage and what Jal had told them when they awakened in Imperiapolis, Loo's capital city. The Imperial Loo-chim, although spoken of in the singular, was composed of a man and woman whose only genetic difference was the y chromosome of the male polarity. They were strikingly similar in appearance—curling indigo hair and pale skin only faintly blue—yet each twin was definitely sexed rather than androgynous. Each twin was also disturbingly attractive, as though the Loo-chim contained the essence of female and male, opposite and alluring sides of the same humanoid coin.

Jal had also told them that a gold-masked furry was the male polarity's favorite slave.

The male polarity spoke first. His voice was as liquid as the captive stream. What he said, however, was not pleasing to Jal. The trader argued respectfully, but adamantly. After a few minutes, he turned toward Kirtn. "The male polarity has decided he prefers his furry paramour not to be pregnant. Bad luck for you."

Kirtn measured the two sensual halves of the Loo-chim whole, then turned back to Jal. "What does his sister say about that?"

Jal made an ambiguous gesture. "She's used to her husband's enthusiasms. They generally don't last long. She has her own diversions, too."

"But she's not particularly pleased by his latest playmate?" persisted Kirtn, looking back at the female polarity.

She returned his gaze with open hostility.

"It's been awhile since the male polarity slept between his sister's sheets," admitted Jal.

"Does she share her brother's lust for . . . furries?"

"Only if they're male," said Jal dryly.

Rheba saw both the satisfaction and the cruelty in Kirtn's smile. She looked away, wondering what he was planning. Fear slid coldly in her veins. It was not safe to be around a vengeful Bre'n.

Kirtn spoke Rheba's name softly, using their native tongue. "Don't worry, sweet dancer. I'll keep you out of the Pit."

Before Rheba could ask what Kirtn planned, the Bre'n began to whistle. The fluting notes were like sunlight on water, brilliant, teasing. The song was as old as Bre'n sensuality. It evoked promises and pleasures gliding beneath the double sun of Deva's spring.

The skin across Rheba's stomach rippled with an involuntary response. She had heard this song as all Senyas children had, at a distance, carried by a scented breeze. She and her friends had speculated on the song's meaning, giggling because they were too young to respond otherwise to the music's sliding allure. But she was no longer a child, and the song was not distant. Resolutely, she tried to close out the sounds, using the concentration that was part of her akhenet discipline.

The song defied discipline. It burned through her will like lightning, incandescent, exploding with possibilities. Almost,

34

she felt sorry for the female polarity who was learning the meaning of the old Senyas saying "as seductive as a Bre'n." All that the song lacked was the female harmony. Rheba knew the notes, but refused to whistle them, fearing to unravel the snare Kirtn was weaving around the female polarity.

Rheba closed her eyes, held her lower lip hard between her teeth and shuddered with the effort of ignoring Kirtn's siren song.

The Bre'n saw Rheba's distress, misunderstood its source, and regretted her reaction. He had hoped she was old enough to understand, if not to respond to, the song. It hurt him to see her shudder, as though appalled by the song's celebration of passion and pleasure. Up to this instant, he had been careful to shield his young fire dancer from a Bre'n's intense sensuality. He mourned her rude coming-of-age, but thought it preferable to dying in the Pit.

Jal listened to the Bre'n song, watched the Loo-chim, and sighed with either envy or disgust. He murmured a counterpoint to Kirtn's song that only Rheba heard. "Just four of the Equality's planets are advanced enough to forbid pairing smoothies and furries. Loo is one of the four. But the Imperial Loo-chim's taste for furry perversity is an open secret. The male polarity's infatuation with the female furry is a scandal. Yet . . . I admit . . . if Bre'ns are as good on a pillow as they are singing, I can understand why the gold-masked furry has such a hold on the male polarity."

Rheba trembled and resolutely tried to think of nothing at all.

The song ended on a single low note that made the crystal ferns quiver and chime. The female polarity remained utterly still for a long moment, then stood up as though she would walk to Kirtn. She got as far as the glass wall before self-preservation overcame lust. UnAdjusted slaves could be carriers of diseases other than physical violence.

The woman's fingertips traced Kirtn's outline on the cool glass. She spoke softly. Rheba did not need Jal's translation to know that Kirtn had won. He would not be going to the Pit.

The female polarity removed her hand from the glass. She looked at Rheba, at the disheveled golden hair and slanting cinnamon eyes, and at the supple, utterly female body. The hand moved sharply. Blue nails flashed. Fingers snapped in contemptuous dismissal.

Disappointed but not surprised, Jal turned to Rheba. "The

35

Loo-chim is not impressed by you. It has prettier specimens that are already Adjusted."

"What would impress it?" said Rheba.

Jal shrugged. "Karenga only knows. The Loo-chim already drinks the cream of the Equality."

"Wait," she said, when he would have turned and led her away. She faced the Loo-chim bubble. As she had done on Onan, she began to build colored shapes within the transparent surface of the bubble. Her hands pulsed in subtle patterns of gold. Her palms itched. She ignored the sensation. The shapes she created were small, few, but brilliantly colored. They winked in and out of patterns like geometric leaves driven by a fitful wind.

The female polarity's blue nails flicked disdainfully against the bubble. She spoke a curt phrase. The male polarity gave her a spiteful look and countermanded the order. The Loo-chim began arguing with itself in cultured, razor phrases.

Jal frowned and watched his feet. Kirtn eased over to Rheba's side and put a comforting hand on her shoulder. "What are they saying?" he asked Jal.

Jal sighed and looked like a man with a toothache. "She's jealous of his furry. He's jealous," he looked at Rheba, "of your furry, both as mate for his furry and as mount for his sister. She's jealous of you, too, because the furry she wants is yours."

Kirtn did not know whether to laugh or swear. He stroked Rheba's hair reassuringly, a gesture that brought a frown to the female polarity's face.

"So?" demanded Rheba, impatient with lusts and counter-lusts.

"So they argue," said Jal simply.

After a time, the female polarity made an imperative gesture and snapped her fingers under her brother's nose. He made an angry, dismissing gesture. She snapped her fingers again. He continued to look angry but did nothing.

Jal sighed. "No luck, smoothie. It's the Pit for you." He turned to leave.

"No," said Kirtn.

The flat denial made the ruby rocks moan. Jal twitched Kirtn's leash. Blood flowed. The Bre'n did not move.

"Look, furry, it won't do any good," said Jal, more discouraged than angry. "You're lucky not to be going to the Pit yourself."

Kirtn ignored the trader. He turned to Rheba and trilled a

36

single phrase in the highly compressed whistle language of the Bre'n. "Whatever I do, don't fight me."

Rheba whistled a single note of surprised assent.

Kirtn turned toward Jal. "You might as well kill both of us here and now. If you separate us, we'll die anyway."

Jal's grip made the training leashes tremble. "I doubt that, furry. Oh, it'll be painful, I suppose, but you'll make new friends."

"You don't understand," said Kirtn harshly. "Bre'n and Senyas are one. Without mutual enzyme transfer, we die."

Rheba succeeded in keeping both surprise and admiration from showing on her face. Jal did not.

"It's a thought, furry. But the other furry didn't say anything about symbiosis with her smoothie kid."

Rheba bit back a sound of dismay. She had forgotten about the Senyas boy; and so, apparently, had Kirtn.

"Did you separate the Bre'n from her Senyas?" asked Kirtn, fear in his voice.

"No." Jal grimaced at the memory. "When we tried, she went berserk."

"You would too, if someone had just condemned you to death by slow torture," said Rheba enthusiastically. "It's ghastly, the worst death in the galaxy."

"Rheba." Kirtn's whistle was sharp. "Enough. The less lies, the less chance of being caught."

She subsided with no more embellishment than a delicate shudder. She watched Jal with huge cinnamon eyes. He frowned, plainly wondering if there was any truth in Kirtn's words. "Stranger things happen in the Equality at least six times between meals," he muttered after a long time. "But— enzyme transfer? How does it work?"

Kirtn turned Rheba until she faced him, no more than a hand's width away. "I'm sorry," he whistled. "It's all I could think of." And the Bre'n spring song had helped to stir his thoughts, he admitted silently to himself. "Don't fight me, little fire dancer," he murmured as he bent over her.

Kirtn drew Rheba to him and kissed her as he would a woman. Shocked, she did not resist. She had known Senyas boys on her own planet, friends whose playful fumblings had ended in transitory pleasures. But she had never thought of her Bre'n mentor as a man. Since her planet had died, she had even stopped thinking of herself as a woman.

Gently, Kirtn freed his dancer, hiding his sadness at her shocked response to his touch. He turned toward Jal. "That's how the enzyme transfer works," he said, his voice toneless.

37

Jal snickered. "More than enzymes could get transferred that way."

Kirtn's gold eyes became as flat as hammered metal. He said nothing. Even so, the trader moved uncomfortably. He turned toward the Loo-chim and stood for a long moment, plainly calculating the risk of Imperial wrath against the profit to be made from selling two high-priced slaves instead of one. He drew a long, slow breath and began to speak persuasively.

Neither polarity seemed to appreciate what Jal was saying. The Loo-chim glared at itself, then at Jal, then at the slaves. Finally the Loo-chim spoke to itself. As he spoke, the male's smile was vindictive. The female spoke in turn, smiling with equal malice. The Loo-chim turned back to Jal and made a twin, abrupt gesture. Jal stopped talking as though his throat had been cut.

The bubble opaqued, then cleared. It was empty. The ferns quivered in musical relief. Even the stream seemed to flow with greater ease. Jal stared at his slaves, waiting for them to ask. They stared back. His hand tightened on the training leashes, sending a warning quiver up their silver links.

"The Loo-chim is generous," said Jal dryly. "Indecisive at times, but still generous. If both of you survive the Loo-chim Fold, the Loo-chim will then address the question of enzymes, separation and survival."

Rheba felt relief flow in warm waves along her nerves. She sagged slightly against Kirtn's strength. His breath stirred her hair as he thanked the Inmost Fire for Its burning benediction.

"You're not safe yet," Jal said sharply to her. "First, you have to survive Adjustment. Then you'll have to find an Act. The Loo-chim has no use for your smooth body, but if you're talented in some other way they'll find a place for you in their Concatenation."

Rheba looked confident. Jal made a contemptuous gesture.

"If you're thinking of your Chaos trick, forget it. You'll have to find something more dramatic than a few colored shapes. The Loo-chim has a six-year-old illusionist who does much better than that." Jal waited before continuing in a hard voice, taking pleasure out of deflating her. "If you survive Adjustment, I'll send someone to help you with your Act."

Rheba's face was carefully expressionless, but Jal was skilled in reading the faces of slaves far more experienced

38

than she. "It won't be easy, smooth bitch. The male polarity bought the furry's boy. What the Loo-chim buys, it keeps. You'll never take the boy off planet. You got yourself turned into a slave for nothing."

# V

The exterior of the Loo-chim Fold was a high, seamless brown barrier capped by a nearly invisible force field. Only the subtle distortion of light gave away the presence of energy flowing soundlessly over the slave compound.

Jal saw that both his slaves had noticed the Fold's deadly lid. He smiled and made a soft sound of satisfaction. "Good. You're alert. You'll need that to survive. There's no real sky in the Fold—only energy. If you try to climb out, you'll die." He stepped up to a wide vertical blue stripe that was part of the fence and began speaking in the language of Loo.

Rheba's gaze was withdrawn as she measured the enormous currents of energy flowing silently so close to her. Her hair shimmered and lifted as though individual strands were questing after energy. Her body quivered, each cell yearning toward the compelling, unseen tide surging just beyond her. To reach it, join it, ride forever on its overpowering waves—

"Fire dancer," said Kirtn roughly, using the Senyas tongue.

Rheba blinked, called from her trance by her mentor's command. She turned toward him, her hair shifting and whispering, her cinnamon eyes incandescent.

"Don't let it summon you," he said harshly. "You can't handle that much energy."

She sighed and let go of the filaments of force she had unconsciously woven. She caught her long, restless hair and bound it at the nape of her neck with a practiced twist. "It's beautiful," she said softly, staring at the invisible energies pouring over the Fold, "so alive, so powerful, always different and yet always familiar, safety and danger at once. Like a Bre'n Face. Like you."

His eyes reflected the light of Loo's topaz sun as he watched his dancer grope toward an understanding of him— of *them*. She was growing up too quickly. One day she would look at her Face and realize what it held. How would she feel then? Would she be mature enough to understand? Would he be able to wait? On Deva she would have been at least ten years older, her children safely conceived, safely born, before she saw the truth in the Face. But Deva had burned, spewing its children out into a galaxy where they had to grow up too soon or die forever.

Jal returned, breaking into Kirtn's bleak thoughts. With a gesture, the trader motioned them toward the indigo slit in the fence. "You aren't counted as a new slave until you drink at the well in the center of the Fold. That is the only water in the Fold. Don't forget what I told you on the ship, or you won't live long enough to get thirsty. When you're inside both concentric circles that surround the well and the center of the compound, you'll be safe from any attack by other slaves. That's all I'm allowed to tell you."

Before they could ask questions they were sucked into the blue stripe. Their bonds fell off as they passed through the wall. When Kirtn looked over his shoulder, the slit was gone, leaving behind a uniform brown fence as tall and obdurate as a cliff. It stretched away on both sides until it vanished into the silver haze that gathered beneath the Fold's invisibly seething ceiling.

In silence, they examined their prison. The haze made distances impossible to estimate.

"How big?" he asked, turning toward her.

She shut her eyes, trying to sense the subtle flow of energy, currents of heat and cold and power that would tell her whether the fence quickly curved back on itself or stretched endlessly into the mist.

"Big," she said finally, blinking her eyes and rubbing her arms where bindings had deadened her flesh. "We could walk the fence for days and not come back here."

His whistle was short and harsh. "Well," he said, flexing his arms, ignoring the pain of returning circulation, "at least we're not tied any longer."

She swallowed. The drug Jal had used to knock her out had left her mouth feeling like old leather. Her throat was sore, her tongue like a dried sponge. She knew that Kirtn had to be as thirsty as she was, but neither of them was eager to take the trail leading off into the center of the mist. Both of them knew instinctively that the most dangerous part of any territory was usually the watering hole, where every living creature must eventually come to drink or die . . . sometimes, both.

But they would never be stronger than they were right now. Delay was futile. Without speaking they set off down the broad path, walking carefully, quietly, side by side. As she moved, Rheba gathered energy, renewing it from moment to moment, even when she was full. She dared not let the energy drain away, or she might be caught empty at the instant of attack. For Jal had left them no doubt that they would be attacked; the only uncertainty was when. And by what.

A small wind gusted, carrying groans and cries to them. Shapes mounded at the edge of the mist. Some shapes moved, some were still, some writhed in a way that suggested ultimate pleasure or ultimate pain. Wind shredded the mist, revealing a small humanoid form.

It was a child. A very young girl, naked and emaciated. Half of her face had been burned away, but still she lived and walked, making small noises that carried clearly on the wind.

Rheba leaped off the path, running toward the child. Knee-high white bushes clawed at her naked legs and mist twisted like cold flames, consuming the ground. She fell once but scrambled to her feet without pausing, her eyes fixed on her goal.

Dark shapes leaped onto Rheba's shoulder, flattening her onto the dank ground. She felt the rake of claws and the burning of teeth in her neck. In a searing burst, she released the energy she had held. Her attackers cried out and scrambled away from her, all except one that clung to her with flexible, clawed hands. Kirtn broke its neck with a single kick. He snatched up Rheba and ran back toward the path. Nothing followed him.

"The child!" screamed Rheba, fighting him. "The child!"

"Bait," he said succinctly. "That was a gtai trap."

Belatedly, she remembered Jal's lectures on board the *Devalon*. The gtai were semi-intelligent pack hunters who used wounded prey as a lure. Whoever or whatever took the bait could be acting as predator or savior; the gtai did not care, so long as what fell into the trap was edible.

She felt the claw marks burning on her back and knew how close she had come to death. Gtai regularly hunted—and caught—armed groups of men. She should have remembered Jal's words.

"But the child," she repeated in a strained voice. "We can't leave it with the gtai. . . ."

Yet they must do just that. She knew it. They had been lucky. The child had not. She must accept that as she had ac-

42

cepted Deva's end. She must put away that burned face, hide it in the dark places of her mind with all the other burned faces, Senyasi and Bre'ns scourged by their own sun. She had survived so much already. Surely she could survive the memory of one more burned child. Just one more.

"I'm all right," she said numbly. "I can walk. Put me down."

Kirtn hesitated. He had first heard that deadness in her voice after Deva burned. He had not heard it so much lately, even in the echos of his mind.

"I'm all right," she repeated. "I won't be so stupid again."

"I was right behind you," he said. "I didn't remember Jal's warning until you were attacked." He set her on her feet and looked at the marks on her back. "Welts, mostly. How do they feel?"

With a shrug of indifference, she reached up to coil her hair once again. Kirtn saw the four puncture marks on her neck. Jal had said nothing about gtai poison, but that was no comfort.

"Light," snapped Kirtn.

Automatically, she wove a palm-sized glow of cool light and handed it to him. He looked carefully at the wounds. There was no sign of discoloration or unusual swelling.

"Hold still."

She stood without moving while he sucked on each puncture until blood flowed freely. It hurt, but she said nothing. She would willingly endure much worse at her mentor's hands, knowing that he would hurt her no more than necessary, and feel it as painfully as she did.

Kirtn spat again as the glowlight died. "Didn't taste anything more than blood," he said. "How do you feel?"

"Like throwing up, but it has nothing to do with the marks on my neck."

He had felt the same way since the first moment he saw the child's face and realized there was nothing he could do. Someday he would not be a slave. When that day came, the creators of the Fold would know hell as surely as Deva had.

They resumed walking down the path, legs almost brushing with each stride. Erratic cries rode the wind, and at the margins of the haze were forms seen and half-seen but never fully known. Her fingers curled among his as they had when she was no taller than his waist. He caressed her fingers and said nothing, enjoying the comfort of familiar flesh as much as she did. The Fold made children or corpses of everything it touched, even a Bre'n.

The mist concealed, but not enough. They saw dead slaves mutilated by scavengers. The diseased, the injured, the despondent, all were clumped near the path, pleas and curses in a hundred languages, despair the only common tongue.

The children were the worst. It was their faces that would scream in Rheba's and Kirtn's nightmares, new faces among the chorus of Deva's dead.

As they walked, the mist waxed and waned capriciously, revealing startling varieties of plants. Occasional cries and complaints punctuated the silence. Rheba and Kirtn taught themselves to hear only those cries that seemed to be following them. No one came out of the mist, however. Either Kirtn's size or the certainty that new slaves had nothing worth taking prevented them from being attacked.

Yet they had the persistent sense of being stalked. The mist was part of their unease, maddening, changing shapes before their eyes, teasing them with half-remembered nightmares. The trail wound between and around low hills covered with thick trees that quivered in every breeze. The brush grew higher and sweet flowers unfolded. Rheba trusted the flowers least of all, for they looked gentle and she had learned that gentleness died first in the Fold of the Loo-chim.

The trail divided around a smooth, wooded hill. They took the side that seemed to be most heavily traveled, the left side. Half-seen shapes condensed out of the mist, blocking the trail. Kirtn stared, counting at least twenty six men and women of every race and size. He waited for one of them to speak. None did. One of the men gestured toward Rheba, then toward his genitals, then toward Rheba again.

Kirtn and Rheba sprinted down the right fork of the trail. Nothing followed them but hard laughter and harsh words of encouragement. Suspicious, they slowed. The voices came no closer. The trail curled off to one side, winding among the beautifully faceted ruins of a small city.

Abruptly, Kirtn froze, afraid even to breathe. From the ruins came an echo of ghostly harmonics. His hand closed around Rheba's arm, silently urging her backward. Jal had warned them most particularly about singing ruins. Other than a Darkzoi brushbat, there was nothing deadlier in the Yhelle Equality than the First People waiting along the trail ahead.

The harmonics seeped into Kirtn's bones, making him ache. It was nothing to what would have happened if they had run innocently into the midst of the faceted city, where buildings were intelligent minerals who spoke among them-

44

selves in slow chords that dissolved organic intelligence with terrible thoroughness.

"No wonder those slaves didn't follow us," she said. "They knew we'd come wandering out sooner or later with no more brains than a bowl of milk." She made a bitter sound. "Trader Jal is a liar. More than one out of two slaves die in the Loo-chim Fold."

"But no one counts you until you reach the well inside the two blue circles," he said softly.

Rheba wished ice and ashes upon Jal's Inmost Fire, but felt no satisfaction. Kirtn measured the surrounding hills with metallic gold eyes, but there was no comfort there either, only traps where First People shone in the sun.

"We have to go back," he said finally.

She did not argue. There was a chance that they could survive the attentions of their fellow slaves. There was no chance that they could survive the resonant speech of the First People.

Slowly, they walked back to the fork in the trail.

# VI

——————◆◆◆———◆◆◆◆——————

The shapes waited at the edge of the mist, shifting restlessly, talking with the many voices of an ill-disciplined pack.
Rheba's hair unknotted and fanned out with a silky murmur
of power. Kirtn felt her hair brush his arm and knew that she
was gathering energy again. A fire dancer, especially a young
one, should not fill and hold her capacity so many times, so
quickly; but neither should a fire dancer die young. He regretted the strain on her, and knew there was no other
choice.

"They have stones, clubs, bones," he said, summing up the
slaves' crude armaments, "no more."

"And a fifteen-to-one edge," she said. "I wonder what
would happen if we tried to go around them."

He looked at the boulders and trees just beyond the grassy
margin on either side of the trail. Many things could be hidden out there. Perhaps even safety. "Do you want to try out-
flanking them?"

The mist swirled, revealing the waiting slaves. They did not
seem worried that their prey would escape. Rheba stepped
boldly off the trail and began to cross the grass. The slaves
watched, smiling in grim anticipation. No one moved to cut
her off. After a few more steps, she turned back to the trail
where Kirtn waited.

"They know the territory better than we do," she said.
"Anyplace they'll let me go, I don't want to go."

He agreed, yet he hesitated. "There are too many of them
to be kind, fire dancer, and you're too tired for finesse."

The Bre'n said no more. In this he could not advise his
akhenet. It cost a fire dancer less energy to kill than it did to
stun. A simple touch, energy draining away; a heart could
not beat without electricity to galvanize its muscle cells. To
stun rather than kill required an outpouring of energy from

46

the fire dancer, energy woven and channeled by a driving mind. She was too tired to stun more than a few people.

Rheba remembered the child in the gtai trap, and the other children she had seen, the lucky ones who had died cleanly. None of them had chosen to die. These slaves, however, had chosen whether they knew it or not. "I'll kill if I have to," she said tonelessly, "but it takes more concentration than making fire. It's not easy to . . ." Her voice faded into a dry swallow.

He stroked her hair. "I know," he said, wishing he could protect her, knowing he could not. "I'm sorry."

"Maybe I could just scare them. They've never seen a fire dancer at work."

He said nothing. It was her decision. It had to be, or she would never trust him again.

She concentrated on a bush midway between the slaves and herself. When the bush finally began to quake, she raised her arm, pointed at the bush, and let a filament of yellow energy course from her finger to the bush. The gesture was unnecessary, but it was satisfying.

The bush burst into flames. The slaves muttered among themselves but did not back away. The leader walked up boldly to the bush, saw that the flames were not an illusion, and began warming his wide body by the fire. Soon the slaves had regrouped around the bush, snickering and congratulating their leader as though he had conjured the fire himself.

Flames whipped suddenly, called by an angry fire dancer. Bright tongues licked out. There was a stink of burning hair. Scorched slaves leaped back, only to find that the fire leaped with them.

Rheba worked furiously. Her hands and lower arms burned gold with the signature of akhenet power at work. Fire danced hotly across the shoulders of the slaves. A few people fled, but most of them had seen and survived too many malevolent marvels to be routed by a few loose flames. With an enraged bellow, the leader called his slaves to attack.

A hail of stones fell over Rheba, stunning her until she could no longer work. Streamers of fire winked out or drained back into the bush. Before she could recover, the slaves swarmed over, swinging wood clubs and fists with rocks inside them.

Most of the slaves who attacked chose to concentrate on Kirtn instead of the woman whose hands had called fire out of damp shrubbery. Even so, she was swept off her feet in the rush, her head ringing from a glancing blow. Screams and

47

curses in several languages showed that Kirtn was a deadly opponent despite being badly outnumbered; but even his huge strength could not survive the onslaught of thirty enraged slaves. He vanished under a tumult of multicolored flesh.

Rheba pushed herself to her knees, head hanging low, hair and blood concealing her view of the fight. Kirtn's whistle sliced through the confusion, a sound of rage and fear. The shrill notes commanded her to run away if she could. Abruptly, the whistle stopped.

His silence frightened her more than any sound he could have made. She lunged toward the melee, heedless of her own danger. One man grabbed her, then another. Instantly they reeled away, numbed by the shocks she had reflexively sent through them. She screamed Kirtn's name, desperately grabbing energy from the still-burning bush, from the sunlight, from every source within her reach. Thin lines of fire sizzled over the slaves who covered Kirtn.

The pile of flesh heaved and a Bre'n roar echoed. Kirtn clawed his way out of the pile with three men and the leader clinging to his shoulders. The leader's pale arm flashed upward as a club took lethal aim of Kirtn's skull.

Even as Rheba screamed, fire flowed like dragon's breath from her hands, more fire than the bush had held, more fire than she had ever called before. Her hands and arms seemed to burst into flames. Lines of molten gold burned triumphantly on her arms, answering and reflecting a fire dancer's will, stealing energy from the day and weaving it into a terrible light.

The leader's squat white body suddenly crawled with flames. He screamed and dropped his charred club, trying to beat out the fire with hands that also burned. The other slaves saw what had happened and fled in panic, leaving dead and injured behind.

Rheba sucked back the flames, but it was too late. The leader had breathed pure fire. He was dead before he fell to the damp ground. She stared, horrified. She had seen others die like that, Senyasi and Bre'ns screaming when the deflectors vaporized in one station after another, Deva's fire dancers blistering and dying . . . Sobbing dryly, she forced down her memories and horror. She knelt by Kirtn and sought the pulse beneath his ear.

"Kirtn?" she said softly, hesitantly, trying not to think of what her fire could have done to him.

After what seemed like a very long time to her, his eyes opened. They were as gold and blank as the lines of power

48

still smoldering on her body. He tried to sit up, groaned, and tried again. On the third attempt he succeeded. He saw the pale, scorched body sprawled nearby and the smoking club that had been ready to smash his skull. He looked at her haunted eyes and knew what she had done. He caressed her cheek in wordless thanks, not knowing how else to comfort her.

Slowly he stood up, pulling her with him. The light from the burning bush washed over his eyes and mask, making them incandescent. "I'm sorry," he said, speaking finally, looking at her. "Not for him. He deserved to die, and die more slowly than he did. But you, little dancer, you didn't deserve the job of executioner."

"It wasn't very hard . . . I didn't even know what I was doing. All I knew was that I didn't want you hurt. I didn't want to live if you died." She rubbed her lower arms and hands where new lines of power had ignited. As the lines faded, the itching began. She was grateful for the distraction from her own thoughts. "Let's get out of here."

She began walking up the trail as quickly as her shaking legs would allow. She lost track of the passage of time. Mist and the trail conspired to create a dream that she moved through long after she wanted to stop. Fatigue became an anesthetic, numbing. She did not fight it, but accepted it as she had accepted her itching hands, gratefully.

Trees loomed out of the mist, their supple, tapering branchlets swaying like grass in a river current. There was no wind. Kirtn and Rheba stopped, staring. When they looked away from the trees, they realized that the trail divided. A small spur took off to wind between the graceful, slim-trunked trees. The spur ended in a liquid gleam of water.

Kirtn stared at the small pool caught among the grove's lavender roots. Water so close he would only have to walk six steps to touch its cool brilliance. As though sensing his thoughts, the pool winked seductively, catching and juggling shafts of light that penetrated the mist.

"Kirtn, something's wrong."

"I know. But what?"

"I wish I weren't so thirsty. Makes it hard to think." She closed her eyes, trying to shut out the seductive pool. Then her eyes snapped open. "We haven't come far enough yet. Jal said there was water in the center of the Fold. This can't be the center."

"You're sure?"

She closed her eyes, reaching out to the subtle currents of

energy that flowed along the Fold's unseen fence. "Yes. The fence is closer to us behind and to the left. We aren't in the center."

Kirtn looked around until he found a fist-sized stone. He measured the distance, drew back his arm, and fired the rock into the pond. Silver liquid fountained up, spreading pungent fumes.

"Acid!" said Rheba, stepping back. Then, *"Look!"*

The trees bent down, sending their branchlets into the disturbed liquid. As the trees sampled the nutrient mix, delicate sipping sounds spread out like ripples from the pond. The rock, however, had contained little of the organic nourishment the grove required. With whiplike grace, the trees straightened again and resumed waiting, patient as all predators must be, especially carnivorous plants.

"Morodan?" asked Rheba, remembering Jal's lecture.

"Or Trykke. Either way, one of the Second People."

She stared, fascinated in spite of her uneasiness. She had never before seen intelligent plants of this size. "I wonder how they got here, and what they talk about while they wait for a thirsty animal to come to their acid pond."

"I don't know, but from their size, they've been talking about it for thousands of years."

"They're insane," she said suddenly, her voice certain.

"Maybe. And maybe they're only Adjusted."

She shivered. "That's not funny."

He turned back toward the main path. She followed. They were still within sight of the grove when a low moan of pain made her stop suddenly. Just off the trail, in a small clearing, a sleek-furred mother huddled with two very young children. She was badly injured, unable to move. Her children cowered next to her, seeking what warmth and safety they could.

When Rheba walked closer, the stranger spoke in Universal, ordering her children to hide in the ubiquitous waist-high shrubs. The children, who were not injured, half disobeyed. They stayed close enough to see their mother, but far enough away to be safe from the trail.

"We won't hurt you," said Kirtn gently in Universal, "or your children."

The woman's only answer was the slow welling of blood from a wound low on her side. She watched Rheba's approach with eyes that held neither fear nor hope, only an animal patience for whatever might come. Slow shivering shook her, fear or chills or both.

Warily, knowing she should not but unable to stop herself,

50

Rheba stepped off the trail. Kirtn followed, close enough to help but not close enough to be caught in the same trap with her, if trap there was. While he stood guard, she crouched by the wounded woman. The stranger's body was thick and muscular, but its power was draining inexorably from the inflamed wound in her side.

There was nothing Rheba could do. She had neither water nor medicines. She did not even have clothes to tear into bandages. The woman's lips were cracked with thirst, her breathing harsh, her thoughts only for her children.

"I'm sorry," whispered Rheba, helpless and angry at her helplessness. "Is there anything I can do?"

The woman's lips twisted in what could have been a snarl or a smile. "My children are cold. Go away so they can come back to me."

"A fire," said Rheba quickly. "Would you like a fire?"

"I might as well ask for water—or freedom." The woman's voice was as bitter as her pain and fear for her children.

Rheba closed her eyes, gathered light and concentrated on a nearby bush. Her hair shook free of its knot and fanned out restlessly. After several minutes the bush quivered as though it were alive. Sweating, she concentrated until the bush ignited. She wove its flames into arches connecting other nearby bushes and held them until there was an arc of burning shrubbery warming the woman and her children. After the first bush, the others burned quickly; it was always easier to use existing fire than to weave random energy into heat.

Kirtn uprooted other bushes, limiting the spread of fire and feeding the flames at the same time. He did not complain that she was spending her energy on a dying woman. He did not say that Loo's period of Adjustment was designed to kill the weak, not to succor them. If you were not strong, lucky, smart and vicious, you died. On Loo, compassion had about as much survival value as a broken neck.

But he kept his conclusions to himself, because he knew what drove his dancer. She had seen too many people die on Deva—and so had he. The need to help others was as deep in her as her akhenet genes.

"Should I cauterize her wound?" asked Rheba in Senyas, her voice trembling with effort and too much emotion.

"No," he said softly. "Soon she won't hurt anymore."

"The children."

"Yes. After she dies."

Wordlessly, Rheba sat down on the trail to wait.

Gray mist moved against the multihued grasses. A vague

51

breeze brought the clean scent of burning leaves. The woman slipped into semiconsciousness, moaning as she would not have allowed herself to do if she were awake. Her children crept back to her side.

Kirtn ached to end the woman's suffering, but did not. She had chosen to cling to life for the sake of her children. Perhaps she hoped for a miracle, perhaps not. All he knew was that he had no choice but to respect her decision . . . and to grind his teeth at her futile pain.

"Someday," whispered Rheba, "someday I'll meet the Loochim again. Then I'll share with them the hell they created."

Kirtn smiled a Bre'n's cruel smile. "Save a piece for me, fire dancer."

"Rare or well done?"

"Ash," he hissed. *"Ash and gone!"*

Her fingers laced more tightly with his. "I promise you that."

The woman's body slumped suddenly, seeming to fold in upon itself. Only that marked her passage out of pain. Kirtn and Rheba rose to their feet and crept toward the children huddled unknowing against their mother's cooling body. A stick shattered beneath Rheba's feet with a piercing crystal sound.

The two small children woke from their daze of cold and hunger with yelps of fright. They saw the forms looming over them and panicked. With a speed born of survival reflexes, both children leaped up and ran away before Kirtn could intercept them.

"Come back," shouted Rheba in Universal. "We won't hurt you! Please, let us help you!"

The children never hesitated. They had learned too well the Fold's brutal lessons. They trusted no one. They raced down the trail and into the shelter of a thick grove of whiplike trees.

"No!" yelled Rheba, recognizing the trap of the Second People. *"No!"*

Disturbed by the two small bodies scrambling over their roots, the trees shivered and stretched. Their limber branchlets hissed through the air.

Rheba raced desperately toward the grove, calling for the children to come back. The first child reached the edge of the gleaming pond and drew away, confused by the acrid fumes. He turned and pushed his sister back from the evil liquid. But when he tried to follow her retreat, the roots that he had used as steppingstones humped up suddenly and sent him staggering into the acid pool.

The boy screamed, warning his sister to flee, then words became agony as the acid ate into his living flesh. The little girl stood frozen for a moment, her eyes like silver coins in the half-light. Then her brother's terror drove her back. As she turned to flee, her thick fur shed light with a ripple of silver that echoed the deadly pool.

Rheba saw the second child stumble away from the pond, dodging to avoid the writhing roots. The first child's terrible screams bubbled and drained into silence. The little girl hesitated again, looked over her shoulder, and saw nothing but ripples on the sullen silver pond. Her brother had vanished into the Second People's communal stomach.

Limber branches whipped down suddenly, scoring the girl's body, driving her back toward the waiting acid. Her dense fur cushioned the blows, but not enough. She screamed as acid-tipped tendrils found her unprotected eyes. Blows rained down on her, jerking her about, disorienting her. Inexorably she was beaten toward the oily shine of the pool.

Screaming with horror and helplessness, Rheba tried to force her way back into the hungry grove and drag the child out. Kirtn held her back, grimly accepting the burns and bruises she gave him in her mindless struggle to follow the child. Any other man would have died trying to hold her, but he was Bre'n, and very strong.

A pale, nimble branch uncoiled, blindly seeking the child's warmth. It found her, wrapped around her body and dragged her toward the fuming pool.

Rheba changed beneath Kirtn's hands. Raw energy enveloped her, as uncontrolled as her rage at losing the child. His hands burned, but still he held her, his mind struggling to channel her fury into the disciplined responses of a fire dancer.

Then she heard him, felt his presence, understood his restraint and his rage equaling hers. Energy leaped at her command, raw lightning that split a pale tree from root to crown and sent thunder belling through the air. The other trees thrashed helplessly, trapped by their own vegetable necessities, unable to flee their most ancient enemy—fire.

Lightning slashed and seared, trunks bled, fragrant blood flowing down pale smooth trunks. A thin cry sprang up from the grove, a sound as painful as the continuous rolling thunder. The Second People keened and writhed and yanked their prey into the pond.

For an instant Rheba and the child and the trees screamed in unison; then all sounds were subsumed in the sheet of lightning and simultaneous thunder that exploded over the grove. The Second People twisted and heaved, tearing out ancient roots, branches flailing so violently that they broke and sprayed purple fluids that vaporized in the instant of release. But there was no escape from a fire dancer's revenge and a Bre'n's savage skill.

The grove of Second People died, and the smoke of their cremation was a thick fragrance over the afternoon.

Rheba breathed in the ashes of her dead enemies and choked.

# VII

With a hoarse cry, Rheba jerked free of Kirtn's grip and ran away, her eyes dry, blinded by fire. She wanted to run until she was free of feeling and memory, responsibility and revenge. But she could only run until her body convulsed from lack of oxygen, and then she crawled into a concealing thicket.

She wrapped her arms around her knees, shuddering and gasping until her breath returned. With breath came memories, Deva and Loo and children burning, a man breathing fire and Second People screaming, dying. She wanted to weep and scream but could not. Her eyes were wild and dry, the color of flames. She sat without moving, holding on to herself in the mist. She heard Kirtn's urgent, questing whistle, but her lips were numb, unable to shape an answer.

And then softly, ever so softly, she heard the velvet murmur of a hunting brushbat. Behind her, the thicket quivered as though at the passage of a large hunting beast.

She remembered Jal's dry voice describing the Darkzoi, certain death on clawed wings and nimble feet, an animal voracious and invulnerable except for eyes and genital slit. She knew she should run or walk or crawl away, should do anything but turn and stare over her shoulder into predatory eyes. Yet she turned, and stared, too numb to do more than see what kind of death had called her name.

The sounds continued, sly velvet rustles, hiss of air over wings, muscular windings of flesh and bone through branches. She stared, but could see only the dark wood of the thicket, its many branches as tangled as her hair. Against the silvery backdrop of the sky, she should have been able to see an animal as big as her hand, much less one fully as long as Kirtn.

Yet she saw nothing except a slight thickening of a branch overhead, a subtle flexing that was too sinuous to be wood.

She leaned closer. Gradually the shape of an animal longer than her arm and as thin as her finger seemed to separate from the angular brush. The snake quivered and enlarged. The brushbat sounds came closer.

"You're not a Darkzoi," she whispered. "You're as frightened as I am, aren't you? Hiding behind brushbat noises and scaring everyone. You should be ashamed." Her words were sharp, but her tone was gentle, as beguiling as a Bre'n whistle. "Come to me. I'll protect you. You don't have to be afraid."

As she spoke, she slowly reached up toward the branch where the snake wound helplessly around cold wood. It opened its mouth and hissed threateningly. The sudden movement revealed delicate scales tipped with metallic copper, silver and gold.

"You're a beauty," she murmured, "and you can't scare me. If your bite was as bad as your hiss, you wouldn't have to hide."

With a deft swoop, she captured the snake. It stiffened, stared at her out of opalescent disks, then gave a soft cry and went limp. She looked at the dark, slender animal dangling lifelessly from her hands. The snake was much heavier than she had expected. And very still.

"Snake?"

With utmost care she searched for a sign of life. There was none. Her touch had frightened the timid creature to death. As she held the animal, she felt its warmth drain into the damp air. She stared at the small corpse and then at her own hands . . . everything she touched died. She sank down to the ground and began to cry, shuddering and coughing, weeping for the first time since Deva burned.

The ragged, tearing sounds of her grief drew Kirtn to the thicket. He slid into the brittle shrubbery quietly, sat near her and took her hand, sharing her unhappiness in the only way he could, for Bre'ns lacked the gift and curse of tears.

While her sobs slowly diminished to little more than an occasional quiver, Kirtn whistled soft consolation in the Bre'n language. It was a language of emotion and evocation, as Senyas was a language of precision and engineering.

"Death is the pause between heartbeats," whistled Kirtn. "The children will live again someday, and someday you will love them again, and cry for them again, someday."

"I know," she whispered in Senyas. "But that is *someday*

and I am *now*. In this *now* everything I touch dies! This shy creature never—harmed—"

Her words became ragged. Her hand traced the outlines of the snake. For the first time, Kirtn noticed the motionless coils in her lap. He whistled a soft, undemanding query.

"It was in the thicket," she answered in Senyas, controlling her tears. "Hiding. It made sounds like a brushbat. You remember the noise Jal described, like velvet on satin, only stronger?"

Kirtn's whistle was both affirmative and encouragement.

"The poor animal imitated a brushbat to scare me away. But I just didn't care enough to run." She drew a deep, broken breath and spoke in a rush. "So I looked and looked and all I saw was a snake hugging cold branches and I thought it must be frightened and I thought I could help it even if I couldn't help the children—the children—"

He waited, fluting sad counterpoint to her words, crying in the only way a Bre'n could. After a time she spoke again, her voice drained of everything but exhaustion.

"So I lifted the snake out of the branches. It hissed at me, but I thought if it was dangerous it wouldn't have to hide behind brushbat noises. I was right," she said hoarsely. "It wasn't dangerous. It was just very, very shy." Gently she gathered up the cool body of the snake. Metallic colors rippled, intricate scallops of light thrown off by quasi-reptilian scales. "This beautiful, nameless creature died of fright in my hands."

The snake's sensors brightened to opal as he said, "My name is Fssa. Do you really think I'm beautiful?"

Rheba was so startled she nearly dropped him. She felt warmth radiate from the sinuous body and sensed the life invigorating him. "You're alive!"

"Yes," said Fssa, ducking his head, "but am I beautiful?"

She received her second shock when she realized that the snake was whistling fluent Bre'n. "You're whistling Bre'n!"

"Yes," gently, "but am I beautiful?"

The snake's wistful insistence was magnified by his delicate use of the Bre'n language. Kirtn smiled and touched the snake with a gentle fingertip.

"You're very beautiful," Rheba said in Senyas, divided between tears and laughter. "But where did you learn to speak Bre'n?"

"And to understand Senyas," added Kirtn, realizing that she had been too upset to whistle Bre'n's demanding language.

"You taught me," whistled Fssa.

Rheba and Kirtn looked at one another.

"Do you mean," said Kirtn in precise Senyas, "that you learned to speak Bre'n and understand Senyas just by listening to us?"

"The whistle language was more difficult," fluted Fssa. "So many colors in each note. But the thrills are exquisite. It's one of the most exciting languages I've ever used."

"Do you understand many languages?" asked Kirtn numbly, beyond disbelief.

"I have as many voices as there are stars," Fssa said, watching the Bre'n with luminous sensors. "Even among my own people, I was called a genius. Fssa means All Voices."

"Not only beautiful, but modest," she said dryly.

Fssa did not miss the nuances of her voice. He wilted. "Should I be modest? Is modesty necessary for beauty?"

Kirtn chuckled, moving his fingertip the length of Fssa's resilient body in a soothing gesture. The muscles he felt were very dense, very strong. Despite Fssa's timidity, measure for measure the snake was far more powerful than even a Bre'n. "Modesty is necessary only for fire dancers," he said with a teasing glance at Rheba. "Do you speak any other languages, Fssa, or can you only make musical notes?"

"I can imitate any sound. Languages are merely sounds ordered by intelligence."

Rheba stared at the shy, immodest creature looped around her hands, and said, "Speak Senyas to me."

Fssa's sensors darkened. "If I do, I won't be beautiful anymore."

"That's ridiculous," she said. "Speak Senyas."

"You won't drop me," pleaded Fssa, "even when I'm ugly?"

"I won't. Now, speak to me."

"All right," whistled Fssa in sad resignation. "But I enjoyed being beautiful. . . ."

Despite her promise, she nearly dropped the snake. Before the last quiver of Bre'n language had faded from the air, Fssa changed in her hands. Sparkling gold quills unfolded along his spine, then fanned out into a flexible ruff. Openings winked between the quills, sucked in air, distributed it to chambers where it was shaped and reshaped by powerful muscular contractions.

"What do you want me to say?" asked Fssa, his Senyas as perfect as hers.

"By the Inmost Fire," she breathed. "He can do it. Do you speak Universal, too?"

The pattern of quills changed. Vanes sprang up, flexed, thickened; other metallic folds of skin opened out, platinum and copper, silver and steel blue. Fssa was like a magic box she had had as a child—once opened, the box unfolded into myriad shapes, each larger and thinner and more beautiful than the last.

"Every educated snake speaks Universal," said Fssa in that language, "but," wistfully, "I would rather be beautiful."

Rheba looked at the glittering, incandescent fantasy looped around her hands. "Fssa, it's impossible for you to be anything *but* beautiful. Where did you get the absurd idea you were ugly?"

"I have no limbs," said Fssa simply.

He folded his vanes and ruff, returning to a more conventional snake shape. Passively, he hung from her hands, waiting for her judgment. She stroked him with her cheek and thought what life must be like for an intelligent, sensitive snake in a world ruled by leggy bigots.

"Poor Fssa," she murmured. "Poor, beautiful snake. Would you like to come with us to the well? We can't guarantee safety, but we'll tell you you're beautiful twice a day."

Metallic glints ran like miniature lightning down Fssa's long body. His answer was a liquid ripple of Bre'n joy. Smiling, Kirtn rose to his feet and held his hands out to Rheba. She looked up, weariness in every line of her body.

"The well isn't far," offered Fssa.

She licked her lips, but her tongue was too dry to do much good. Thirst was another kind of fire burning in her body, like hatred and memories of death. "I could hate the Loos, Bre'n mentor."

"I could help you." He looked at the snake. "We may have a new language to teach you."

Fssa whistled a query. "What language?"

"It's called revenge."

Fssa's laugh was a sibilant, sliding sound. "I'd like to learn that one. Yesss. That would be fun."

Rheba smiled grimly as she coiled Fssa around her neck. After a few moments, the peculiar snake vanished into her hair, an invisible presence balanced around her skull. Silently, she and Kirtn walked back to the trail. Soon it became broader, smoother, almost a road, and the mist thinned in the slanting afternoon light to little more than a golden veil. On each side of the road small shelters appeared, inhabited by slaves who plainly preferred to live beyond the concentric rings of sanctuary surrounding the well.

The slaves were of many races and sizes, but there was only one type—shrewd, strong, and as hard as necessary to survive. They ignored the road and the new slaves who wearily walked on it.

Rheba stepped over a blue tile line that curved off on both sides of the road. Just beyond it was another strip of tile, curving in parallel to the first. She hesitated, then remembered Jal's words. *When you're inside both concentric circles you're safe.*

Safety? Did such a thing exist in the Loo-chim Fold? Perhaps not, but the well did. She could hear it calling to her in liquid syllables. She quickened her stride, hurrying toward the chest-high cylinder of the well. Half of it was blue, half was white. Random patterns of holes spouted water.

Then four people walked around from the far side of the well. Two men and two women. Loos. They wore clothing and an air of utter assurance.

Kirtn watched them, measuring the obstacle between him and water. His reflexes were slowed by thirst, hunger and drug residue. His body was bruised and scraped and sported crusts of blood barely concealed by his brief copper plush. The pain he felt was attenuated, a distant cry held at bay by discipline and a Bre'n heritage that would not be ruled by pain short of death.

Beside him Rheba gathered energy once again. Her hair crackled, random noise that told the Bre'n his protégé was dangerously tired. Several times on Deva he had pushed her to this point, pushed her until her mind reacted rather than reflected. The result could be a breakthrough to a new level of fire dancer achievement, or it could be fiery disaster. He was too tired now to safely control her energy. She was a threat to everything around her, most of all to herself.

Rheba's hair twitched, spitting static. She did not seem to notice. Gold lines pulsed unevenly from her fingertips to her shoulders in intricate designs.

"Do you understand Universal?" asked one woman, looking at Rheba.

"Yes," said Kirtn, not wanting Rheba to break her concentration to speak.

"I was talking to the human," said the woman.

Rheba whistled a savage retort in the Bre'n language. Kirtn touched her arm warningly and received a hard shock. Startled, he looked at her. He was even more disturbed to realize that she had allowed the energy to escape without intending to or even noticing it.

"We're both human," said Rheba in Universal.

"Maybe you were where you come from, but you're on Loo now." She watched Rheba with impersonal interest. "We are the Four. We represent the Divine Twins."

Rheba waited, weaving power that leaked away almost as quickly as she could gather it.

"You two," continued the woman, "must have been strong, quick and lucky to have come this far."

"And human?" suggested Rheba acidly.

The woman ignored her. "Now you have to prove that you're also smart. Listen and learn. There are three classes of life on Loo. The Loo divinity is highest, ruled by the Loochim. Humans are second. Animals are third. If it wears fur, it's an animal." The woman's voice was impersonal. She was relating facts, not insults.

"Do 'animals' get to drink?" asked Kirtn.

"Animals drink on the white side," said the woman to Rheba, answering Kirtn's question without acknowledging its source. "Animals get food and water so long as they obey their keepers."

"What about clothes?" asked Rheba, shivering in the increasing chill.

"Animals don't need clothes. They were born with fur. That's why they're animals."

Anger blazed visibly along Rheba's arms. Her hair slithered over itself disturbingly. Fssa stirred, but did not reveal himself. He remained invisible, his body as gold as her hair.

"It's not worth fighting about," said Kirtn in rapid Senyas, "as long as they let me eat and drink."

Her only answer was a crackle of leaking energy. Kirtn gave a whistle so high that it was felt more than heard. She flinched at his demand for her attention. The whistle slid low, coaxing and beguiling her. She fought its power, then gave in. She hugged him hard.

"We could take them," she whispered in Senyas. "They're only four."

"They're too confident," he replied. "They know something we don't—like that mob where the trail divided."

Reluctantly, she admitted that he was right. She had also been bothered by the Four's total confidence. "I'll drink on the white side with you."

"No. We'll follow Loo's diagram until we learn more about its social machinery."

"All I want to know is the best place to pour in the sand."

Fssa laughed softly, a sound that went no farther than her ear. But Kirtn's sudden, savage smile brought the Four to attention. They watched very closely as the Bre'n walked to the white side of the well and drank. Rheba followed, but kept to the blue side as she had agreed to do.

While they drank, the woman continued her spare instructions in the same impersonal voice. If she was pleased, repelled or unmoved by their obedience, she did not show it. She pointed to various white or blue stations as she spoke. "Water there, food there, clothing there. If you stay inside the circles you'll be safe. You have been counted."

The Four winked out of existence.

"Illusion?" asked Kirtn in perplexed Senyas.

"I don't think so," said Rheba. "When they left, the ceiling funneled down where they stood." She waved a hand at the seething energy that acted as a lid on the compound. "It must be some kind of transfer system."

"Is it controlled from here?" asked Kirtn, looking around with sudden eagerness.

"No. It called *them*. They didn't call *it*."

"Outside the wall," he sighed, not surprised. It would have been careless of their jailers to leave keys inside the cell. The Loos did not seem to be a careless people. "You're shivering," he said, turning his attention back to her. "Get some clothes."

"If you can't wear clothes," she said tightly, "I won't."

"I'm not cold. You are."

The Bre'n's pragmatism was unanswerable. Without further argument, she went to the clothing station. A beam of energy appeared and traced her outlines. Seamless, stretchy clothes extruded from the slit.

She pulled on the clothes, shivering uncontrollably with cold. She hurried over to the place where Kirtn had made a bed out of grasses while she was measured for clothes. His arms opened, wrapping around her, warmth and comfort and safety. She curled against him and slept, too exhausted to care if Jal and the Four had lied about the sanctuary of the inner circle.

Kirtn tried to stay awake, distrusting any safety promised by the Loo-chim Fold. Despite his efforts, exhaustion claimed him. He slumped next to Rheba, sliding deeper into sleep with each breath.

Fssa slid partway out of Rheba's hair, formed himself into a scanning mode, and took over guard duty. It was little enough to do for the two beings who had called him beautiful.

# VIII

Kirtn awoke in a rush, called out of sleep by an alien sound. His eyes opened narrowly. His body remained motionless. Nothing moved in the dull gloaming that was the Fold's version of night. He listened intently, but heard only Rheba's slow breaths as she slept curled aginst his warmth. Then, at the corner of his vision, he sensed movement like another shade of darkness.

Slowly, he turned his head a few degrees toward the area of movement. He saw nothing. He eased away from Rheba and came to his feet in a soundless rush. He crept forward until he recognized one of Fssa's many shapes silhouetted against the soft glow of the well. While he watched, the snake shifted again, unfolding a structure that looked like a hand-sized dish. Quasi-metallic scales rubbed over each other with eerie, musical whispers. Kirtn relaxed, recognizing the sound that had awakened him. Overhead the sky/ceiling changed, presaging dawn. He stretched quietly, too alert to return to sleep.

"Kirtn?" The snake's whistle was barely more than a breath, but very pure.

"There's something out there. Something sneaky. More than one. Many."

"Close?"

Fssa's dish turned slowly, scanning. The dish hesitated, backtracked a few degrees, then held. "Beyond the sanctuary lines," he whistled, referring to the twin blue tile strips that encircled the well and food stations. "They're moving off now. Scavengers, most likely. Wild slaves."

Kirtn listened, but heard nothing except his own heartbeat. "You have sensitive hearing."

"Yes." There was a subdued sparkle of scales as the dish

64

folded in upon itself. "On my home planet, discriminating among faint sound waves was necessary for survival." Fssa seemed to look upward, questing with the two opalescent "eyes" that concentrated energy bouncing back from solid substances. He sighed very humanly. "The sky reminds me of my home."

Kirtn looked overhead where muddy orange sky seethed, nearly opaque. "Where is your home?" he asked, responding to the tenor of longing in the snake's soft Bre'n whistle.

"Out there." Fssa sighed again. "Somewhere."

"How did you get to Loo?"

"My people were brought here long, long ago. We're the Fssireeme—Communicators." He fluted sad laughter. "We're debris of the Twelfth Expansion. I think that's the Makatxoy Cycle in Universal. In Senyas, it would translate as the Machinists Cycle."

"Do you mean that you're a machine?" asked Kirtn, whistling loudly in surprise.

Fssa did not answer.

Rheba murmured sleepily, then became quiet again. Even after Loo's long night, her body was still trying to make up for the demands that had been made on it since the Black Whole. Kirtn watched her. He was careful to make no sound until he was sure that she was asleep again. He wished he could teach her how to restore herself with energy stolen from the sun, but he did not know how, only that it was possible. He did know that it required complex, subcellular adjustments. It was much more demanding—and dangerous —than merely channeling energy. Only the most advanced fire dancers could weave light into food.

Quasi-metallic scales rustled musically. Kirtn looked up as Fssa scanned a quadrant for sound. Dawn rippled over the unorthodox snake, making him glitter like a gem sculpture.

"You're beautiful, snake," whispered the Bre'n. "Machine or not, you're beautiful. Thank you for guarding our sleep."

Fssa changed shape again with a subdued sparkle of metal colors. "I'm not a machine. Not quite. My people evolved on a huge gas planet—a failed star called Ssimmi. Its gravity was much heavier than Loo's. The atmosphere was thick. It was wonderful, a rich soup of heat and life that transmitted the least quiver of sound . . ." His tone was wistful. "Not like this thin, cold, pale world. At least, that's what my guardian told me at my imprinting. I've only been to Ssimmi in my dreams."

Kirtn waited, curious, but afraid to offend the sensitive

snake by asking questions. Fssa, however, was not reluctant to talk about his home and history. It had been a long time since anyone had listened.

"Am I keeping you awake?" asked Fssa.

Kirtn smiled and stretched. "No. Tell me more about your home."

"It's uncivilized, even by the Yhelle Equality's standards. We aren't builders. We're . . . we just live, I guess. If we're lucky. There are lots of predators. My people became illusionists in order to survive at all."

"Illusionists? But you're blind!"

"You see better than you hear, don't you?" asked Fssa.

"Yes. Much better."

"I thought so. Most of the Fourth People are like that. We Fssireeme use sound the way you use light. Our illusions are aural. They're the only kind that matter on Ssimmi. Light and heatwaves are useless in our soupy atmosphere. The predators are blind."

"They hunt with soundwaves, like sonar?"

"Sort of. It's more complicated though. They use different wavelengths to find different things. Whenever we hear a predator coming, we send out sound constructs that make the predator believe we're its own mate. If we're good enough, we eat its warmth. If not, we get eaten. Life on Ssimmi is very . . . simple."

"If you weren't builders, how did you get off the planet?"

"By the time the Twelfth Expansion found Ssimmi, we were galactic-class mimics with just enough brains to realize that we couldn't fool the invaders. They had hands, and machines, and *legs*." Fssa was silent for a long moment. "When they finished sorting out our genes, we were intelligent, organic translators. Less bulky and far more efficient than the boxes they had before or the bodies we had used originally. We aren't machines, Kirtn, but they used us as if we were."

"A lot of races have been enslaved and genetically modified," he whistled gently. "Most of them outlived—and outshone—their conquerors."

"Yessss." Scales rubbed musically over each other. "It happened so long ago that it hardly matters now. Only one thing matters. I want to swim the skies of Ssimmi before I die."

Kirtn's body tensed in response to the longing carried by the snake's Bre'n whistle. "I understand," whistled Kirtn in return. "I'd give my life to see my planet blue and silver again."

"Maybe we'll both get our wish," whistled Fssa, misunderstanding Kirtn's meaning.

"I won't," said the Bre'n, speaking unemotional Senyas. "Deva is a scorched rock orbiting a voracious sun."

Fssa's whistle was like a cry of pain. "I'm sorry!"

"It's in the past," Kirtn said, his voice flat, almost brutal. "But if we escape Loo, I'll take you to Ssimmi. I promise you that, Fssa. Everyone should have a home to go back to."

"Thank you," softly, "but I don't know where Ssimmi is."

"How long ago did you leave?"

"My people left thousands and thousands of years ago. But that doesn't change our dream of swimming Ssimmi's skies. We have perfect memories, perfectly passed on. Guardians imprint the history of the race on their child. Their memories are ours, right back to the first guardian to leave the gene labs wrapped around the wrist of an Expansionist trader. Before that . . ." Scales rustled as the snake shifted. "Before that there is only the Long Memory . . . swimming the ocean skies of Ssimmi."

Suddenly the snake seemed to explode. Quills and vanes fanned out from his long body, combing the air for sound waves. Kirtn froze, trying not to breathe or make any movement that would distract the snake.

"New slaves," sighed Fssa after a moment.

"How can you tell?"

"The rhythm of their walk is erratic, as though they're tired or injured."

"Probably both."

"Yes."

Fssa sparkled, showing a sudden increase in copper color as he switched the angle of his attention back toward the well. Faintly, Kirtn heard the sounds of high, shrill voices coming from a nearby grove of trees. There were many such groves within the sanctuary. He remembered seeing a family there at dusk, three adults and five children. He had wondered how the adults had managed to bring such young children unharmed into the center of the Fold.

In the growing light, children darted in and out of the grove. They moved with surprising speed, chasing and catching and losing each other in a bewildering game of tag. Casually, four tackled one. The result was a squealing, squirming, bruising pile. An adult emerged from the grove, watched the brawl for a moment, then walked back to the darkness beneath the trees.

Fssa laughed sibilantly. Kirtn made an appalled sound.

"They're Gells," whistled Fssa. "To hurt one, you have to drop it off a high cliff on a six-gravity planet. Twice."

"That explains how they got this far."

"They lost one adult and three children. The Gell family unit is usually four and eight."

Kirtn looked at Fssa. The snake seemed unaware of him as he scanned the heaving pile of Gell children.

"Do you know a lot about the Yhelle Equality and its peoples? Trader Jal didn't have time to tell us much before he dumped us in the Fold."

"Whatever my guardians back to the Twelfth Expansion labs knew, I know, plus whatever I've experienced since my guardian died. I've been in the Fold for a long time, but I haven't learned much. It's so cold. I dreamed most of the time. If people came too near, I frightened them off with my Darkzoi sounds." The snake's coppery quills shivered and turned to gold as he faced away from the Gell children and shifted his attention to the sanctuary's perimeter again. "We didn't learn much from our owners. They thought of us as machines. Machines don't need to be educated, much less entertained. We dreamed a lot, the slow dreams of hibernation. And we went crazy from time to time." The quills stretched and thinned, fanning out with a rich metallic glitter. "So I don't know much and I talk too much. It's been very lonely."

"You don't talk too much, snake. And you're beautiful."

Fssa whistled with pleasure, but the sound was lost in the angry shrieks of Gell children. One of them had tripped over a rock and was digging it out of the dirt with the obvious intention of smashing the rock to pieces. The rock was head-sized and irregular, almost spiky. Where dirt had been dug away, the rock glinted with pure, primary colors. The sudden display of color caught the rest of the children. Immediately, each child was determined to own the rock. They began to fight in earnest under the indulgent eyes of an adult.

Fssa's sharp whistle called Kirtn's attention back to the area beyond the curving blue lines dividing safe from unsafe territory. The whistle woke Rheba. Slowly she sat up, stretching and scratching the new lines on her lower arms, looking at the new slaves in the distance.

There were seven people, three furred, four unfurred. All of them walked slowly although at that distance Rheba could not see any injuries. All of the people were of medium height with compact, sinewy bodies. Despite their labored steps, there was a suggestion of muscular suppleness in each person's body.

68

"Do you know their race?" asked Kirtn.

Fssa did not answer. His whole body shifted and seethed with his efforts to scan the sounds and shapes of the new people. Kirtn looked back at the group. They were at least five minutes away from sanctuary. As he watched, one of the furred ones staggered and fell.

Kirtn started forward, only to be stopped by Fssa's urgent warning. "No! Look!"

From the bushes just beyond the lines, figures began to emerge. There were three, then five, then nine, ill-assorted races like those Kirtn and Rheba had met near the trap of the First People. The nine made no move to attack. They simply watched the new slaves limp toward safety, supporting the woman who had fallen.

Behind Kirtn, coming closer, the shrill anger of Gellean children drowned whatever sounds anyone else might have made, frustrating Fssa's attempts to scan the two groups. Kirtn made an impatient noise. He felt Rheba's hand on his arm, lightly restraining.

"Some cultures are violently insulted by interference, even when it's well meant," she said, watching the new slaves slowly approach. "And they're not badly overmatched."

"And there aren't any children at stake?" asked Kirtn, his voice lighter than the expression on his face. He understood the implication beneath her words, but he did not like to preserve his safety at the expense of others. Tension narrowed his eyes until they were almost invisible in his gold Bre'n mask.

"I don't like it any better than you do . . . but, yes, there aren't any children in danger."

Yet even as she spoke, her hair began to whisper with gathering energy. Tiny sparks leaped where her hand rested on Kirtn's arm, but she did not notice. He did, and was frightened that she did not.

"No!" he whistled sharply. "You're not recovered from yesterday. Your control is gone."

She withdrew her hand and said nothing. Her hair moved disturbingly. She lost almost as much energy as she gathered. She could accomplish nothing at this distance. If she crossed the lines she would be doing well to defend herself, much less others.

Seven people limped closer, as though drawn by the shrill cries of Gellean children. The nine slaves who had slunk out of the bushes shifted restlessly, but waited for the new slaves to come to them.

"The clearing," said Kirtn angrily. "They're waiting in the clearing so that none of the new slaves will be able to run away and hide."

Fssa writhed. Quills were replaced by a light-shot, steel-colored dish that was trained on the approaching slaves. He made a whistle of frustration when one of the ambushers moved, unknowingly coming between him and his targets. Kirtn snatched the snake off its knee-high boulder and held him high. Instantly the dish shifted its angle downward.

Adult Gellean voices joined the angry children's shrieks. The fighting children simply screamed louder. Obviously the fight was getting out of hand. Children snatched at the coveted rock, but no one child managed to hang on to it for more than a few seconds. The screams subsided as children saved their breath for chasing whoever managed to grab the colorful trophy.

Into the relative silence came the rough voice of one of the men who was waiting. It took a moment for Rheba to realize that it was Fssa's translation, rather than the man himself, that she was hearing.

"—told you they were J/taals," he said in Universal. "The men are smoothies and the women are furries. Wonder if they're furry on the inside, too."

"We'll find out soon enough," said a short man. Then, nervously. "But if they're J/taals, where are their damn clepts?"

"What?"

"Their war dogs."

"Oh. Dead, I guess." Dryly. "This planet is hard on the new ones."

"Nothing's *that* hard. Clepts are *mean*."

The tall man turned to the short one. "Do you see any clepts?"

"No."

"Then there aren't any."

"You sure the J/taals aren't employed?" asked the short man.

"If they were employed, they sure as sunrise wouldn't be in the Fold, stupid. Nobody takes them alive if they're employed. But if they aren't," he laughed, "they can't fight at all."

The seven J/taals kept on walking toward the promised sanctuary beyond the blue lines as though no one stood between them and their goal. If they understood Universal, they gave no sign of it.

"What do they mean about not fighting?" whispered Rheba.

"I don't know," said Kirtn softly. "It doesn't make sense."

They watched the J/taals reform into a wedge-shaped group with the injured woman in the center. After a moment, they began a ragged run toward the blue lines of sanctuary.

"Watch it!" yelled the tall man. "They're trying to run through. Grab them! Once you lay a hand on them, they can't—"

Enraged shrieks from Gellean children overrode Fssa's translation.

The J/taals rushed their ambushers, only to be peeled away from the protective wedge formation one by one. Once caught, they did not fight, no matter what their captors did to them. Ambushers who had been bruised in the first rush began methodically beating captives into unconsciousness. No J/taal retaliated. When two men dragged a furry shape down to the ground and began mauling her, hoarse sounds from her friends were the only response.

Kirtn and Rheba watched in stunned disbelief. The J/taals were tired, injured, yet obviously strong. Why didn't they fight?

Another J/taal woman was tripped and dragged to the ground. The few J/taals still conscious screamed in frustration and anguish at what was happening to their women . . . and did nothing.

A Gellean child streaked past Kirtn, holding a bright rock in her arms. She turned and called insults over her shoulder, goading her slower siblings. They howled after her in a ragged pack. The adults cuffed their way through the children, yelling at the fleet girl. She looked back over her shoulder again—and ran right over the blue lines of sanctuary. Within seconds, she was grabbed by a scavenger slave.

Tenuous lightning flared from Rheba's hands, but the distance was too great for a tired fire dancer. "The child!" she screamed. "Save the child!"

# IX

Reflexively, Fssa translated Rheba's cry into a form the J/taals could respond to. The result was incredible. Only one J/taal was still conscious, but it was enough. She killed her rapists with two blows, then leaped to her feet, moving so quickly among the scavenger slaves that she was more blur than fixed reality.

Within moments the nine attackers were dead. The Gellean child, frightened by the J/taal's ferocity, dropped the multi-colored stone and fled back across the lines to the sanctuary of the well. The J/taal woman watched until the child reached its own kind, then she turned to face Rheba. As the J/taal spoke, Fssa translated.

"She asks if you believe the child to be safe now."

"Tell her yes."

The woman spoke again. Again, the snake translated so quickly that his voice came to Rheba like a split-instant echo overlaying the J/taal's hoarse voice. Very quickly, Rheba forgot that her words were being translated, as were the J/taal's words. Fssa was like having one of the fabled Zaarain translators implanted in her skull.

"May I have your permission to check on the other J/taal units and call in the clepts?" asked the woman.

"My permission—" Rheba turned toward Fssa. "Do you know what she's talking about?"

"They are J/taals. Mercenaries. You hired them."

"I—what?" Then, before Fssa could whistle a note, she turned back to the J/taal. "Do what you can for your friends. If they need more than food, water and warmth, I'm afraid we can't help you." She returned her attention to Fssa. "All right, snake. Explain."

Fssa smoothed out his body until he shimmered metallic

72

gold and white. Among Fssireeme, it was considered a shape of great beauty. Rheba waited, sensing that the snake was uncomfortable with something he had done.

"When you called out for someone to help the child," Fssa whistled in seductive Bre'n, "I . . . ah . . . phrased your request in such a way as to hire the J/taals. They can't fight unless they're employed, and they were the only ones close enough to save the child. Do you understand? The J/taals have to be employed, even to defend themselves. It's built into their genes the way translation is built into mine."

"And the need to have and protect children is built into mine," sighed Rheba. "Yes, snake, I understand." She closed her eyes and saw again the lethal efficiency of the J/taal woman. "Mercenaries. But I can't pay them. I'm a slave."

Fssa rippled in the Fssireeme equivalent of a blush. "Well, yes. Of course. Money isn't any good to slaves anyway."

She began to understand. "Snake, what did you promise the J/taals?"

"Freedom. A ride home."

Rheba said several things that Fssa would have blushed black to translate. He began to shrink in upon himself until he was as small as he had been when she plucked him out of hiding in the thicket. There was silence. Then she spoke again in a voice that trembled with the strain of being reasonable. "I can't give them freedom."

The snake's whistle was soft and very sweet, begging understanding and patience. "The J/taal woman knows that. I merely told her that if we and they survived the Fold, and found a way to be free, you would take them home if we could steal back your ship."

"Oh." She cleared her throat. "Well, of course. Ask if she needs help with her friends."

Fssa whipped into a shape that allowed him to speak J/taal. The woman looked up. She bowed her head toward Rheba and spoke in a low voice. "I thank the First and Last God for your kindness. My units would have been honored to die at your hands. Few J/taaleri—employers—are so kind. But it won't be necessary for you to bruise your hands on J/taal flesh. I've freed those who could not heal or kill themselves."

"You've killed—by the Inmost Fire—*snake, stop translating my words!*"

Fssa fell silent. Rheba watched as the woman caressed the face of a fallen male, stroked the dark fur of an unmoving

73

female, and knelt by another male. Her hands moved slowly, touching his face as though to memorize it with her fingertips. With an obvious effort, she looked away from the dead man and forced herself to her feet. Her black fur was dull with blood and dirt. She swayed, then caught herself.

"With your permission, J/taaleri, I'll guard the living units until they can guard themselves again."

Rheba looked toward Fssa. The snake's bright sensors watched her. "I don't want to say anything that will harm the living J/taals," she said. "Would it be all right to offer to move the wounded inside the sanctuary?"

"Yes! Scavengers are gathering, both human and animal. Tell her to call in her clepts. Now that she's employed, she can use the war dogs. And tell her to hurry!"

"You tell her. You're the Fssireeme."

Fssa relayed a babble of hoarse sound. Immediately the woman sent out a ululation so high it made Rheba's head ache. The sound pulsed and swooped, then soared to an imperative that could shatter steel. Suddenly, Fssa began undergoing an astonishing metamorphosis. When he was finished, a number of bizarre listening devices were centered on the ground between himself and the J/taals. She stared, but saw nothing except the sparkling rock that had nearly cost a child's life.

Uneasily, Kirtn watched the bushes and trees surrounding the clearing where scavenger slaves had faced J/taals. Although he lacked the snake's ultrasensitive hearing, the Bre'n sensed that there were unseen people in the brush, as well as animals gathering courage, waiting for an unguarded moment.

"I'm going to help her bring them in," he said suddenly. "She may be death on two feet, but she's nearly dead herself right now. She can't hold off another attack."

As he crossed the sanctuary lines, the agonizing clept call stopped, much to Rheba's relief. She rubbed her aching head and started after Kirtn.

"Woman," said a voice suddenly. "You've helped us. How may we help you?" The speaker's Universal was harsh, but understandable.

Rheba turned and saw one of the Gellean men standing at a polite—safe—distance. "It was a small thing," she said quickly, wanting to go with Kirtn. "I don't need repayment."

"Wait!" The man's face changed in obvious distress. He seemed to be struggling with words he could not speak. Fssa began whistling urgently in Bre'n.

"Unless you want a Gellean child, you'd better let him repay you."

"What?"

"It's the Gellean way. You saved the child. If they can't help you, they forfeit the child."

"Ice and ashes!" swore Rheba, turning to look at Kirtn, farther away now, halfway to the fallen J/taals. "Tell him to help Kirtn bring in the wounded J/taals. And make sure the J/taal woman knows they're trying to help!"

Fssa spoke quickly to the man in his own language. He bowed deeply and smiled. Another adult Gellean joined him, moving with a speed that would have impressed Rheba if she had not seen a J/taal woman in action. Very quickly, the four unconscious J/taals were transferred to the sanctuary. Rheba turned to thank the Gelleans, then thought better of it.

"Fssa," she said in Senyas, the language of precision. "Tell the Gelleans whatever is polite, but don't make or break any bargains. Can you manage that?"

The snake hissed to himself for a moment, confused. "Is there anything wrong with a simple thank you?"

"How would I know? You're the Gellean expert."

"I only know what everyone knows about Gelleans," whistled Fssa with overtones of exasperation.

"Snake—just don't make any bargains that you, personally, can't keep!"

Whatever Fssa said seemed to satisfy both Gelleans. They bowed again and returned quickly to their grove.

"In the future," she said to Fssa, "when you interpret for me, don't say anything I didn't say first, and don't let me say anything that will get us in trouble. Understand?"

Fssa's hide darkened until it was almost black. "Yes."

"How are they?" asked Rheba as Kirtn walked up to her.

"Bruised. Broken bones. Knife and energy-gun wounds partly healed. They're tough people. Their flesh is as dense as Fssa's. One of the men is conscious. She's working on him now." He turned and watched the J/taal admiringly. "If they hadn't been badly wounded to start with, those scavengers would have had to work all day to beat them to death."

Rheba watched the black-furred J/taal as she checked on her companions. She raced with vision-blurring speed to the white fountain, drank, then raced back. She bent over one of the men and began patiently dripping water from her mouth into his.

"Can we help her?" asked Rheba.

75

"She was uneasy when I touched them," answered Kirtn.

She watched for a moment longer. "The bodies," she said to Fssa. "Should we just leave them there?"

"J/taals always leave the dead where they fall. They burn their dead when they can." The snake rippled with metallic colors. "They can't, here. They won the battle, but there's no fire."

She looked at the woman tending her comrades, then back at the bodies. "Do they put much value on the burning?"

"Yes. If J/taals aren't moved after death and if their bodies are burned, they'll be reborn. Otherwise, they're lost in eternity."

Whether or not the J/taals' beliefs were accurate, they determined how the survivors felt about their dead and about themselves. Kirtn glanced at Rheba. She tipped her head in agreement. He began gathering fragments of wood and dried leaves. When he started across the lines toward the bodies, Fssa shrilled suddenly.

"Scavengers! It's not safe! Once you're beyond the lines the Fold won't protect you!" When Kirtn ignored him, the snake turned to Rheba. "Stop him! It's insane!"

"The J/taal woman saved a child. That was more than we could do on Deva . . . or Loo. We're akhenet, snake. Children are our Inmost Fire."

Fssa hissed in confusion, then turned toward the J/taal. Hoarse words poured out of him. Instantly the woman abandoned her comrades and went beyond the lines to protect Kirtn while he scrounged for inflammable debris. Rheba stayed within the lines, gathering strength until the last moment. Her hair whipped and sparked erratically. Slowly, she brought herself under control. By the time the bodies had symbolic pyres built on them, she was ready.

She walked over the lines, seeing nothing but the pyres. They were barely adequate for her purpose, but it would be easier to begin with them than with flesh. Once started, the flames could be guided within the bodies until they were no more than ashes lifting in the Fold's fitful wind.

When the air around her began to shimmer, Kirtn stepped into position behind her. His hands went to her shoulders, long fingers spread to touch points of greatest energy flow. Beneath the level of her consciousness, Bre'n savagery flowed, coiling around fire dancer's desire.

The pyres exploded into white flame. Rheba did not see it. She sensed only the incandescent wine of energy flowing molten in her mind, becoming lightning in her veins. She felt the eager flammability of wood, the tiny bright flashes of fur evaporating into fire, the slow deep surge of heat as the bodies sought to become ash.

She guided the forces, holding them beneath the threshold of fire until bone and sinew alike were ready to ignite. It was a complex shaping of energies, but all fire dancers learned it. It was their duty to see that the dead envelope of human flesh received a fitting transformation. Few fire dancers enjoyed performing the ritual; but all learned how in their fifteenth year.

She let the fire go.

The bodies vaporized in a white flash that left no odor and very few ashes. The J/taal fell to her knees, her hands over her blinded eyes. She made small sounds Fssa translated as joy.

"Tell her," Rheba said in a ragged voice, "tell her I'm sorry I had to use the pyres as a crutch. It's the first time I've ever had to burn my own dead." In that, at least, Deva's sun had not failed its children. It was small comfort, but she clung to it all the more for its scarcity.

As Kirtn guided Rheba and the J/taal back inside the lines, eerie, harmonic howls issued out of the bushes. Waist-high, muscular, lean, three clepts converged on the scorched ground where their masters had died. The J/taal ululated briefly. The silver-eyed, tiger-striped reptiloids loped over the sanctuary lines to the woman's side. She gestured blindly toward Rheba.

"Hold still," said Fssa urgently. "It's all right, but *don't move*."

The clepts licked, sniffed and very gently tasted their way across Rheba's and Kirtn's bodies. When the J/taal was satisfied that the new scents were indelibly imprinted on the clepts, she made a low sound. The animals fanned outward, ranging nearby in restless circles that had the J/taaleri as its center.

"We'll be safe tonight," said Kirtn, noting the reptiloids' soft-footed, deadly strength.

"I'm not going to wait that long to sleep."

Without another word, she curled up on the ground and went into the profound restorative unconsciousness all akhenets learned. Despite the clepts, Kirtn sat protectively beside her, watching her with luminous gold eyes. From time to time he touched her lips lightly, waited, then withdrew, reassured by the warmth of her breath on his fingertips.

77

After a long time he lay beside her, one finger resting lightly on her neck, counting her pulse as though it were his own. No impatience showed on his face; exhausted akhenets had been known to sleep for five days at a time.

# X

It was less than a day before Rheba awoke with a headache that made her grind her teeth. She scratched her arms furiously. The quasi-metal lines of power still itched as her body accommodated itself to the new tissue. Pain stabbed at her temples, then subsided.

"How are you feeling?" asked Kirtn.

"Should have slept longer. Headache." She stifled a groan and grabbed her forehead.

"Mine aches too," he said.

She winced. "Disease?" Her voice was ragged, fearful.

"The J/taal has a headache, but it could have come from the beating she took." He rolled his head on his powerful neck, loosening muscles that were tensed against pain. "No fever, though, and no nausea."

She muttered something about small blessings. She looked around very slowly, for quick moves brought blinding knives of pain. The clepts lay at equidistant points of a circle with her at its center. The J/taals appeared to be sleeping. Fssa was nowhere in sight.

"Where's our magic snake?" she asked, looking around again.

"Over there. At the lines."

She looked beyond Kirtn's long finger. At first she could not see Fssa. Then she realized that what looked like a bizarre fungus was actually the snake. "What's he doing? Is that his sleeping shape? Is he sick?"

"He's not sick, not even a headache. Of course," dryly, "that could be because he doesn't have a head to ache at the moment."

She stared. Fssa altered shape abruptly. A quiver went through one part of his body. She closed her eyes and knuckled her temples. The pain intensified, then subsided.

79

From behind her came a low groan. The J/taal woman was waking up. Rheba turned to ask how the J/taal felt, then realized that conversation was impossible without the snake.

"Fssa," she called through clenched teeth. "Fssa!"

The Fssireeme whistled to her without visibly changing form. Whistles were the simplest mode of communication for the snake.

"I need you," she called. "The J/taals are waking up." Then, hands yanking at her hair, "By the Last Flame, *my head is killing me!*"

Kirtn, his lips flattened across his teeth in a silent snarl, said nothing. He closed his eyes and listened to J/taal groans. Gradually, agony subsided to a dull ache, like that of nerves that have been overstressed. Fssa slithered up with a cheerful greeting. Kirtn managed not to strangle the snake. Rheba's fingers twitched, but she, too, restrained herself.

"Ask the J/taals if they need anything. We'll bring water if they'll accept it from our mouths," she said hoarsely.

Fssa flexed into his J/taal speech mode. As the answer came, he simultaneously translated for Rheba. His skill made it easy for his audience to forget that there was a translator at work.

The J/taal female bowed to Rheba, hands open and relaxed, eyes closed, utterly at the mercy of her J/taaleri. "Thank you. As soon as they all wake, we'll complete the tkleet."

"Tkleet?" said Rheba.

"The employment ritual," murmured Fssa in Senyas.

Rheba looked at the snake as a way of telling him that what she said was for him only, not to be translated. "What's going on?"

"I don't know. I'm merely a translator, remember?"

"You're an insurbordinate echo," snapped Rheba.

"Is that unbeautiful?" whistled Fssa mournfully, deflating before her eyes.

She smiled in spite of herself. "No. But what is tkleet?"

"I don't know," admitted the snake.

"Can you find out?"

She waited while Fssa and the J/taal exchanged hoarse noises.

"It's a simple naming ceremony," said Fssa. "She presents herself and the other units and then you give them names."

"Don't they already have names?"

A shrug rippled down Fssa's lithe body. "Most J/taaleris

apparently like to give the units names. It marks the J/taals as their employees."

Rheba grimaced. "That's too much like slavery. If they don't have names, they can choose their own." She came slowly to her feet, expecting a resurgence of her shattering headache each time she moved. "Tell her that we'll have the . . . tkleet . . . after her friends are cared for."

Fssa spoke rapidly, then turned his opalescent sensors back on Rheba. "Will you need me until then?"

"No."

Fssa slithered off in the direction he had come. When he reached the lines marking the end of sanctuary, he stopped and unfolded into the same bizarre fungal mode he had previously used. She watched for a moment, then turned toward the well.

As she, Kirtn and the female J/taal carried water to the injured, their headaches returned. Other than groaning and grinding their teeth, there was little to be done. Movement seemed to set off the pains, but the wounded J/taals needed water. Finally, the J/taals could drink no more. Kirtn gently checked their injuries. They were healing with remarkable speed. Where bones had been broken, the swellings were gone and the bruises had faded to smears of indeterminate color concealed by dark fur or skin.

"At this rate, they'll be on their feet by sunset."

"At this rate," Rheba said, teeth clenched, "I'll be dead by sunset."

He almost smiled. "No you won't. You'll just wish you were."

"I was afraid you'd say that."

The pains stopped, then came with redoubled force. She cried out involuntarily. So did Kirtn and the J/taals. The clepts howled. Paralyzed by pain, she clung to the Bre'n. The agony stopped, leaving her sweaty and limp.

*What's wrong with us?* she cried.

Kirtn held her, stroking her hair. Though he was affected by the pains, he was much less susceptible than she was. "I don't know. It's no disease, though. We felt it at the same time. So did the J/taals and clepts."

"Is it Loo torture? I thought we were supposed to be safe inside the circles."

"I don't know." Kirtn gathered her against his body as though he could shield her from whatever caused pain. "Maybe Fssa knows. He's been here a long time." He covered her ears and whistled a Bre'n imperative.

81

Fssa answered after a long pause. Overtones of reluctance were clear in the snake's Bre'n whistle. Whatever he was doing, he preferred not to be disturbed.

"Then stay there, you cherf," muttered Rheba, counting each heartbeat like a knife turning behind her eyes.

Kirtn, however, did not give up. "Listen to me, snake. We're all in pain, even the clepts. It's not a disease. Have you ever heard of the Loos torturing their Fold slaves by giving them mind-splitting headaches?"

Fssa wavered, then folded in upon himself until he was in his ground-traveling mode. He undulated over to Rheba and turned his sensors on her. "Torture? Is it that bad?"

"Yes!" Slowly, she uncurled her arms, clenched around Kirtn's neck in a hold that would have been too painful for a Senyas to bear. "It comes and goes." She winced, rubbing her temples with hands that shook. 'Even when it goes, it aches. I feel as if an army of cherfs were using my brain for slap ball."

Fssa cocked his head from side to side, bringing the opalescent pits to bear on her from various angles. Then he began a startling series of changes. He moved so rapidly that he resembled a computer display showing all possible variations on the theme of Fssireeme. "If there's an energy source pointed in your direction, I can't sense it," he said at last. "And if I can't sense it, either it doesn't exist or it isn't turned on now."

"Stay here and keep listening," said Kirtn.

Fssa whistled mournfully.

The Bre'n's whistle was shrill, a sound crackling with impatience. "The fire dancer hurts," he said, as though that ended all possibility of argument. And for him, it did.

"So do the rest of you," she said.

"So does it," whistled Fssa softly, "I think."

"It? What are you talking about?" asked Kirtn.

"The rock."

"The rock," repeated Kirtn, looking around quickly. There were rocks of all sizes and shapes nearby. "Which rock?"

Fssa whipped out a pointing quill. "That one," he whistled, indicating the rock the Gellean children had fought over.

"Is it one of the First People?" asked Rheba, pulling herself up to look over Kirtn's shoulder.

Fssa hesitated. "It could be, but . . ." His body rippled with metallic highlights as he shifted into a half-fungus position. "It just doesn't *feel* like one of them. Yet it feels as if it's alive. It's distressed. I keep getting images of pieces of it

82

being torn off and ground to colored dust." His sensors turned back to Rheba. His Bre'n whistle was both wistful and seductive, pleading with her emotions. "Could you save it, fire dancer? It's not a child—at least I don't think it is—but it feels alive."

Kirtn smiled as Rheba muttered about magic snakes and menageries. She sighed. "Tell the J/taal to send the clepts to guard Kirtn while he picks up the damn rock."

Fssa, who had listened to the J/taal speak to her clepts, went directly to the animals. He galvanized them with a curdling ululation. They formed a moving guard around Kirtn as he went toward the rock. The instant he crossed out of sanctuary, the bushes began to rustle. As he bent down to pick up the rock, three men rushed out. A clept leaped forward in a blur of speed. Fangs flashed. One man fell, another screamed. All retreated to the concealing brush. The clepts watched, but did not follow; they had been told to guard, not to attack.

Holding the rock, Kirtn watched the wounded scavenger crawl back under cover. The closest clept turned and regarded Kirtn with oblong silver eyes. Blood shone against its pale muzzle. It resumed its guard position at a point equidistant from the other clepts.

"Glad you're with me," muttered the Bre'n. "I'd hate to be against you." He looked at the rock in his hands. It was a grubby specimen, unprepossessing but for an occasional flash of pure color. "Alive or not, you could use a scrub."

Light winked across the few crystals that were not obscured by dirt.

"Was that yes or no?"

Sun glittered across the stone as he turned it.

"A definite maybe," he said. "To the well with you. The white side, of course. Even though you aren't furry, I doubt if the Loos would like you bathing at their precious blue well."

Ignoring the waiting people, Kirtn went to the well, grabbed a handful of twigs for a scrubber, and went to work on the stone. Mud fell away in sticky clots. When he was finished, he whistled with surprise and delight. The stone was an odd crystal formation that contained every color in the visible spectrum. Rheba, who had walked up halfway through the stone's bath, was equally impressed. Fssa, dangling around her neck, was not.

"It's beautiful!" she exclaimed. "Like a rainbow, only much more concentrated."

"As useless as a rainbow, too," whistled Fssa, using a minor key that was as irritating as steel scraped over slate.

"It was your idea to rescue this bauble," pointed out Kirtn. "So keep your many mouths shut."

"Fssireeme don't have mouths," Fssa snapped. "And it doesn't look as pretty as a rainbow."

Kirtn laughed. "You're jealous."

"Of your mouth?" whistled Fssa indignantly.

"No. Of the stone's beauty."

The snake subsided. He slid down Rheba's arm, dangled from her wrist and dropped onto the ground.

"You're beautiful," whistled the Bre'n, squatting down beside the snake and balancing the stone on his leg.

Light rippled and gleamed across Fssa's body. Colors seemed to swirl into the sensors that were trained on Kirtn. "That's the third time you've told me that today. Our bargain was only for twice."

Fingertips traced the snake's delicate head scales. "You're beautiful more than twice a day."

Fssa quivered. A superb Bre'n trill filled the air with color. Rheba sat on her heels next to Kirtn and watched Fssa.

"You really were jealous, weren't you?" she asked.

"It's not easy to give up being beautiful." Fssa's whistle was mournful but resigned.

"More than one thing at a time can be beautiful. Rainbow's beauty doesn't subtract from yours."

"Rainbow? Oh, the rock." Fssa sighed. "You're right, I suppose. And I wouldn't have left it out there even if I'd known how pretty it was. It was frightened. At least I think it was. Maybe," he continued hopefully, "maybe it isn't alive after all."

He assumed his fungus shape. After a few moments he rippled, then quivered violently. Instantly, Rheba cried out in pain. Agony sliced through her brain in great sweeping arcs that threatened to blind her.

"*Stop!*" screamed Rheba. When Fssa seemed not to hear, she lashed out with her hand, knocking him off balance. "*Stop it!*"

Abruptly the agony ended. She slumped to the ground, dazed by the absence of pain. Fssa's sensors went from one to the other of his friends. "What's wrong? I wasn't doing—I didn't mean—are you all right?"

Kirtn answered the urgent whistle with a reassuring touch. "Whatever you were doing to scan that rock was causing us a lot of pain."

"I?" whistled the snake. "After my first question, I didn't focus a single sound wave. I was only listening." Then, "Oh. Of course. It's alive after all. Rainbow. A very difficult frequency, though. Complex and mulitleveled, with resonances that . . . I wonder . . ."

Fssa snapped into his fungus shape, only thinner this time, and more curved. Slow ripples swept through his body. Rheba screamed as Rainbow answered. The fungus collapsed into a chagrined Fssireeme.

"I'm sorry, but I had to be sure. Rainbow is alive. I still don't think it's a First People, but I can't be sure until I learn its language. Now that I'm collecting its full range, things should go more quickly."

"No," she said raggedly. "I don't care if that's the First People's Flawless Crystal in person. Every time it talks my brain turns to fire. Keep it quiet or I'll—*oh!*" She grabbed her head. "To think I called it pretty! Shut it up, snake. *Shut it up!*"

The fire in her mind slowly burned out. She opened her eyes and stared warily at the rock. Luminous colors flashed from every crystal spire. Pure light pooled in hollows and scintillated from crystal peaks. The crystals were lucent, absolutely flawless. Rainbow was a crown fit for a Zaarain god.

She groaned and wished she had never seen it.

# XI

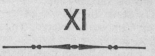

"All right," Rheba said, looking around at Kirtn and the J/taals. "You've had several days to think about it. Now, how do we get out of here?"

Fssa translated her words like a musical echo, leaving out only the undertone of strain that was the legacy of Rainbow's bizarre frequencies. This was the first day she had felt able to string together two coherent thoughts, much less plan an escape from the Loo-chim Fold. The snake did his translations from his favorite place, hidden in her long hair, revealing only enough of himself to speak. As J/taal required little more than a flexible orifice, a pseudo-tongue, and bellows to pump air, he was hidden but for the stirring of her hair with each of his "breaths."

The J/taals listened, then turned and looked at the woman they called M/dere—Strategist. She was the one who had accepted employment in the name of all the J/taals. Rest, water and food had restored her health, a fact that was reflected in the vitreous luster of her black fur. Her four friends were wholly recovered also, and had proved it by spending many hours doing intricate gymnastics that both toned and relaxed their bodies.

M/dere looked at each of the J/taals in turn, silently gathering information from them. They had a species-specific telepathy that greatly aided them in their mercenary work. They used their voices only to communicate with non-J/taals. As a result, their language was simple and their voices unrefined.

"As you asked, we have shared our memories." She hesitated. "I'm sorry, J/taaleri. No one has ever escaped from the Fold that we know of. Not even in legend. Once outside the Fold, some might have escaped from their slave masters and either hidden themselves in the wild places or managed to get off planet in a stolen ship. There are at least rumors pointing toward such escapes."

"Fine. Now, how do we get out of the Fold?" asked Kirtn.

"Excuse me. M/dur has special information about the Fold." She exchanged a long silence with M/dur, the male whom she had nursed with special care. He was their best fighter; as such, he had the second-strongest vote in their council. M/dere blinked, revealing eyes as green as aged copper. "Slaves of potential value are kept in the Fold until they are Adjusted."

"Yes, but how long does that take?" asked Rheba.

"It varies with each slave. Adjusted slaves stay within the sanctuary lines. UnAdjusted slaves stay outside the lines except to eat or drink."

"But don't the Loos care which slaves do which?"

Fssa translated Rheba's tangled question with a hiss of reproval that only she heard.

"Loos," answered M/dere, "don't care about unAdjusted slaves."

"Makes sense," said Kirtn. "If you're too dumb, mean or stubborn to survive on Loo terms, they don't want you as a slave. You'd be more trouble than you're worth. UnAdjusted."

M/dur snapped his fingers together, the J/taal way of expressing agreement.

"All right," said Rheba. "We're inside the sanctuary, healthy, and willing to eat ashes in order to get out of the Fold. In short, we're Adjusted. How do we get their attention so they'll take us out of here?"

The J/taals exchanged looks, but M/dere remained silent. No one had an answer for Rheba.

Fssa whistled sweetly in her ear. "In the time I've been in the Fold, I've noticed that every thirty-eight days there's a lot of activity around the well. The ceiling changes and people come down. Slaves who are gathered around the well divide into groups. The ceiling comes down again. People and some slaves leave."

"But how are the slaves who leave chosen?"

"I don't know. I could ask Rainbow. It knows a lot of—"

"No!" said Kirtn and Rheba together, not wanting a rebirth of her debilitating headaches. She added, "I doubt if that rock learned anything buried in the ground." Frustration crackled around her in a display of temper that would have brought a rebuke to a much younger fire dancer than she was. "Why in the name of the Inmost Fire didn't Trader Jal teach us something useful?"

"He made it plain that you would have to play more spectacular fire games if you wanted the Loo-chim to buy you," said Kirtn, remembering the Loo-chim's dismissal of her creation of fire images on their transparent chamber walls.

"Fine," she snapped. "But how will that help you to stay with me? How will that help the J/taals to stay with us so we can keep our promise to them? And Fssa? What about him?"

One of the clepts snarled chillingly. M/dur looked up and spotted a small, angular man lurking around the edge of the piece of ground they had marked off as their camp. The clept snarled again, showing a flash of blue-white teeth.

"Please," said the man in hurried Universal. "Not to harm this miserable slave. I'm born of a weak species, no more aggressive than flowers, not a bit."

M/dur looked at Rheba. The J/taal did not understand Universal, and Fssa had not been told to translate for the stranger.

"What do you want?" said Kirtn, standing up.

The man made a low sound of fear as he measured Kirtn's size. He turned to Rheba and said pleadingly, "Gentleher, all I want is out of this kaza-flatching Fold!"

Some of the words might be unfamiliar, but the sentiment was not. Rheba's lips twitched in a barely controlled smile. "Come away from the bush. We won't hurt you." Then, to Fssa, "Translate for the J/taals, snake."

The man came forward with tiny steps, bowing to her every other instant until he looked like a stick bobbing in a wild current. "Gentleher, my name is Yo Kerraton Dapsl. Dapsl, please. So much easier among friends and I very much want to be your friend," he said fervently.

She looked at the small, sticklike figure moving crabwise out of the brush. His skin was very dark, more purple than brown, stretched across bones barely softened by flesh. He stood no higher than her breast, making even the J/taals' compact bodies seem tall. His eyes were the color of white wine, with no pupil. The Fold's murky light seemed far too bright for him. It was a miracle that he had survived the trek from the wall to the well.

"How did you get this far, Dapsl?" said Kirtn, echoing her thoughts.

Dapsl moved in obvious distress, closing his eyes and bowing his head. A clept growled. "I—that is—it was—" He ran his hands over his thin face and frail arms. "It was—I don't—"

"It's all right, Dapsl," she said gently. "It must have been terrible for you, but you survived. You're safe, now."

Dapsl shuddered so violently that his Fold robe quaked. "Yes, that's right," he said quickly. "I survived, didn't I? After all, I'm here so it's obvious that I survived. Yes. Quite clever. Yes."

Rheba looked at the man, then at Kirtn. "He's a little mad, isn't he?" she asked in Senyas.

Two clepts snarled, then howled, watching Dapsl with hungry silver eyes. He made a frightened sound and began muttering prayers to purple gods.

"Silence the clepts," said Rheba to M/dere. "He's about as threatening as a flower."

M/dur muttered to a clept. Fssa's acute hearing translated the comment, but only for Rheba's ear. "He says that he's known some pretty deadly flowers."

"Yes," said Rheba impatiently, "but what can Dapsl do to us here?"

M/dere and M/dur exchanged a long silence, then he made a gesture that was the J/taal equivalent of a shrug. She turned toward Rheba. "Whatever the J/taaleri wishes."

Rheba turned back toward Dapsl. "What do you want from us?"

"A simple exchange, gentleher. My information for a place in your Act."

"I don't understand."

He smiled, revealing ivory teeth. "I know. Is it a bargain, then?"

Kirtn's hand moved to her arm, subtly restraining. "He may be child-sized, and nearly as helpless," whisted Kirtn, "but he plainly is an adult of his species. Don't let your instincts rule you."

She looked into Kirtn's eyes. The impatient comment she had been about to make died on her lips. "Mentor, will I ever stop learning from you?" she whistled in Bre'n.

He smiled and stroked her arm beneath the loose Fold robe. "No one is mentor here. We all learn from each other—or die."

She rubbed her cheek against his shoulder. Dapsl made a sound that could have been distress or disgust. Kirtn looked up with clear golden eyes.

"Is it a bargain?" repeated Dapsl.

"How long have you been in the Fold?" said the Bre'n.

"What do you know about the Loo that might help us? Why can't you help yourself with all your information? Why do you need us?"

An emotion that could have been anger or unhappiness distorted Dapsl's thin face. "If I answer all your questions, I won't have anything to bargain with, will I?"

"If you don't answer some of our questions, you won't have any bargain," shot back Kirtn.

Dapsl hesitated. "My information is good. I've been out of the Fold. I'm back here as . . . punishment. But I know what you need to know. I know how to get out of the Fold!"

"As slaves or as free men?"

Dapsl's laugh was shrill. "Slaves, of course. The only free men who leave here are dead. Didn't you know, furry? There's no escape from the Fold—except one."

Kirtn grunted. "Keep talking, small man. We want to get out of the Fold."

"Then you have to be chosen. And to be chosen, you have to have an Act that is good enough to perform at the Loochim Concatenation."

"What does that mean?"

"Our bargain." The voice was prim, inflexible. "I won't say more without a bargain."

Kirtn and Dapsl stared at each other.

"I could peel the truth from it," said M/dere calmly, her eyes as cold as a clept's. "I could peel it one layer at a time. That wouldn't take long. It's such a little thing."

Fssa's translation went no farther than Rheba's ear. "In return for information," she said hastily, "you want to be part of our Act?"

"Yes," said Dapsl eagerly. "It's my only way out of the Fold."

She stared at Dapsl, weighing him. She closed her eyes. It was easier that way. His voice was adult; his body that of a child. Akhenet instincts were inflexible where children were concerned. "Kirtn?" she whistled. "Shall I put it to a count?"

He whistled a brief note of agreement.

"J/taals," she said. "Count yourselves for and against Dapsl's bargain."

The silence was brief. M/dere spoke, but her eyes were on Dapsl the whole time. "We must have information, J/taalleri. And if he causes trouble, we can always feed him to the clepts."

Dapsl shuddered, for Fssa had made sure that the translation carried to the little man.

"Kirtn?" she asked.

"Yes. We need information."

Fssa whistled a soft affirmative in her ear, a sound both Bre'n and Fssireeme at once.

"Then it's done," she said, turning toward the frail, frightened man. "Your information for a place in our Act—whatever that might be."

Dapsl sighed and sidled closer to her, trying to stay as far away as possible from the clepts and the J/taals. As he sat down next to her, his hand slid up beneath the sleeve of her robe. She flinched away. Instantly two J/taals closed in. Dapsl squeaked.

"Don't sit so close to her," said Kirtn. "And don't touch her at all unless she invites it. Otherwise, you'll make them nervous"—he gestured toward the J/taals—"and me angry. We're very careful of her, you see."

Dapsl licked his lips and looked at the large hand so close to his throat. "Yes, of course, she's something to be careful of, very luxurious, soft and golden." He looked up. "But I'm a man, not a furry. Surely she prefers a man's touch to—ahhhk!"

Kirtn's huge hand closed around Dapsl's robe, lifting him up and then thumping him down on the other side of the Bre'n, away from Rheba. Air whuffed out of the little man's lungs. The J/taals' blue-white smiles flashed as Kirtn bent over the frightened man.

"No," said Rheba gently. "Let me." The fire dancer leaned across Kirtn's lap until her face was on a level with Dapsl's. "You're less attractive to me than those prowling clepts." She pointed to Dapsl's long, intricately braided cranial hair and his smooth, purple-brown skin. "That no more makes you human than Kirtn's beautiful velvet body makes him animal." Her hand caressed Bre'n lips, stroked across his muscular shoulders, savored his textures with obvious pleasure. "Do you understand me, small Dapsl?"

"Perversion," he whispered, swallowing.

Her hair seethed. Fire danced on the fingertips that reached for Dapsl. It was Kirtn who intervened with a clear, derogatory whistle that made Fssa quiver in admiration. The snake hissed soft laughter beneath her restless hair.

She smiled despite her rage, but her voice was not gentle when she spoke. "Don't touch me, Dapsl. Ever. You won't like what happens. If you can't accept that, walk away. Now."

Dapsl's eyes narrowed to pale horizontal slits. She thought

91

suddenly of the J/taal's comments about deadly flowers. Then his eyes relaxed and it was as though the moment of anger had never been.

"I would never touch a female who kaza-flatches," he said, his smile not at all pleasant.

Fssa refused to translate the little man's words when she asked what "kaza-flatch" meant. He directed a burst of sound to Kirtn, however, and his skill was so great that she did not hear kaza-flatch defined. The Bre'n did, however. His hands flexed with eagerness to be around the small man's throat.

"Start talking," snarled the Bre'n, "before you choke on your information."

Dapsl looked at Kirtn's hands and began talking in a high, rapid voice. "All the slaves in the Fold potentially belong to the Loo-chim. But the Loo-chim won't take just any slave. You must have an Act that is good enough to be performed at the Loo-chim Concatenation."

Rheba started to speak.

"It will be quicker if you don't ask questions until I'm finished," said Dapsl sharply. "The buyers come to the Fold, review the Acts, and decide who goes and who stays. Getting out of the Fold is only the first step. Then you have to compete with all your owner's other Acts. Only the top three Acts go to the Concatenation. The rest are broken up and sold to whoever has money to buy. But once you've appeared at the Concatenation, the Act can only be sold as a unit, and can only be bought by a member of the Loo aristocracy—perhaps even the Loo-chim itself. It's a great honor to be owned by the Loo-chim," he added, pride clear in his voice.

Kirtn muttered something graphic and unflattering in Senyas. Fssa translated with embellishments until Rheba shook him and told him to behave. The snake subsided with a flatulent noise directed at Dapsl.

"I don't expect animals to appreciate what I'm saying," Dapsl muttered. "Why didn't Jal send you to the Pit instead of the Fold?"

"Jal?" said Kirtn sharply. "How did you know that we were put here by Trader Jal?"

"Why—ah—it's—" Dapsl squeaked and scuttled away from Kirtn's hands. "It's the talk of the city! Everyone knows that a new gold-masked furry was brought in and that the male polarity is hoping the animal dies before it can practice its furry perversions on the female polarity." He glanced frantically from clepts to J/taals to Kirtn, then moaned and regretted his birth. "Gentleher, please! Control your animals!"

Rheba's eyes glowed with unborn firestorms, but all she said was, "You were speaking of Concatenation, Acts, and aristocracy. Keep talking on those subjects, small man. If you speak about animals again I'll burn your greasy braids off."

"If your Act is good enough to get you out of the Fold, but not good enough to get into the Concatenation, we'll be sold to people too poor to buy machines." Dapsl moaned softly. "It's a terrible loss of caste. And hard, very hard. Even the strongest don't live long. You're crippled in one leg and chained in the other. No escape, no rest." He moaned and put his head in his hands. "No escape, no escape, no . . ."

Rheba sighed and felt her rage drain away. It was hard to be mad at such a pitiful creature. Just because he had the personality of a cherf with a broken tooth was no reason to frighten him half out of his ugly skin. "The Act," she prompted gently. "What makes a good Act?"

"Why, displaying your Talent, of course." Dapsl's voice was high, surprised. "You must have a Talent or you would have been sent to the Pits."

Rheba looked at Kirtn, remembering the female Loo-chim's lust. "Is mating in public considered an Act?" she asked dryly.

Dapsl smiled eagerly. "Oh, yes. When performed by ill-matched animals it's considered a high form of comedy. The Gnigs and the Loradoras, for example. The female is so huge that the male has to—"

Rheba cut him off with a gesture of distaste. "No. That has nothing to do with our Act." She frowned and looked at the J/taals. "M/dere, were you chosen as gladiators?"

"I don't know. When our J/taaleri's ship was captured, we fought until he was killed. Then we were unemployed, and could not fight."

Fssa's murmur continued even after the J/taal woman had stopped talking. "If the slaver saw them fight, I'm sure he brought them here for blood sports."

"Did you fight for the Loo-chim to see?" asked Kirtn.

"No. The slaver merely displayed a construct of his capture of the ship."

"That would be enough," murmured Fssa.

The J/taals did not answer, except to say, "We'll be gladiators for you, if you want. You are the J/taaleri, and fighting is our Talent."

"No," said Rheba quickly. "If the Loo found out that you were employed by me, they would probably kill all of us. Besides, blood sports aren't much better than public mating.

93

I'd rather not have to participate in either." She remembered the J/taal's graceful, swift and intricate exercises. "Gymnasts! I'll make fire shapes, Kirtn will sing, and you'll do a tumbling act." She turned toward Dapsl. "Is that the sort of thing the Loo-chim would enjoy?"

"Too cluttered. Just you and the big furry would be much better."

"No," said Kirtn and Rheba together.

"All of us," she continued, "or none of us. That's the way it is."

Dapsl grimaced. "A variety Act. They're the hardest kind to stage effectively. But," he brightened, "they *are* unusual. Most slaves don't get together. Language problems or fear or both. Yes," he said, absently chewing on the end of one of his thirty-three intricate braids, "it just might work."

"And you," said Kirtn, "what will you do for our Act?"

"Me? Why, I'll manage it, of course."

# XII

"No, no. no!" shouted Dapsl, yanking on a handful of braids in frustration. "All that grunting might impress barbarian enemies, but the Loo-chim will find it extremely unaesthetic. Do it again. *Quietly!*"

M/dur said something that Fssa wisely failed to translate. After the first few days, Rheba had made it clear to the snake that his job was to prevent rather than to incite trouble. So the Fssireeme ignored Dapsl and fluttered a metallic blue ruff that was as functionless as it was pretty. Kirtn smiled, but did not tease Fssa; like the snake, the Bre'n had been on the receiving end of a sharp lecture from Rheba about the necessity of being civilized to one another. Unfortunately, Dapsl had not learned the lesson.

"Ready?" said Dapsl, beating time with two sticks he had scrounged. "On four—a-one and a-two and a-three and a-four."

The J/taals formed a diamond with M/dere in the center. In time with Dapsl's beat, they executed an intricate series of backflips, leaps and lifts that ended in a pyramid that was three J/taals across and two high. On the next beat the pyramid exploded into five J/taals doing individual gymnastics that wove in and out of each other with dazzling ease. At least it appeared easy, and so long as the J/taals smothered grunts of effort, the appearance remained intact.

"Better," said Dapsl grudgingly, "but must you women sweat so much? Ugh. It mats your fur."

In lieu of translating M/dere's response, Fssa preened his sparkling new ruff.

Dapsl sighed and pulled halfheartedly on three of his braids. "Again. On four. This time do it s-l-o-w-l-y. Try to make it appear that you are f-l-o-a-t-i-n-g. And don't frown.

You're enjoying yourselves, remember? Sweating, grunting, grimacing beasts are for the fields, not the Loo-chim stage."

M/Dere snarled and looked toward Rheba, but the fire dancer was deeply involved in building stage props made of flame. She did not notice the J/taal's silent appeal.

When Rheba raised her hands, a line of fire followed, creating an arch. She moved her fingers. Brilliant blue vines writhed up the arch, held trembling for a moment, then exploded into a shower of golden blossoms. The arch became an incandescent cage big enough to hold a Bre'n. Her hands danced, braiding light into silken lines with which to hold a raging beast.

She looked from her creation to Kirtn. The lines changed subtly as she measured them against his breadth and height. Frowning, she looked from the Bre'n to the cage again. She kept misjudging his size: it did not seem reasonable that even a Bre'n should have such wide shoulders. Yesterday she had singed his fur. She had wanted to make the cage out of cold light, but Dapsl had wanted the drama of living flames. She had told him—falsely—that hot fire was nearly impossible for her to make. He had told her that nothing was too much work for a Concatenation Act. She had given in with a silent prayer that the Loo-chim would not be upset by a few tendrils of flame.

Still frowning, she scratched at her arms. The developing lines of power itched constantly, both irritant and warning. She should stop working with fire until her arms healed. A scratching fire dancer was an overworked fire dancer. Deva had pampered its akhenets for practical as well as altruistic reasons. A fatigued akhenet was often irrational, and thereby a danger to everyone.

"A-one and a-two and—no, no, no! Lightly! *Float*, you kaza-flatching mongrels!"

Dapsl's demands were simply a buzzing around the edges of Rheba's concentration. She flexed her fingers. Flames leaped upward, twining into the shape of a demon that was supposed to represent Kirtn. The demon's mouth expanded like death embracing the audience. At this point, Fssa was supposed to give forth some truly curdling sounds, but the snake was too busy translating—selectively—for J/taals and Dapsl.

She sighed and the demon vanished. Idly she began making cool, colored shapes, lithe manikins that imitated the motions of the J/taals. To one side she made a purple light that expanded and contracted with Dapsl's exhortations. The little light bounced madly, trailing purple braids, foaming from its lavender mouth, bouncing higher and higher in an attempt to be impressive in its rage. Farther away, removed from the hubbub, she created a slim silver snake admiring itself in a golden mirror.

Kirtn's chuckle sounded beside her. "I didn't know you could do that."

She glanced up guiltily, caught playing when she should have been working. His hand smoothed her vivid, crackling hair.

"I haven't seen much mimicry since Deva," he said, "when a master dancer would while away the icy night with laughter." His eyes looked inward to a time when Bre'ns and Senyasi had lived in myriads on a world not yet ash.

The figures winked out, leaving only memories like colored echoes behind her eyes. "Deva . . ." she whispered. "Children." Her head bowed, she looked at her glowing hands and arms without seeing their intricate lines of power. "I'm afraid I'll never stop seeing the people. All my potential mates, fathers of my unborn children, standing dazed while the sun poured down, burning . . ." She leaned against Kirtn's hard warmth. "We've got to get out of here. _We've got to find the boy Senyas and his Bre'n_." She looked up at him with eyes that had seen too much fire. "We're akhenet. How can we live without children?"

He pulled her into his lap, stroked her, giving her what comfort he could. Silently he cursed the overriding need for children that had been built into Bre'ns and Senyasi alike, instinct squared and then squared again, that akhenets would not become so bound to their cross-species mate that they refused to mate with their own kind. Bre'n and Senyas akhenets alike had nearly died out before a gene dancer had been born who could substitute instinct for personal preference. Myth had it that the gene dancer was neither Bre'n nor Senyas, but both, one of the few viable hybrids ever conceived between the two species.

He wished he could share his knowledge with Rheba, giving her some of the history she had lost, helping her to understand the needs built into her . . . but she was too young. She had not yet discovered the depth of Bre'n/Senyas sharing. Despite her forced maturity since Deva died, she had shown no interest in him as a man, nothing but tantalizing flashes of sensuality that also were part of a fire dancer's genetic heritage. It was possible that she would never turn to him as a lover. Not all akhenet pairs mated physically as well

97

as mentally. But of those mismatched pairs, few lived long or easy lives. Bre'ns in *rez* were an indiscriminate destructive force.

Pushing aside his bleak thoughts, Kirtn whistled sweetly, softly, coaxing her out of her despair. Another whistle joined his in sliding harmony. He felt Fssa coiling around his arm. The snake wove from there into Rheba's hair and began singing into her ear. Some of the tension gradually left her body. She smoothed her cheek against Kirtn's chest, shifting her weight until she fitted perfectly against him. Her hair lifted and curled around his neck, hair that was silky and warm and alive as only a fire dancer's could be. Though she did not know it, the soft strands wrapping around him made a fire dancer's caress that was usually reserved for lovers. She did not know, and there was no one left alive to tell her except Kirtn—and he could not.

"If you're quite through," said Dapsl indignantly, "I need that bizarre snake. The J/taals pretend not to understand me unless that slimy article wrapped around your arm talks to them."

Rheba felt Kirtn's muscles tense as he gathered himself to lunge. For an instant she was tempted to let him shred Dapsl into oozing purple fragments, but the instant passed. Even the youngest fire dancers learned that an akhenet *never* abetted Bre'n anger. She allowed electrical impulses to leak from her body wherever she touched Kirtn, disrupting his muscle control. At first he fought her, then he gave in.

Deliberately, she stroked Fssa. The snake was dark where he had been incandescent. She had discovered that the darker forms of Fssireeme, as well as being a heat-conservation mode, indicated shame, embarrassment, or discomfort.

Dapsl reached to snatch away the snake. Kirtn's big hand shot out. Dapsl squeaked and tried to pull back, but the Bren's grip on his lower arm was too firm.

"If I squeeze," said Kirtn conversationally, "you'll lose your arm from the second elbow down. Stand still. Apologize to Fssa."

Dapsl stood. He apologized.

"Now, tell him he's beautiful."

"That thing? Beautiful? I've seen prettier mudholes! In fact—"

Dapsl's arm turned pale lavender where the Bre'ns fingers were. "Tell him," said Kirtn gently, "that he's beautiful."

"You're beautiful, lovely, perfect," Dapsl said hastily. With each word he eased more of his arm out of Kirtn's grasp.

98

"You can't help it if you were born without legs. Be grateful," he said triumphantly, jerking free of the Bre'n, "you weren't born with stinking fur all over your animal hide!"

Rheba came to her feet in a lithe rush that reminded Kirtn of the J/taals. Fire blazed from her hands, licking toward Dapsl with hot intent.

"Our bargain!" said Dapsl, backing away quickly. "Stay away from me!"

"Fire dancer." Kirtn spoke in Senyas, his words precise, his tone that of a mentor.

She stopped. Flames licked restlessly up and down her arms, and her hands shone with dense lines of gold. With a long sigh, she released the flames.

"If you hadn't been so stubborn," said Dapsl in a high voice, "about committing kaza-flatch on stage with your furry pet, none of this would have been necessary. The female Loo-chim would have leaped up onstage with you. Your problems would have been over! You and your pet would never be separated, because not even the Loo-chim would break up a Concatenation Act. But no, you have to hold out for *group* kaza-flatch, and I tell you right now, you tight-rumped little—"

Whatever Dapsl had been about to say was forgotten in his rush to evade Kirtn's feint. Rheba and the Bre'n watched as the small purple man raced back to the J/taals. After a few moments, Fssa followed, coiling through the dust like a cobalt whip.

"If I cooked him first," she said tightly, "do you think the clepts would eat him?"

"They don't eat carrion."

She sighed. "Even if I burned off his oily braids?"

"Doubt it."

"Damn." She scratched her arms absently. The elbows were particularly itchy. She longed for some salve, but it was aboard the *Devalon*, as out of reach as Deva itself.

"On the count of four." Dapsl's irritating command and Fssa's soft translation came across the campsite. "A-one and—"

"He may be a limp stick," she said, "but he knows what he's doing. Our Act would have been chaos without him. That doesn't mean I like the cherf."

Kirtn's long fingers rubbed through her hair, massaging her scalp until she sighed with pleasure. "Once we're out of here," he said, "we'll shed Dapsl like a winter coat."

She arched against his strong hands. Her hair shimmered

with pleasure, curling around his arms, mutely demanding that he continue. He laughed softly and extricated himself before she could sense his reponse to her innocent sensuality. "Back to work, akhenet. And this time, please, make the cage big enough."

She groaned. "How many more days before the buyers arrive?"

"Three, if Dapsl's memory is right."

"It would be the first thing right about him." She stretched languidly, rubbing her shoulders against her Bre'n. "Itches."

"All the way up there?" he asked, concerned. His hands slid beneath her Fold robe. Gently he explored her shoulders and neck with his fingertips. Lines of power radiated faintly beneath his touch. "Too soon . . ." he whispered. "Slow down, fire dancer. Don't burn so hard."

For a moment she leaned her weight against him, letting down barriers of instinct and discipline until he could sense the exhaustion and despair that lapped like a black ocean just beyond the shores of her control. He closed his eyes, accepting her emotions until the edge of his mind overlapped hers lightly, very lightly. Then he let strength flow into her, a coolness that washed over the intricate patterns covering her arms, calm radiating through her from the Bre'n hands touching her skin. The shores of her control expanded, throwing back the black ocean.

"I didn't know you could do that," she murmured. "Thank you, mentor."

"I didn't do it. We did. You're changing so quickly, little dancer," he said, his voice divided between hope and fear. "Sharing strength is just one thing a Bre'n does for a Senyas. Just one small thing."

"What do you get in return?"

He hesitated, wondering if it was too soon, too much. In the end he gave her only half the truth, and not the most revealing half. "A channel."

"Channel?"

"An outlet for Bre'n emotions, Bre'n energy."

"*Rez,*" she whispered, shivering beneath his hands.

"No," he said fiercely. "I'll never do that to you."

She did not argue. Both of them knew that *rez* was a reflex, not a choice. Kirtn would do what he had to. He was Bre'n. And she was Senyas. She forced a smile.

"Stand over there," she said, pointing to a bush, "and I'll see if I can build a cage big enough to hold a Bre'n."

# XIII

Rheba awoke with a headache that made her want to weep. Overhead, the Fold's ceiling was dull gray with a hint of brass, an hour away from full light. She shivered, rearranged her robe, and snuggled closer to Kirtn's warmth. He shifted in his sleep, gathering her against him. She rubbed her cheek against the velvet of his chest fur, wishing her back could be as warm as her front. It seemed that she had been cold since she landed on Loo.

Her headache redoubled, faded, then returned. Kirtn awoke with a grimace, though his headache was but a shadow of hers. "Fssa. Where is that damned snake? Is he talking to Rainbow again?"

She looked around, then felt carefully through her hair. "Gone," she groaned.

He sat up. "When I get my hands on that Fssireeme I'll bend him into a new shape!"

The headache diminished. She sighed and felt herself go limp in response to less pain. At the same instant, both she and Kirtn spotted Fssa coiling across the dark ground. He sparked silver and copper, gold and steel. He was beautiful—when he was not splitting her brain.

"Fssa." Kirtn's hand swept out to scoop up the snake. "I told you what I'd do if you caused Rheba pain again!"

Fssa turned black and hung limply from Kirtn's hand. The Bre'n gave him an impatient shake. The snake remained limp and very, very black.

"What is it about Rainbow that's so irresistible?" demanded the Bre'n.

Fssa's whistle was pure and beguiling. "It's so old, friend Kirtn. It's older than my guardians' memories. It's older even than the Long Memory." The snake's body changed, more pearl than black, streaks of gold dividing the most dense ar-

101

eas of gray. The whistle became eager. "It knows more than I dreamed was possible. Languages," the whistle soared ecstatically, "languages that were extinct before the Long Memory, and languages to me are like fire to you. And Rainbow knows fragments of other things, but I can't make those fragments whole. The languages, though—I can make them whole for Rainbow and then it's more at ease. It's lost so much of its knowledge. It's had pieces of itself broken off and scattered, made into baubles for two-legged idiots."

Rheba's curiosity grew as her pain diminished. "How old is Rainbow? Is it one of the First People?"

Fssa's whistle was tentative, then slid into a negative. "I don't think so. Its energy is similar in some ways, but it was created by man. At least it says it was, and I can't think why a rock would lie."

"Created." Kirtn frowned. "When? By whom? For what?"

Fssa changed colors, becoming lighter, rippling with confidence now that his friends were no longer angry. "Rainbow was made by the—" An impossible sound came out, one that meant nothing to his listeners. The Fssireeme became darker with embarrassment. "Names are very hard to translate. I think you would call it Zaarain. Does that sound right?"

Kirtn and Rheba looked at one another. "We know the name," said Kirtn finally, "but are you sure?"

"That's the only possible translation of Rainbow's frequency, especially since it used the *kfxzt* modulation. It's a difficult modulation to reproduce," whistled Fssa, his tone divided equally between earnestness and pride. "I'm the first one who has talked to Rainbow for a long, long time."

Rheba shook herself as though waking from a dream. "Zaarain . . . if the Loo-chim find out, Rainbow will be taken away."

"But—but—" Fssa writhed, then changed into his Senyas mode and spoke with precision, as though to be sure there could be no possibility of misunderstanding. "But no one else can talk to Rainbow. *It needs to communicate.*" Fssa writhed, so upset that he could not hold his Senyas shape. "It was made to be a—library? Yes, that's close enough—library, and it needs to communicate with intelligent minds," he whistled urgently.

She winced and covered her ears at the shrillness of Fssa's tone. "It may need to communicate, but that hurts! Shut up, snake!"

Fssa's volume diminished. "I, too, was lonely for a long time," he whistled in oblique apology/appeal.

Kirtn looked over to the lump of gleaming darkness that was Rainbow at night. "Library?" he murmured. "A Zaarain library? What wonders could it tell us?"

Fssa sighed, a long susurration. "A fragment of a library," he amended. "It used to be much larger. It was looted from an old installation and broken into trinkets for barbarians."

"How big was it before that?" asked Kirtn.

Copper streaks rippled through Fssa in his equivalent of a shrug. "At least as big as the blue well. Perhaps bigger. Rainbow isn't sure. It's just a conglomeration of random fragments, not even a whole segment of the original library. It barely gets enough energy to hold itself together, now that it's no longer connected."

"Still," said Kirtn, "a Zaarain library . . ."

"A Zaarain headache, you mean," she said, rubbing her temples. "I hope the damn thing doesn't talk in its sleep."

"It doesn't sleep," said Fssa primly. "And it won't talk unless you ask a question or scare it to death by threatening dismemberment as those children did."

"Good. Then if I get a headache, I'll know that it's your fault for asking questions."

Fssa's glitter faded into dark gray. "Could you . . ." His whistle was tremulous, then it broke. He started over again. "Would you include it in our Act? Otherwise we'll have to leave it here, or some Loo will discover it and hack it up into jewelry and it will die. Please, Rheba? Surely a creature as beautiful and warm as you can find room in your emotions for a lonely crystal."

She stared at Fssa, then laughed. "Don't flatter me, snake. When it comes to beauty, I'm a distinct fourth to you, Kirtn, and that Zaarain rock."

Fssa waited. Slow ripples of black consumed his brilliance as the silence stretched into seconds, moments, a minute.

"Ice and ashes!" snarled Rheba. "Brighten up, snake. We'll fit that damn mind breaker into our Act."

"What will you tell Dapsl?" said Kirtn, smiling at how the snake had won.

She smiled in return, but not pleasantly. "Nothing. If he objects, I'll burn the braids right off his head."

Fssa suddenly shone with bright metal colors. He puffed out his most incredible ruff in a shower of glitter. "Thank you!" he whistled exultantly.

Kirtn laughed. "Too bad Rainbow doesn't have as many shapes as you—then it would be easy to put in the Act."

The ruff vanished in a flash of silver. "I think—" He began

to change into his Rainbow communication mode, then turned his sensors on Rheba hesitantly. "I think Rainbow can make different shapes. It's just an assembly of fragments, after all. If it assembled itself, it can unassemble itself. Should I ask?"

She groaned and glared at Kirtn. "What shape did you have in mind for the Act?"

"Oh . . . a crown, a necklace. Something bright and barbarous for me to wear," said Kirtn. "I'm supposed to be a vicious demon king, after all, according to Dapsl's Act."

She frowned. "That might work. We'll tell Dapsl that Rainbow is one of the First People, and thus a legitimate, intelligent part of the Act. Then no one could take it away from us, once we appeared in the Concatenation. But—ice and ashes! How I wish that rock didn't split my mind!"

Fssa waited, a study in subdued metal colors.

She ground her teeth. "All right. Ask it. But make it short."

Fssa whipped into his Rainbow communication mode. She closed her eyes and tried to ignore the lightning that lanced through her brain while Fssireeme and the Zaarain library talked. As she had hoped, the exchange was brief. She opened her eyes and stared coldly at Fssa, her head still shattered by alien modulations.

"Rainbow doesn't want to rearrange itself, but it will. It's terrified of dismemberment, you realize."

"Yes," she said grimly. "I understand. If you hadn't told me it was alive, I'd have torn it facet from facet the first time it curdled my brain."

Fssa's sensors winked as he ducked and turned his head: "It's very sorry that it hurts you. We've tried to find a frequency that doesn't, but we haven't been successful."

She sighed. "I noticed."

From across the camp, the J/taals stirred. If they were bothered by headaches, they gave no sign. Dapsl rolled out from beneath his robe, shrugged into it, and began cursing the clepts. The ceiling turned to sullen brass, then slowly began bleaching into smoky white.

"Another day," muttered Kirtn, flexing his hands suddenly. "I don't like being a slave, fire dancer."

"I'm unAdjusted myself," she said, watching Dapsl stalk over to the blue fountain to drink. "When I think that animated purple ashcan is considered human and you aren't—" She did not finish. Nor did she have to.

Suddenly her hair leaped and writhed like dry leaves

caught in a firestorm. She staggered, her eyes blind cinnamon jewels alive with energy.

"What—?" Kirtn caught her and tried to calm her frantically lashing hair. "Rheba!"

She did not answer nor even hear. She was caught in a vortex of energy building, twisting, spinning rapidly and then more rapidly until it was a solid cone of raw power dipping down from the ceiling. Abruptly, the turmoil ceased. A large group of people stood by the well. They were richly dressed, arrogant of expression, and Loo to the last tint of blue in their skins.

"The buyers," said Kirtn, shaking Rheba. "Fire dancer. *Fire dancer!*"

His command for attention ripped through her daze. She blinked, held by untrammeled energy that had come down, touched. She stretched yearningly toward the ceiling, as though she would touch it with her fingertips. Her hair crackled with the wild power of a fire dancer who was overflowing with energy. Then she turned toward the Bre'n, who watched her with concern shadowing his yellow eyes.

"I'm all right," she murmured, smiling dreamily. "That felt . . . good. I'm renewed. I haven't felt like that since I sat in the center of a fire dancer circle."

Slowly, Kirtn's concern became relief. "Good. But be careful. Energy like that can ruin you as quickly as it can renew you."

She blinked again, as though awakening after a long sleep. "There would be worse ways to die. I wonder if that's what the other dancers felt when the sun bent down and seared them to the bone. . . ."

Dapsl's screech cut through the air. "Line up! Line up! The buyers are here! Line up!"

Four guards stepped out from behind the group of buyers. In clipped Universal, they spelled out the rules of what was to come. The ceiling amplified their voices so that everyone within the two-circles sanctuary could not avoid hearing the words.

"You will perform your Acts for the buyers within that circle." An area the size of a large Loo stage suddenly glowed in front of the well. "Those Acts that are chosen will leave with their buyers. Line up!"

People from all over the sanctuary began walking toward the well. Within minutes, nearly one hundred people had gathered. Rheba and Kirtn stared, for they had not seen a quarter of that number coming and going from the well. All of the people appeared healthy—at least, they moved easily enough. She counted fourteen distinct racial types before she gave up. Then with a sudden surge of hope she looked among the people again. As though he shared her thought, Kirtn stared through narrowed eyes. But no matter how hard they both searched, they saw no one that resembled either Senyas or Bre'n.

Dapsl's shrill enjoinders to action grated on their ears. "Get that snake under control before someone steps on it and ruins our Act. You—Kirtn! Listen to me! Be sure those clepts stay out of the way during the Act!"

Kirtn ignored the little purple man and picked up Rainbow. It disassembled in his hands. Crystal faces shifted slowly, as though pulled by magnets, then reformed along new alignments. When it was finished, Rainbow looked like a rough crown. New facets glittered in the light in a suitably barbarous display. Some of the facets were patterned with engravings. All were vivid, colorful.

"Good for you," muttered Kirtn, although he doubted Rainbow could understand him. Gently, he set the crown on his head. Rainbow shifted subtly, fitting his head with a grip that was both secure and comfortable. Very soon Kirtn no more noticed Rainbow's presence on his head than Rheba noticed Fssa's presence in her hair.

The clepts moved between Rheba and the watching Loos.

"The clepts!" shrieked Dapsl. He turned on Rheba and the snake, who was invisibly woven into her hair. "Get those kaza-flatching clepts out of the way!"

Her lips parted in a smile that was more warning than reassurance. "The clepts are part of the Act."

"But they can't—we haven't practiced—it's impossible!"

"They worked while you slept. Whether the results please you or not, they are part of the J/taals and therefore part of our Act. Now shut up, little man. If Fssa can overhear the Loo buyers—" Abruptly she stopped speaking. Dapsl did not know the extent of the Fssireeme's skill. Nor did she want the irksome little man to find out. She did not trust him. He thought like a slave and she did not.

Dapsl chewed angrily on the frayed end of his longest braid, muttered a comment in a language that Fssa did not know and went back to harrying the J/taals. Beneath the cover of Rheba's hair, the snake transformed a part of himself into a sensitive receiver aimed at the gathering of Loos.

"Can you hear anything?" she murmured, her voice so low that it was little more than a vibration in her throat.

106

Fssa, who had left a coil of himself around her neck, picked up the vibrations as easily as he did her normal speech. He could speak in a soft whistle to her, listen to her answer, and still not lose track of the Loo conversations. He shifted, reforming the listening extension of himself until it bloomed like a spiky silver flower below her left ear. "Nothing yet. I'll try a different mode." The flower widened, petals reaching toward the Loo. "Got them!"

She was silent then, letting Fssa drink up every foreign syllable he could.

"Line up!" snapped Dapsl. "Only an unAdjusted slave would keep a Loo waiting. These buyers are aristocrats only one birth away from the Imperial Loo-chim."

As though summoned by Dapsl's words, the Loos walked forward, pacing the line of waiting slaves like generals reviewing troops. At intervals one or another of the Loo signaled. The guards stepped forward then and summarily removed one or more slaves from the line of hopeful Acts.

"Rejects," hissed Dapsl. "Their smell probably offended, or their color, or perhaps the Loos are merely bored with that particular race. Get those kaza-flatching clepts in line!"

Rheba ignored Dapsl's nervous dithering and watched the approaching Loos. Their flimsy robes turned and flashed in the cold sunlight, revealing embroideries in tiny precious stones across the very sheer cloth. She wanted to believe that the robes were barbaric, but could not. Like the room where she and Kirtn had first seen the Imperial Loo-chim, the robes were luxuriant without being crass.

Two by two the traders passed, each pair composed of a chim, a man and a woman so like each other as to be identical twins. Rheba looked at their faces—shades of blue, broad-cheeked, high-nosed, arrogant. There was neither sympathy nor simple interest in those paired dark eyes, until the eleventh buyer, a male with no twin female on his right hand.

"Jal," breathed Rheba. *"Trader Jal!"*

# XIV

Jal smiled and bowed sardonically. "Lord Jal," he correct-ed. "All buyers in the Fold are lords and ladies of Loo."

Rheba looked from Jal to the blue-skinned pairs appraising the ranks of slaves. "But there's just one of you."

Jal's expression revealed a loss so terrible it almost made her forget how cruelly he had used her and Kirtn. She under-stood what it was to have everything and then lose it in a single irrevocable instant. She looked away, unable to face herself reflected in his dark eyes.

"My chim died," said Jal. It was all he said. It was enough. He looked coldly at Dapsl. "What's this, Whip? A me-nagerie?"

"An Act, my lord," Dapsl said quickly, bowing so low that his purple braids danced in the dust. "A unique Act for the amusement of the Loo-chim and the lords and ladies. We have a story to tell in song and motion that will make you laugh and cry and sigh with wonder. It's the tale of—"

Jal cut off Dapsl's prepared speech with a curt motion. The Loo lord who had been known to them as Trader Jal looked over the gathering of Bre'n and Senyas, Fssireeme, and J/taals and clepts. An expression that could have been rage distorted his features. "*All* of you?" He moved as though to motion the rejection of J/taals and clepts.

"Lord—" said Dapsl softly, urgently, twisting his braids in distress. "Lord, this is a unique Act, one that will gain you much pride at the Concatenation, and much wealth after-ward. Before you decide, please, let us perform."

Lord Jal looked at Dapsl for one long, unwavering mo-ment. The small man tugged silently at his braids, holding Jal's eyes for an instant, looking away, then looking back with silent pleas.

"Done," said Jal. "But if I don't like the Act, Dapsl, you will never leave the Fold."

Dapsl made a small sound of despair and looked at Rheba. "Please," he said, speaking so quickly that his words tumbled over one another, "please think again about including the animals. Just you and the big furry, a single dance of kazaflatch, even the songs. Yes—the songs. You can even keep the snake. No one will notice and then I'll—"

"No." Rheba's voice was as smooth and hard as a river stone.

Dapsl wilted. He glanced at Lord Jal, but found no comfort in that broad blue face.

The lords finished their review of the slaves. Whether they had previously divided the slaves among the aristocracy, or whether each chim only reviewed slaves it had captured, no one else spoke to or even looked at the Act that included Rheba and Kirtn. When the lords turned away and walked back toward the blue chairs that had appeared along one curve of the stage, Rheba let out her breath in a sigh. Kirtn looked over and touched her arm in mute understanding. Each had been afraid of being rejected for no better reason than the whim of one of the blue chims.

Dapsl waited until the chims had withdrawn beyond the range of normal hearing. Then he turned on Rheba. His voice was so tight with rage that it squeaked. "If your perverted tastes have cost me my freedom, I'll make your life as short as your ugly little nose!"

Rheba looked at Dapsl's own long, slender nose. It was quivering with his bottled rage. She smiled. "You're a Fold slave. You couldn't leave the Fold without an Act. How am I responsible for your freedom or lack of it?"

"Because Lord Jal sent me here to help you, you ungrateful kaza-flatch!" He breathed deeply. "Now, bitch, stand here and watch the Acts. There shouldn't be any real competition here, but watch anyway. You're so stupid that anything you learn has to be an improvement!"

Kirtn's hand dropped onto Dapsl's shoulder. The touch was gentle. The possibilities were not. "Cherf," said Kirtn, "I'm tired of your voice."

Dapsl's small face turned unusually purple but he said nothing more. Instead, he pointed toward the stage. One of the groups had walked into the half-circle reserved for the Acts. The lords and ladies conferred among themselves briefly, then a chim waved for the Act to begin.

There were three people standing on the Act place, facing

the semicircle of indifferent chims. The three were smooth-skinned, with an abundance of red hair that grew like a crest down the median line of the skull and fell in long waves down the back to the hips. They were not obviously male or female, and alike enough to be clones. At an unseen signal they began to sing. Their voices were pleasant, their harmony good, and their songs . . . uninteresting. The beat was invariable, more like a chant than anything else. Like the red crest flowing to their hips, the trio's songs were not far removed from barbarism. After the third song, one chim snapped its fingers suddenly. Another chim leaned closer to the first and began speaking in low voices.

Rheba felt Fssa stretch toward the conversation with senses that were far more acute than any human and most machines. She waited with outward patience, as did everyone else, while the chims talked. At last she dared a soft whisper to Dapsl.

"What's going on?"

Dapsl answered without moving his head to look at her. Even his lips barely moved. His voice was softer than hers. "The chim who captured this trio revoked Concatenation hold."

"Explain."

The small man's eyes flicked to Rheba at her curt demand, but his face did not turn. "All Fold slaves are potential Concatenation Acts. The chim just signaled that it no longer believes this captured trio good enough for the Concatenation. You see, each chim can enter only three Acts at the Concatenation."

"Is that other chim trying to buy them for its own Acts?"

Dapsl made a sound of disgust. "No chim would buy another's rejected Act. They'll be sold for pleasure or work or pain, whichever the buyer wants." He looked critically at the three. "Separately, they might be quite a novelty among kaza-flatchers. That hair has possibilities. . . ."

Rheba did not ask what the possibilities were. She was sorry she had asked anything at all. She watched while the two chims bargained over the three slaves. Then, apparently, a deal was struck. Two guards stepped forward and separated a pair of red-haired barbarians, leaving one behind.

At first the slaves seemed too stunned to respond. Then they realized that they were being sold separately, and not as an Act. They turned to the chim who had first enslaved them and spoke rapidly in a language that Fssa either did not know or did not want to translate. Their voices became thin-

110

ner and higher, more desperate, but neither the chim who had enslaved them nor the chim who had bought them seemed to notice.

The ceiling came down in a simple flick of power that licked up one guard and two barbarians in the time it took to blink. When the remaining barbarian realized what had happened, he went berserk. His scream of rage and pain made Rheba's hair stir in reflexive sympathy to another creature's agony. Before the cry was complete, he leaped at his guard. His unsheathed claws seemed to gather light at their sharp tips.

There was a surge of energy from the ceiling. The barbarian froze in mid-leap, feet off the ground, claws extended, screaming silently, imprisoned in a column of raw light. His hair rippled and writhed, replicating the currents that tormented him. His lips peeled back, revealing serrated teeth and a tongue that bled from being bitten through in the first instant of agony. But the blood never touched the ground and the screams were silent, imprisoned in the column as surely as he was.

"Stupid," said Dapsl, watching the barbarian writhing silently, tortured and held by currents of pure force. "He was told not to attack anything within the two circles. Now he knows why."

"Will they kill him?" said Kirtn, his own lips peeled back in a silent snarl.

"Oh, no. They don't have their price for him yet."

Rheba shuddered and willed herself not to collect any of the energy that seethed around the barbarian. She thought she could bleed off some, perhaps even enough to prevent his torture, but she suspected that if she was discovered it would be her death sentence. Yet she did not know how much longer she could watch and do nothing.

"No," continued Dapsl, "they won't kill him. They won't even damage him."

The column of energy sucked back into the ceiling with no more warning than it had come down. The barbarian fell to the stage in a boneless sprawl. The guard who had been attacked looked at the chim who had bought the barbarian. The chim spoke softly. The guard picked up the barbarian, waited an instant, and the ceiling came down again.

The two remaining guards brought out the next Act. The rest of the slaves stood without moving, afraid even to breathe. Rheba remembered the time she had first entered the

111

two circles, when she had considered attacking the guards at the well. She was profoundly glad that she had not.

The guards stepped off the stage, leaving behind four small people who looked like racial cousins of Dapsl. From their hair they drew long purple strands, wove them together with dazzling speed, and presented for the chims' inspection a hand-sized tapestry.

"Is weaving considered an Act?" asked Kirtn, his voice too low to carry beyond Dapsl's ears.

"Any skill can be made into an Act. Namerta," he added, "Is known for its weavers." He stroked his intricately braided hair with pride.

The various chims fingered the Namertan's creation. Special care was taken by the chim who had captured the Namertans. That chim stroked, examined, and picked at the hand-sized patch, then spoke to the guards. The ceiling flexed and the Namertans vanished.

"Accepted," said Dapsl, his face proud. "Namertans are almost always taken to the Concatenation. No other race can equal our skill at weaving." He added a phrase in his own language.

Rheba hummed to Fssa, but the snake still did not have enough clues to unravel Dapsl's speech. The Fssireeme darkened with embarrassment for an instant.

"You're beautiful," whispered Rheba. "Do you have the Loo language yet?"

"Almost," he whistled very softly, brightening. "There are at least four forms of it and not much relation between them."

"Slave, master, middleman and equal," guessed Rheba.

Fssa hissed soft agreement.

The next act was a very pale-skinned male. His features seemed neither handsome nor ugly, just as he was neither tall nor short. He looked so unremarkable that Rheba found herself wondering what he could possibly do that would be up to the standards of a Concatenation Act.

Then the man changed before her eyes. He became taller, broader, darker, velvet-textured. His eyes burned gold in a golden mask. He seemed to reach out to her, compelling her body to respond to him. Soon he would touch her and she would burst into flame, touching him, igniting him until they burned together in a consummation of passion that she could not imagine, much less understand.

With a moan, she forced herself to look away.

"What is it?" asked Kirtn, touching her. Her skin seared

112

his fingertips with a kind of heat she should not have generated at her age. His own response was instantaneous, almost uncontrollable, a reflex as ingrained as hunger. But he was Bre'n, and must control the sensual heat that would otherwise destroy them both. Too soon. Everything had happened too quickly after Deva. "Rheba!"

Kirtn's harsh whisper broke the Act's hold on her. She shuddered. Heat drained from her skin, bleaching the patterns of power. "I'm—all right," she said, breathing brokenly. "I don't—I don't know what happened."

Kirtn knew; dreams of just such an awakening on her part had haunted him more frequently of late. Yet she was at least ten years too young; and she had neither Senyas mother nor Bre'n sister to gently lead her to understanding.

Dapsl looked over at her. When he saw her flushed face, he smiled. "So you can respond to something besides a furry—or did he look like a furry to you?" His smile widened at her confusion. "Is that the first time you've seen a Yhelle illusionist? His Talent is unusual, even among the Yhelle. He makes you see whatever would most inflame you sexually." Dapsl looked around the audience. "He's not very good, though. Only the women responded. And you were able to break his illusion. He's probably too young for full control."

Apparently the Loo lords agreed. There was a brisk bargaining session but apparently no price was reached. The guard led the illusionist out of the circle and abandoned him. The man hesitated, then walked back to wherever he had come from before the Loo lords had condensed out of the Fold's ceiling.

Dapsl made a satisfied sound. "Next time he'll be ready. He'll be able to reach men as well as women. Then he'll be a prize for any chim to buy and use."

Rheba looked at the ground and hoped she would never again be within range of the man's illusions. She had known pleasure and laughter and simple release with her Senyas friends, but she had never suspected the existence of such consummation as she had seen in him. She wondered how much had been illusion, how much a reality latent within her that she had not yet experienced. She wondered . . . but was oddly reluctant to ask the only one who might be able to answer her. Kirtn.

The guard stopped in front of Dapsl and spoke curtly. Rheba did not need Dapsl's translation to know that it was their turn on the stage. She wiped the illusionist from her mind, thinking only of the Act.

113

# XV

Dapsl bowed low to the Loo lords and ladies. His braids brushed his bare feet and the hard-packed earth of the stage. "Lords and ladies," he said, his voice ringing, "I have a tale for your astonishment and amusement, a tale about a time long ago when demons were kings and the Devil God created the First Woman as punishment to an unruly king."

Kirtn listened to Dapsl with only half his attention. The first few times he had heard the Loo's creation myth, he had been amused: at one time in the past, the Loo had apparently gone furred; even today it was whispered that some children were born with pelt rather than smooth blue skin. Those secret children were the legacy of the First Woman's victory over the Demon King.

"—came to the furred king. He was strong and fierce, his minions were swift and vicious—"

On cue, the J/taals and their clepts swept into the ring in a leaping, swirling entrance that required both strength and split-instant timing. The five J/taals moved as one, doing back flips and somersaults while the clepts wove through with fangs flashing. The clepts appeared on the edge of wounding the J/taals—and that would have happened, had not the timing been perfect.

There was a final, closely choreographed burst of movement, then J/taals and clepts froze into a savage tableau, animal fangs echoed by the shine of J/taal teeth.

"—Demon King had heard of the Woman made by the Devil God. The King had been told that if he conquered her, she would give him a furred male child who would rule the world. But if she conquered him, her children would be two, and smooth, founders of a superior race.

"He was only an animal, a demon. The thought of siring his superiors enraged him."

Lord Jal snapped his fingers twice. Instantly Dapsl speeded the presentation. "In time, he succeeded in capturing the Woman. Capturing, but not conquering."

Rheba felt a quick pressure on her hand as Kirtn strode away on cue toward the stage. When he was inside the circle, Fssa began creating soul-curdling sounds, as though a gathering of demons dined on living flesh. The snake projected the sounds so that they seemed to come from Kirtn. For her part, Rheba concentrated on Kirtn's body, changing the quality of the air around him until he seemed to walk wrapped in sable smoke that licked out toward the audience.

While the Loo's attention was on Kirtn, she stole onto the stage. She stood close to him, looking angry, wrapped in thin flickers of flame. A leash of black connected her to him, but the leash was no more substantial than the smoke that clung to his copper body. Fssa produced sweet cries of distress for her to mouth, sounds that would have wrung compassion from any audience but Loo-chims.

The next part of the Act was supposed to be a ballet of advance and retreat where the J/taals menaced and tormented the First Woman while the Demon King watched. Dapsl, however, did not give the cue. He summarized swiftly, then cued in the culmination of the battle between Woman and Demon. Because he had warned the Act that the performance might be shortened at the whim of the Loo, they were ready. Rheba formed balls of blue energy and flicked them at the J/taals and their clepts. They froze in place, paralyzed by cobalt light.

With the "minions" disposed of, she advanced on Kirtn. Her footsteps were outlined in red flames, and fire leaped from her flying hair as she sought to change his demon soul, thus making him a fit mate for her. A demon head grew out of Kirtn's skull. The ferocious face expanded and expanded until its mouth was large enough to devour the stage. Out of that mouth—courtesy of Fssa—rose a caterwauling that was enough to freeze the core of a sun.

A cage of fire sprang up around Kirtn. He struggled terribly against it, but could not break free. It was a difficult part of the Act for Rheba; she had to sustain the cold blue fire around the minions, the rippling demon head that filled the stage, and the moving cage of hot fire around Kirtn.

Fssa switched from screaming to a pure whistle that was like water in the desert to the listening chims. The whistle was the opening note of a Bre'n courtship song, but such was its power that people of all races were compelled by it. Had

115

Rheba not been so busy holding various kinds of fire, she would have sung the female part of the duet. As it was, the notes only seemed to come from her lips.

Slowly, as though drawn against his will, Kirtn stopped struggling. The demon head above him waxed and waned, changing with each beat of song until the grim mouth closed with a long series of moans which were also supplied by Fssa.

Rheba felt the snake change to meet each need of the Act, at the same time holding his surface color so that he exactly matched her hair. Fssa was justifiably proud of his performance. Neither whistle nor demon cries could be traced to the hidden Fssireeme.

The demon head puffed out, releasing one drain on Rheba's energies. Kirtn appeared to test his immaterial cage. It held, and he howled in fear. Still Fssa/Rheba whistled beguiling notes that danced like moonlight on a waterfall, presaging the fiery dawn yet to come. Unwillingly, the Demon King answered.

When Kirtn's lilting whistle slid into harmony, weaving a world of sensual possibilities out of pure song, the Loos stirred and leaned forward. The contrast between the savage Act and the lyrical duet was so great that it was almost incomprehensible. Even Lord Jal seemed caught, body keeping time to alien rhythms, imprisoned by uncanny music.

The fire that had flickered over Rheba's body leaped forward, joining with Kirtn's cage in a soundless explosion. The duet simultaneously reached its peak. Then Fssa/Rheba sang alone, coaxingly, luring the Demon King, promising him ease and beauty in marriage to the First Woman. Step by slow step, the Demon King crossed the ground separating him from the First Woman, drawn by a passion that consumed him. She waited, arms raised, demanding and inviting his touch. Then his arms folded around her and he bent toward her.

For a moment all Rheba could see was his gold eyes burning over her, head bending down, arms hard around her. She was as shaken as she had been by the Yhelle illusionist, caught in a chaos of needs she was not prepared to understand.

"It's almost over, fire dancer," he murmured against her flying hair, holding her tightly. "Just a bit more."

As she heard his words she realized that she was stiff, unbending, as though she still fought against the illusionist. But this was Kirtn who held her, Kirtn who had soothed her smallest hurts since she was a toddler, Kirtn who always had

116

a smile and a gentle touch for his little fire dancer. Kirtn, not an alien illusion.

She tightened her arms around him, clinging to him with sudden fierce heat. She felt his hesitation, then his body molded to hers, answering her embrace.

Lines of power smoldered over her body, searing him where he touched her, but he did not flinch or protest. He knew that she was unaware of herself and what she did to him, what she was becoming. Too soon. . . .

"It's over," he whispered. "You can let go of the fire."

Despite his words, he held her even after the last random flame flickered free of the clepts. Then, with a reluctance he could barely conceal, he released her. As she stepped away she looked up at him. Her eyes were red-gold, luminous, searching his for something she could not name.

A murmur of Loo language washed over the stage. Fssa tickled her neck as he changed into listening mode. Her confused feeling about Kirtn evaporated when she heard Fssa's satisfied hiss.

"Got it," he murmured. He began sumarizing the Loo mutterings for her. "They like you and Kirtn. They think that you veiled the obscenity nicely by using Loo creation myths."

"What obscenity?" whispered Rheba. Then, "Oh. Furry and smoothie, right?"

Fssa whistled soft agreement. "The J/taals and clepts are competent, but unnecessary. They distract from the central necessity—the Demon King's conversion. Several of the chims are trying to buy the J/taals as guards. The J/taals are well known in Equality. Theirs is one of the few languages other than Universal that I learned from my guardian."

"He can't sell them!" she whispered harshly. Fear made gold lines flare on her arms.

Fssa did not bother to make the obvious statement that a slave master could do whatever he wanted with his slaves.

"But we're an Act. He wouldn't separate an Act," she said, as though the snake had contradicted her.

"Only *after* you appear in the Concatenation are you an Act. Until then, you're a collection of slaves."

She wanted to argue with the snake, but knew it was futile. Fssa was right. She realized she was squeezing Kirtn's hand with enough force to hurt. She looked up at him, and saw from his expression that he had heard Fssa. "They saved the child when we couldn't," she said. "I can't abandon them."

"I know."

"What are we going to do?"

"Jal hasn't told them yet."

Lord Jal raised his arm, pointed at Dapsl, and snapped his fingers impatiently. Dapsl hurried forward and made a deep obeisance at the hem of Jal's sheer robe. Fssa changed shape again, tickling Rheba's ear. She waited, breath held, but the snake said nothing.

"Translate," she snapped.

"They're using Dapsl's language," responded Fssa. "Others are talking at the same time. It's hard to separate, much less learn."

She took the hint and stopped bothering him. Several chims joined in Jal's conversation, but they spoke only master Loo. Still Fssa said nothing. Dapsl hurried back to the stage.

"The clepts," he said, "are unnecessary and ugly. The J/taals are little better. They are rejected."

"Then the Act is rejected," said Kirtn before Rheba could speak.

Dapsl stared at Kirtn. "The Act is *not* rejected. Just the J/taals and the clepts. Lord Jal will graciously allow you to keep that flatulent snake and the ugly First Person you are pleased to call a crown."

The Bre'n touched Rainbow, forgotten around his forehead. The rock had changed itself until it matched the color of Kirtn's hand-length hair. Fssa had told them that it would be better if Rainbow did not excite any greed or unusual interest until it had appeared with them at the Concatenation. Rainbow had obliged by pulling its colored facets inward and altering the remainder until it appeared to be a battered, primitive, gold-colored crown.

"Lord Jal," said Rheba quietly, "takes us all together or not at all."

Dapsl's color deepened, then bleached to lavender when he realized that Rheba meant what she said. "Do you want to spend the rest of your life in the Fold, until they tire of feeding you and send you to the Pits? No one is that stupid—not even a kaza-flatch bitch!"

"We haven't had much time to prepare our Act," said Kirtn. "When the buyers come again, the J/taals and clepts will be a vital part of the Act."

"But you could be free of the Fold right now! All you have to do is leave the—"

"No," said Rheba and Kirtn together.

"But if you miss this Concatenation, you'll be at risk of separation for another year!"

"No."

118

With a furious, inarticulate sound, Dapsl turned and stalked back to Lord Jal. Whatever was said was very brief. Jal knocked Dapsl to the ground, then walked toward the stage. He looked curiously from the J/taals to Rheba.

"What bond do you have with these?" Jal asked. "Is it simply that kaza-flatchers stay together, the better to enjoy their perversions?"

"Nothing that complex," said Rheba, her lips thin but her voice even. "Honor. A promise kept."

Lord Jal looked at his blue-black fingernails, his eyes hooded, his expression bored. "And if I separate you from them?"

"I'll be unAdjusted. You can't take an unAdjusted slave out of the Fold."

Kirtn leaned forward. "And I'll be unAdjusted, too. How will you explain that to the female cherf who is half of the Imperial Loo-chim?"

Lord Jal looked up. Despite herself, Rheba took a step backward. Defensive fire smoldered on her arms, waiting to be used.

Jal smiled. "Do you still share enzymes?" he asked, his voice as cruel as his eyes, reminding her that he could take away more than the J/taals.

She blinked, forgetting for a moment what Jal meant. Then she remembered the ruse she and Kirtn had used to stay together. "Of course," she said quickly. "Didn't you see us onstage?"

Jal's laugh was soft. "I see everything, kaza-flatch bitch. Remember that." He stared at her for a long moment, then shifted his regard to Kirtn. "You, furry, are worth a great deal of money to me, but not enough to risk humiliation. A man without a chim is . . . vulnerable. The Act is embarrassing." He tapped one long nail against his nacreous teeth. The sound seemed very loud in the silence.

Fssa stirred against Rheba's neck and whistled low Bre'n phrases. Kirtn listened, then turned to Jal. "To be part of the Act, the J/taals and clepts simply have to appear with us on the Concatenation stage, correct?"

Lord Jal gestured agreement. And waited.

"Surely the Loo still have some equivalent of hell in their mythology?"

Again the gesture. And the silence.

"A flaming hell?"

Gesture. Silence.

119

"Rheba will make the J/taals and clepts into fire demons. Our Act will be a vision of hell."

The silence stretched. The taps of nail on tooth slowed, then stopped entirely. Jal's expression was not encouraging. Fssa whistled like a distant flute, enlarging upon what he was hearing the chims in the audience say. Kirtn listened without seeming to as the snake eavesdropped on chims speculating upon ways to improve the Act they had just seen.

"If you have a hell myth," the Bre'n continued, "then you must have a myth about a man trapped and distorted by devils, then finally rescued by somebody who symbolizes pure innocence."

"Saffar and Hmel," said Lord Jal, startled. His eyes looked through them, focused on one of the Loo's favorite myths. "Yes . . . mmm." His glance narrowed and returned to the Bre'n. "A happy choice. The female polarity's favorite story." His eyes closed, then snapped open. "It's worth the risk. We'll try it. You surprise me, furry. But if it's not good enough to be one of my three Acts—and the trash I just saw certainly was *not!*—we'll have another talk about honor and unAdjusted slaves."

Kirtn, relieved Jal had not noticed that Fssa was feeding him information about Loo culture, did not object to the threat in the blue lord's words. Then, before Kirtn could feel more than an instant of relief, a funnel of energy came down, engulfed him, turned him inside out, and spat him onto the top of a ramp outside the Fold.

The ramp was long, curving, and quite high where he stood. A walled city stretched away from him on either side of the ramp. People, curious or idle or simply cruel, lined the walls, waiting for the new crop of Fold slaves to appear.

Behind him he heard a gasp and low cries as the rest of the Act materialized out of the savage energy so casually employed by the Loo. He turned to help Rheba, then froze, riveted by a single clear sound.

The Bre'n whistle called to him again and yet again, peals of joy rising from farther down the ramp. Without thinking he spun and ran toward the sound, not even seeing the guard who had come through with the new slaves. He never heard the warning shout, nor saw the brutal flash of energy that cut him down.

# XVI

Rheba watched while two guards peeled off the filaments of force net from Kirtn's slack body. Bre'n and guards blurred in her vision. She scrubbed away tears angrily but could not control the fear that shook her body, fear such as she had not felt since the morning Deva died. She pushed past the guards and knelt next to Kirtn, checking for his pulse with a hand that trembled too much to do anything useful.

Gently, M/dere lifted Rheba's hand and replaced it with her own. Fssa, tangled in Rheba's hair, watched with sensors that were incandescent against the black of his body.

"He's alive," said the J/taal.

Rheba did not know whether Fssa had translated or she had snatched the hoped-for words out of the air. She felt a rush of weakness overwhelm her. She clutched M/dere's arm, taking strength from the J/taal's hard flesh.

Lord Jal entered the room, shoved the women aside and went over Kirtn with a hand-sized red instrument. It chimed and clicked, giving Jal information that Fssa could not translate. With a grunt, he put the instrument into a pocket of his filmy robe and turned toward the guard who had shot Kirtn.

"Your chim is very lucky. She won't spend the rest of her life mourning a dead male who had no more brains than a handful of shit."

The guard went pale, but he knew better than to interrupt a Loo lord.

"Tell me very clearly," said Jal icily, "and very quickly, why you struck down a slave that is worth more than you and your chim cast in gold!"

"It—it ran down the ramp."

Jal waited, obviously expecting more. Much more.

"That's all, lord. It ran down the ramp."

Jal spoke vicious phrases in the master language of Loo. Fssa's translation faltered, then stopped entirely. After a few moments, Jal controlled his vindictive tongue and the Fssireeme began translating the slave master's words into softly whistled Bre'n.

"*Fool*. Who could have been harmed if that slave ran up and down the ramp for the next ten-day? Sometimes the transfer energies overload the nerves of inferior species. That's why we built the ramp and the walls! Slaves can go berserk and not even endanger themselves, much less others. *Fool!*"

Lord Jal clenched and unclenched his fists. Then he sighed, wiped his face with a sheer, voluminous sleeve, and turned his back on the guards who had carried Kirtn into the Concatenation's spacious slave compound. He pulled out the instrument again and moved it slowly over Kirtn's head. The crown glowed oddly against his broad forehead, as though the transfer energies had in some way affected whatever passed for Rainbow's metabolism.

"Odd," muttered Jal. "That ugly thing really is alive. Hmmp." He repeated his motion with the instrument, and the instrument repeated its chimes and clicks. "Well, the wonders of the Equality are endless. I thought Dapsl was just trying to pass off a double handful of gold as one of the First People."

"I?" said a shaky voice. "I'd never deceive my lord." Dapsl limped into the crowded room. The left side of his face was swollen and darkened where Lord Jal's fist had struck him. "I told you that was one of the stone people."

Lord Jal ignored both the little man's words and his deep bow. With a swirl of his rich robe, the Loo turned toward Rheba. "It"—he gestured toward Kirtn—"will wake up soon. It will be sore. See that it walks around or the soreness will get worse."

Rheba imitated the Loo gesture of agreement. Jal looked startled, as though he realized for the first time that he was speaking master Loo, not Universal—and she was understanding every word. He stared at the slender snake body barely visible beneath her hair.

"Dapsl didn't lie about that, either," Jal said in Universal. "How many languages does it know?"

Unhesitatingly, Rheba lied. "Loo, a bit. Universal, a bit more. Enough so that we get by. He says he knows J/taal, but I have no way to be sure. The J/taals obey well enough,

122

so the snake must know something." She shrugged. "He's quite beautiful, but I'm afraid he's not at all bright. As much a mimic as anything else."

She whistled sweet Bre'n apologies to Fssa and hoped that Jal would not see through her lies. Until the Fssireeme performed with them on the Concatenation stage, he could be snatched away at the whim of a Loo Lord. Fssa's linguistic genius must be kept secret for a few more weeks.

Lord Jal stared at the snake. He did not entirely accept Rheba's glib explanation. On the other hand, the snake obviously was necessary to the smooth performance of the Act. Besides—if the beast were truly valuable, the chim who had captured it in the first place would have claimed it long since.

He turned back toward Dapsl, dismissing whatever small mysteries surrounded the snake. "The new year begins in two weeks. I'll choose my Acts two days before. Organize your Act around the Saffar and Hmel myth. Weave right this time, or you'll die in the Pit."

Dapsl swayed as though Jal had struck him again. "No, lord," he whispered. "Not the Pit. Please, lord."

Jal was indifferent to the trembling in the smaller man's voice. "The Pit. What else can a failed weaver expect?"

"But—but—" Dapsl stuttered hoarsely. "They d-don't respect me, Lord. They d-don't obey. They laugh. They ignore. How can I weave an Act with such c-creatures?"

"The most stubborn threads make the most satisfying pattern," Jal said blandly, quoting a homily of Dapsl's people. "And . . . I'll give you a nerve wrangler to use on the J/taals and clepts." He looked at Rheba, who was stroking Kirtn's face while tears ran down her own. "I wouldn't recommend using it on either of them, though. The Bre'n would kill you before the nerve wrangler disabled him."

"Lord, are you saying he's *unAdjusted?*"

Jal smiled. "So long as he's with his kaza-flatch, he's Adjusted. Walk lightly, manikin. If you goad them into breaking Adjustment and I have to have them killed, you'll die first and very badly."

Dapsl swallowed several times but still was not able to speak. Lord Jal measured the purple man's distress, smiled, and swept out of the room.

Kirtn groaned. His body jerked erratically, aftermath of the nerve wrangler the guard had used on him. M/dere and Rheba worked over him, trying to loosen muscles knotted by alien energies. After a few moments he opened his eyes. They

123

were very dark gold, glazed by pain. Remembering Jal's words, Rheba urged the Bre'n to his feet and guided him on a slow circuit of the room.

He seemed to improve with each painful step. Finally he shook himself, as though to throw off the last of the nerve wrangler's disruptions. Then he remembered what had happened before the world became a curtain of black agony.

"What is it?" asked Rheba, feeling his body stiffen suddenly. "Jal said the pain would get less, not more, if we walked. Do you want to stop?"

Kirtn answered in Senyas, his voice as controlled as the language itself. "There is a Bre'n woman here, in this city. She called to me while I was on the ramp."

Rheba was torn between elation and dismay. She ignored the latter emotion, not even asking herself why the news of a Bre'n woman would bring less than joy to her. "You're sure?" Then, immediately, "Of course you are. No one could mistake a Bre'n call. Is she well? Is she akhenet? If so, is her akhenet with her? Is he well? How old——" She stopped the rush of questions. Kirtn would not have had time to speak to the woman before he was cut down by the guard.

"Her name if Ilfn. She used the major key, so she and her akhenet are as well as slaves can be. She didn't use an adult tone to describe his name, so I assume that Lheket is a child. She didn't use the harmonics of gathering to describe herself, so I have to assume that she doesn't know of any other Bre'ns on Loo."

Rheba thought quickly, grateful for the compressed, complex Bre'n language. Few other languages could have packed so much information into a few instants of musical sound. "It must be Lheket's earring that Jal stole." Her voice changed. She reached up to touch her right ear, barren of Kirtn's gift, the Bre'n Face. Jal had taken both earrings, Lheket's and her own, before he dumped her and Kirtn into the Fold. "May his children turn to ashes before he dies," she said, a fire dancer's curse. Her voice was frightening in its hatred. Her arms smoldered beneath the robes. Lines of burning gold glowed on her neck and her hair twisted restlessly.

For once, Kirtn did not attempt to calm her. The earring was the symbol of all that Bre'n and Senyas could be, the Face of the future, catalyst to Rheba's understanding of herself, and him. He felt its loss as acutely as she did; perhaps more, for he understood more.

"We'll have to find out where she's kept," said Rheba

124

slowly, "then we'll have to figure out a way to free her and her akhenet—and ourselves," she added in bitter tones, "ourselves first of all." She looked around the room. It was large, contained simple furniture and simple house machines. There was nothing that could be used as a weapon.

"At least we found the boy," said Kirtn, understanding her scrutiny of the room. "Part of our goal is accomplished."

"Did you . . . see him?" she asked, oddly reticent. She felt uncomfortable discussing the child who was the only possible male to father her children. On Deva such reticence would have been impossible; she and Kirtn would have thoroughly discussed the choosing of each other's mates. But Deva was gone, choice narrowed to nothing. "Is he very young?"

Kirtn stroked her hair, enjoying the subtle crackle of stored energy clinging to his fingers. "I don't know. I hope so," he said absently. Then, hearing his own words, his hand stopped. "I mean—you're young, fire dancer. There's so much—" Abruptly, he was silent. There was no way to tell her that it would be better for him if she could accept him as a lover or at least a pleasure mate before she began bearing Lheket's children.

"I'm frightened," she whispered. "What little peace we've gained since Deva died—it's been so hard, my Bre'n. If you mate—if I—it will all change again. Oh, I know it will be better. Won't it? But you're all I have—" She heard her own words and stopped, miserable and ashamed to speak such small thoughts to her beloved mentor. "I'm sorry, akhenet," she said in cold Senyas. "I'm unworthy of your time."

Kirtn laughed humorlessly. "Then I'm unworthy of yours. I have the same fears you do."

She looked up, unable to believe him until she saw his face pulled into grim lines beneath the sleek gold mask. Absurdly, she felt better, knowing that he accepted and even shared her fears. She put her arms around his neck and whispered fiercely, "You're mine, Kirtn. I'll share you, but suns will turn to ice before I let you go!"

He returned her hug with a force that surprised her. His strength always took her unaware, reminding her of how much he held in check. She buried her fingers in the thick hair that covered his skull.

"Trading enzymes again?" asked Jal from the doorway.

Rheba felt deadly anger bloom in Kirtn at Jal's unexpected return and cutting words. Deliberately, she put her mouth over Kirtn's and held the kiss for a long count. She meant to

125

insult Jal by ignoring him, but her intention was lost in a swirl of unexpected emotions. Her lines of power flared, a surge of energy that was the first signal of a mature fire dancer's passion.

Kirtn felt fire lick along his nerves where he touched her, fire that burned without hurting, ecstasy instead of agony. She was older than he had thought, maturity forced by a life no fire dancer should have to lead. Her body was ready for him but her mind was not. That could not be forced. With an effort that made him ache, he ended the kiss and turned to face the blue lord who watched so insolently from the door.

"Trading enzymes," agreed Kirtn, his voice as utterly controlled as his body.

Jal snickered. "Then you should be ready for Lord Puc's furry bitch. She'll give you an enzyme transfer that will crisp your *nuga*."

"Lord Puc?" said the Bre'n. "I thought that the Imperial Loo-chim owned the Bre'n woman."

"Lord Puc is the male polarity of the Imperial Loo-chim. When he conducts business that has nothing to do with governing the planet, he's referred to as Lord Puc. His chim is Lady Kurs. The lady doesn't want to wait until after the Concatenation for you to impregnate the Bre'n female. She's afraid that her brother might change his mind. So you'll go to the bitch every night for ten nights—or whatever part of the night is left after Lord Puc finishes with her."

Equal parts of anger and sickness coursed through Rheba at the cold usage of the Bre'n woman as both whore and breeder. She felt ashamed of her earlier jealously; if Kirtn could bring any comfort at all to the Bre'n woman, his Senyas woman would not begrudge it.

She squeezed Kirtn's hand gently, trying to tell him what she felt, that she could share him with the unknown woman and not be ruined by jealousy. "Despite Loo myths," she said coolly to Jal, "Bre'ns aren't animals. They don't mate indiscriminately."

"If your furry can't bring himself to fertilize the bitch, we'll take the sperm from him and do it ourselves. Lady Kurs wouldn't like that. She's hoping to blunt the Bre'n bitch's appetites with a male of her own species. Later, when the bitch is pregnant, Lady Kurs will enjoy her own revenge on her chim with the male furry." Jal smiled at Kirtn. "If you can't perform, Lady Kurs will assume that your kaza-flatch is draining you. Then you'll be separated until you can perform."

126

"Rheba and I aren't lovers, or even pleasure mates," snapped Kirtn.

"Lady Kurs doesn't believe that. Neither do I. A guard will come for you later. Be ready."

# XVII

Kirtn followed the silent chim of guards through the Concatenation compound. It was very late at night, yet people stirred throughout, nocturnal races from planets he had never heard of. Some of the people worked as drudges. Others rehearsed their Acts, their bodies rippling with natural fluorescence and their eyes brilliant with reflected light.

The compound was a warren of hallways, turnings, rooms, dead ends and ramps. As he walked, he got the impression of age, great age, millennia that had worn building stones into rounded blocks. Beneath his feet stone was smoothed to a semblance of softness by the passage of countless barefoot slaves. The air was neither chill nor warm, damp nor dry, yet he was certain he had smelled brine in the instant before one of the outer doors closed.

Breathing deeply, sifting the air for scents, he walked behind the guards. The hint of sea smell remained, or it could have been simply his hope that both Fold and Concatenation were located in the same equatorial city where the *Devalon* had first landed. If that was so, his ship was within reach, or at least within possibility. Unless Jal had slagged the *Devalon* out of anger when he realized it would respond only to Rheba and Kirtn.

The guards paused before a portal. Energy shimmered across it until the chim spoke a command. Like the compound's other safeguards, the key to the doorway was simple. There was nothing to prevent an intelligent, determined slave from escaping—nothing but the knowledge that there was no way off planet and the punishment for an unAdjusted slave was death. The Loos assumed that a slave clever enough to escape was also clever enough to know that it was committing suicide. Those who survived Pit or Fold were invariably intelligent. The Loos had to kill very few slaves in any given year, and most of those had gone mad.

Even so, Kirtn watched and learned, weighing and memorizing alternate routes through the ancient compound, remembering verbal keys to each doorway. What he did was not difficult for a Bre'n; their memories were as great as their ability to withstand pain. It could not be otherwise for a race that guided the dangerous mental energies of Senyas dancers.

Another door, another shimmer of energy, another set of commands. He walked through into a night that was fragrant with flowers and a nearby sea. Wind ruffled over him, bringing with it the sound of surf created by two of Loo's moons. He wished for a window or a hill or even a peephole, anything to give him a view of the surrounding area. But all he had was a walled courtyard that was crossed in seventeen steps. A door gleamed, winked out. In the gold light of an open room stood a Bre'n woman. Ilfn. Her whistle was one of the most beautiful sounds he had ever heard.

Ilfn stepped forward and led him through the archway. The guards did not follow. Behind him energy leaped up again, sealing him within the room. At the moment it did not matter; he was standing close to a Bre'n woman.

A hand brushed his gold mask, smoothing the short, sleek hairs around his gold eyes in a Bre'n gesture of greeting. He returned the touch. Ilfn was smaller than he, smaller than the Bre'n women he had known, barely taller than a Senyas. Her mask was pale gold against the dark brown of her hair and fur. She trembled beneath his touch.

"I hoped, but I never really believed I would see another Bre'n," she whistled. "I hoped. And I survived, because it isn't for a Bre'n to die and leave behind an akhenet child. Are you akhenet, too?"

"Yes. Her name is Rheba. She's a fire dancer from the Tirrl continent."

"Tirrl." The word was like a sigh. "Half a world away from Semma-doh. But we all died just the same."

"Not all. You're here, and we're here. There must be others. Rheba and I will find them. We'll gather them up and take them to a new world. Bre'ns and Senyasi will dance again."

Ilfn's smile was unbearably sad, but she did not say aloud that slaves had no right to dreams. "Fire dancer. Lheket is a rain dancer. Very strong." Her whistle slid into a minor key. "Too strong for a child only eleven years old."

He whistled sympathetically. "Rheba is strong, too. And too young to have lines of power touching her shoulders."

With a last smoothing of Kirtn's gold mask, Ilfn's hand fell. "I think only the strongest dancers survived." Her eyes were pale brown with green lights, but little except darkness moved within them when she remembered Deva's end. "I'm glad that Lord Puc listened to my plea."

Kirtn's whistle rose on a note of query.

"I asked him if you were alive," she explained, "and he said yes. Then I asked him if I could see you. He shouted and hit me." She made a dismissing gesture when she saw Kirtn's face change. "No Loo can make a Bre'n hurt with just bare fists. And Lord Puc is weaker than most." Her lips thinned into a bitter smile. "Lord Puc is very soft in my hands. When the time comes, he's mine. I've earned him."

The last was spoken in Senyas, and was as flat as the light in her eyes.

"When the time comes . . . ?" he whistled.

Ilfn hesitated, then whistled softly. "I suppose I must trust you." Then, defiantly, "If I can't trust the last Bre'n man alive, I'll be glad to die!"

He waited, then hummed encouragement.

"Rebellion," she said in Senyas.

"When? Where? How many?" He spoke Senyas, too, a staccato rush of demand.

"Last Year Night, the final night of the Concatenation, during the Hour Between Years. It's an hour of chaos. We know the gate codes of the compound. There's a spaceport just a few *mie* from the Concatenation amphitheater. We'll steal a ship and get off this mud-sucking planet."

He hesitated, not knowing how to criticize the plan without seeming ungrateful for her confidence. She smiled again, and he realized that she was old, much older than he.

"It's not as foolish as it sounds in Senyas," she said. "On the night of Concatenation there is an extra hour of time after midnight when they adjust their yearly calendar. It's a time of no-time, really, when all rules are suspended and slaves wander the streets. When the hour is up, the New Year Morning begins. Until then, the highborn Loo and their guards stay in the Concatenation amphitheater, bidding for various Acts."

He stood quietly, absorbing the information and its implications for escape. "What's the amphitheater like?"

"It's an ancient place connected to this compound by a tunnel." She switched from Senyas to Bre'n, emotions ringing in her whistle. "There aren't any guards in the tunnel, and there are many rooms, many turnings before the tunnel reaches the amphitheater. We'll stay in the tunnel until the last Act is over. No one will notice old slaves mixed with the new Acts. When the last Act ends and the Hour Between Years begins, we'll escape. We'll seal the exits behind us, go to the spaceport, grab a ship and lift off."

"If it were that easy, there wouldn't be a slave left on Loo," Kirtn said in dry Senyas.

"Easy or hard, we'll do it."

He looked narrowly at her, hearing the desperation that lay just beneath her clear whistle, coloring it with echoes of despair. "What is it? What aren't you telling me?"

Her whistle shattered, then she was in control again, and it was as though the instant had never happened. "Lheket. He's only a boy, but already he's as tall as my shoulder. Lord Puc is jealous. He can't believe that no Bre'n akhenet would touch a Senyas child. He sees my love for Lheket and calls it lust. Someday it might be, if Lheket grows into a mature love of me. But that day is twenty years ahead. Lord Puc can't believe that. He sees only Lheket's height and beauty and the boy's love for me." Her eyes closed, then opened very dark. "He'll take Lheket from me soon. Then there will be a time of *rez* and death." She looked up at him, lips tight around precise Senyas words. "So you see, I've nothing to lose by rebellion, no matter how badly planned."

He had no response. There was no way to change her mind, and no reason to. She understood her choices, few and bitter as they were. "Can you trust the other slaves not to betray you?"

Ilfn's whistle was double-toned, indicating that the question was unanswerable. "They came to me because I've heard the outer-door codes when I go to Lord Puc. Their plan required the right key."

"You."

"Yes." She turned her hands palm down and then palm up. "They trust me because they must, but I don't think they've told me their whole plan. I think many slaves are involved, in and out of the compound. But I know only two names, and those the least important. I don't know how many slaves they expect to take with them. At least one of the two I've met is a pilot. She recognized the ships I described to her."

"Ships? Are you allowed to go to the spaceport?" demanded Kirtn.

"No, but I can see it from my window at the far side of

131

this building. That's how I knew you were here. I saw the shape of a Senyas ship against the dawn. Since then, I've waited by that ramp every time newly Adjusted slaves were released. When I saw you—" Her hands clung to him suddenly with a strength he had not felt since Deva, Bre'n strength. "And then the guard scourged you and you fell. I was afraid you were dead, that I had killed you with a welcoming whistle."

Kirtn held Ilfn while she shuddered. It was the Bre'n way of crying, and it was as painful to him as it was to her. Even when she stopped, he continued to hold her, knowing that it had been too long since anyone had comforted her.

The thought of her being used by Lord Puc made anger uncurl in Kirtn like an endless snake. Even though he probably would not have chosen her for a mate on Deva, she was a good woman, brave and akhenet. She did not deserve to be a Loo-chim toy.

"If we get to the *Devalon*," he promised, "you'll be safe. And Lheket—" He hesitated, switched to unemotional Senyas. "Lheket will have a mate when he's old enough to give my dancer a child. It's not how we would have done it on Deva, but Rheba is akhenet and knows her duty."

"Duty," murmured Ilfn. "A cold companion, but better than none at all." She looked up, measuring him with pale-brown eyes. "I don't think we would have chosen each other on Deva. You're much younger, yet much harder than the men I loved . . . but as soon as we're off this planet I'll bear our children, akhenet. Do you agree?"

"I'm akhenet," he said simply. "Of course I agree."

"But? Don't tell me you're too young to father children?"

Kirtn smiled. "Young, yes, but not that young."

"And your akhenet? How old is she?"

"Neither child nor yet akhenet woman," he said bluntly.

Ilfn pushed away from him with an embarrassed whistle. "I'm sorry. I didn't mean to disturb your desires. My sympathy, akhenet. You've a hard time ahead." She smiled ruefully. "Your whistle didn't describe her as a child."

"I'm afraid I don't often think of her that way."

"How old is she?"

"Twice your boy's age."

"Then she won't be ready to accept you for at least ten years," she said thoughtfully, switching to Senyas. "Yet you already think of her as a woman . . . ?"

Kirtn's whistle was harsh, answering her unspoken questions. "I've never touched Rheba as a woman—except once, to fool the Loo-chim into believing that she and I had to trade enzymes in order to survive. Then she—once—to irritate Lord Jal." His whistle deteriorated into a scathing Senyas oath. "It doesn't matter. She is what she is—*too young!*" In his anger, he lashed out at Ilfn. "And I'm not here at Lord Puc's demand, but at his sister's. I'm supposed to breed you so that Lord Puc will go back to his whore-sister's bed!"

The Bre'n woman looked at him for a long time, understanding his anger without being angered in turn. "You can't. With your akhenet neither child nor woman—no. Mating with me would only heighten your desire for her. Impossible. You'd risk *rez*."

"If I don't mate with you, my fire dancer will be taken away from me. You know what that would do."

"*Rez*," she whispered. Her hands knotted around each other. "Did we survive Deva and the Fold just to be driven into *rez?*"

"I don't know." His whistle was flat and very penetrating. "But of the four of us, I'm the least vital to our future."

"What? What are you saying?"

"If you carry Bre'n babies, the race won't die. Your akhenet must survive until he can give Rheba Senyas children. Rheba must survive until she can bear those children. But I—once you're pregnant, I'm the least important of us."

"Hard," she whistled in a keening tremulo. "I saw it in your eyes, like hammered metal."

"Do you want children who will wail and die at the first obstacle," he said brutally, "or will you mate with a man who can give your children the strength to survive?"

"You misunderstand. I'd have no other Bre'n, now that I've measured you. You're the Bre'n the Equality demands. I'm too old and you're too young, but together we'll breed a race of Bre'n. Survivors, Kirtn. Survivors breeding survivors." She looked at him for a long, silent time. "And perhaps . . . perhaps your fire dancer will understand your need before *rez* claims you."

"Perhaps," said Kirtn.

But neither one believed it.

# XVIII

Fssa hummed soothingly, overriding the sound of Dapsl's complaints. Rheba caressed Fssa with her fingertip, then turned her whole concentration back on the J/taals and their clepts. M/dere looked over, saw that Rheba was ready and signaled the beginning of the Act. Dapsl yelled several phrases that Fssa ignored; the snake was bored by the purple man's lack of invention in epithets.

"Stop! *Stop!* You don't begin until *I* give the signal!" screamed Dapsl. The body-length nerve wrangler in his left hand lashed back and forth as though it were alive. The flexible tips dripped violet light, warning of energies barely held in check. The nerve wrangler licked out, rising against M/dere; violet fire ran up her arm. "Listen to me or we'll all end up in the Pit!"

M/dere stood unmoving, though her eyes were wide and dark. She did not look at Dapsl. She looked only at Rheba, her J/taaleri. Rheba badly wanted to suck the energy out of the deadly whip and send it back redoubled on Dapsl. The only thing that restrained her was the fact that he already suspected that she was more powerful than she appeared. He was afraid of her. If she disarmed him, he would probably run away screaming to the lords about powers she desperately wanted to hide. The Concatenation was only seven days away. She could hold on to her temper for seven more days. She had to.

The nerve wrangler hissed outward again, setting fire to M/dere's arm. Rheba's hair whipped and seethed as she leaped to her feet in rage. Fssa turned black with fear.

"*No more,*" said Rheba, her voice low, frightening. "If you use that whip on J/taal or clept, I won't work for you. The Act will be nothing and you'll be sent to the Pit!"

"So will you, kaza-flatch!" spat Dapsl, more afraid than

134

ever of the alien whose hair was obscenely alive, dripping fire like the whip in his hand.

"I'll survive the Pit," she said. "You won't."

Dapsl hesitated for long moments while the nerve wrangler responded to his unconscious commands by writhing sinuously, bleeding violet fire. "Lord Jal won't like this. He gave me the whip because those lazy animals wouldn't work any other way."

"Make your choice. The Act or the whip."

With a savage twist of his hands, Dapsl broke the nerve wrangler. It sputtered lavender sparks, then died. He threw it into the corner of the room and turned back to Rheba.

"Whenever you're ready," she said calmly, returning her attention to the Act.

Dapsl's lips flattened into thin black lines, but all he said was, "On four."

M/dere took her cue from Dapsl this time, and the Act began smoothly. The J/taals were in a loose group on one side of the area that was marked off as the stage. Rainbow, very subdued, was at their center. They were in contorted positions, moving very slowly, their faces anguished and fierce. They and their silently snarling clepts were the very image of souls caught and tormented in hell. They moved as though swimming up out of an infinite black well, bodies straining. Yet for all their effort, they went nowhere; this was hell, the core of nightmare in which man fled but could not move his feet.

Rheba watched without really seeing. Her whole mind was focused on gathering energy in the dim room, taking that energy and shaping it into uncanny flames that coursed over the straining bodies of the J/taals.

In her hair, Fssa transformed himself into a musical instrument. His sounds were eerie, sliding into minor harmonics and then dissolving into screams as primitive as the fear of death. Fssa's screams broke suddenly, regrouped into a keening harmony that made her skin tighten and move.

The keening was Kirtn's cue to come onstage in his role of Hmel, seeker of lost innocence. But Kirtn was not there, had not returned from his nightly excursion to Ilfn's bed. That was the reason for Dapsl's ragged temper, and her own. She sucked in more energy, drawing from a window high in the ceiling, the only source of energy in the darkened room. Where Kirtn should have been she created an outline of him that was the color of molten gold.

Dapsl gasped and stepped back before he caught himself.

135

His fingers curled, longing for the feel of the nerve wrangler. It was one thing to see her draw lines of fire around a living Bre'n; it was quite another to see the lines without the Bre'n.

The outline keened softly, a soul held in an immaterial cage of fire. Slowly, with great effort, the outline quartered hell, looking for his sister's crown. Hmel had given it to a demon woman in return for a night of passion such as a human woman could never give him.

By increments Rainbow, in the role of the missing crown, brightened to draw attention to itself. It was surrounded by J/taals and clepts, each straining upward, each never leaving its place.

The outline of Kirtn/Hmel turned toward the crown with a cry of hope. But when Hmel tried to penetrate the ring of demons around the crown, a sheet of purple fire flared. The outline screamed, agony as pure as the color of the flames. The outline of Hmel reached for the crown again, and again violet lightning leaped. Hmel was not strong enough to brave the fire demons surrounding his chim's lost crown.

A sound of despair came from Hmel's incandescent form, a cry that began as a groan and ended in a scream so high that it was felt as much as it was heard.

Rheba waited until there was only silence and flames and echoes of despair. She walked onto the stage as though in an exhausted daze. Feigning exhaustion was not difficult. The effort of holding fire on J/taals, clepts, and also creating an outline of Kirtn was enough to reduce her to mumbling and stumbling. It would have been easier to wait for Kirtn, to use his body to shape the bright outline; but he was not here and there was no more time to wait. Jal was choosing his three Concatenation Acts tonight. Some of those Acts had been rehearsing together for nearly a year. Her Act could not afford to waste one instant of practice time.

A tall form slipped by her in the dimly lit room. Kirtn. The outline shimmered, then reformed subtly. Her fire creation was more alive now. It moved with greater grace and conviction, for it was the result of Bre'n and Senyas working together.

Relief was like a tonic to her. She felt energy course through her, expanding the intricate lines of power on her body. Her head came up—and she saw that Kirtn had not come into the room alone. Lord Jal was in the archway. Next to him was the male polarity of the Imperial Loo-chim.

"I must protest, Lord Puc," said Jal in a low voice. "This

136

Act is all but unrehearsed. To decide now whether or not it is good enough for the Concatenation stage is unreasonable."

"It's the right of the Imperial Loo-chim to review any Act at any time," said Lord Puc. "If what we see pleases us, you're assured of a place on the Concatenation stage. And if it doesn't please us, you're spared the embarrassment of presenting an inferior Act to the gathered chims."

Fssa's whispered translation from the master Loo language went no farther than Rheba's ears. She had only to look at Kirtn, however, to realize that he already knew. Something had gone very wrong, and the male polarity was at the center of it.

"And your chim?" Jal said. His voice was clipped, as close to disrespect as he could come without further antagonizing his lord. "Doesn't your chim want to judge this Act with you?"

Lord Puc's glass-blue eyes fixed on Jal. After a long moment, Jal bowed and turned toward the Act. When he spoke, it was in Universal, a language the Imperial Loo-chim did not deign to understand.

"You did your job too well," Jal snapped at Kirtn. "The bitch has been listless in Lord Puc's bed these last nights. The female polarity is pleased. The male polarity is not."

"Ilfn is pregnant," Kirtn said. "She won't willingly accept sex with him again until her children are born."

"So she told him. He took her anyway, of course, but he didn't have much pleasure of it."

Kirtn's expression shifted as his lips flattened into a silent snarl. Immediately, Rheba went to his side. Her hand rested lightly on his arm. Gradually his eyes lost their blank metallic sheen.

"Now," continued Jal, "Lord Puc is after revenge. All that is available at the moment is a command performance of your Act."

"If he doesn't like it—and he won't—we go to the Pit," said Rheba, more statement than question.

Lord Jal's mouth pulled into a frown. "Crudely put, but accurate. I've sent word to the female polarity." He shrugged. "She should have been here by now. I hope she hasn't changed her mind about bedding your pet."

Lord Puc looked at Kirtn with a hatred that needed no translation. Jealousy had eaten at the lord until he was barely sane. Rheba could not help wondering what the Bre'n female had that apparently all other women lacked—and did Kirtn feel the same way about her that the Loo lord did?

137

"Begin," said Lord Puc to Jal. "Now."

"Don't be in such a rush, chim," said a silky voice from the archway. "Don't you want your leman and her pet to watch? She should know how well you keep your promises."

With an audible snarl, Lord Puc turned on his chim. The sight of Ilfn with Lheket brought an ugly sound out of the male polarity. "I said she was never to see the boy unless I was present!"

"But you *were* present, my chim, my other half, my petulant nonlover. Where I am, you are. Soothe yourself, chim. The bitch hasn't touched her blind pet." Lady Kurs smiled, then turned her shattered blue eyes on Jal. "Begin." She turned back toward her own chim, bane and treasure of her existence. "Of course, dear Puc, you won't let the fact that your *nuga* is stuck in the furry bitch affect your judgment of an Act's worth."

Lord Puc made an effort at self-control that showed in every sinew of his body. "Of course not. Acts are sacred."

Lady Kurs smiled. "Then begin, Lord Jal. Now."

The command was issued in such silky tones that it took Jal a moment to realize what Lady Kurs had said. Hurriedly he summarized the central conceit of the Act, the story of Saffar and Hmel. Lady Kurs listened, but her eyes never left the swell of muscle beneath Kirtn's velvet plush. His fur was so short, so smooth, that it defined and enhanced rather than concealed the body beneath.

Watching, Rheba realized anew that Kirtn, like all furred slaves, was naked, accorded no more dignity than a draft animal. She felt a sick rage rise in her at Lady Kurs' lustful inspection of the Bre'n's body. For an instant Rheba's rage broke free, lighting the lines of power beneath her muffling robe. Kirtn felt power flow, saw Rheba's hot glare at Lady Kurs, and guessed what had triggered his fire dancer's rage. With an inner smile, he turned his back on the female polarity's intrusive stare.

"—finds the crown but can't penetrate the demon fire," summarized Jal hurriedly, silently cursing the unbridled lusts of the Imperial Loo-chim. "His chim, meanwhile, has descended to hell in search of him. She has forgiven him for his unnatural desires, knowing that he was under the spell of the furred bitch demon. Together, the chim fights the demons and wins back the crown. He's freed from hell, but to remind him of his sins, he's forced to wear fur for the rest of his life. And to this day, Loo children sometimes bear the curse of fur, sign of our ancestor's unnatural mating so long ago."

Lady Kurs licked her lips with a long blue tongue. "Unnatural mating . . . the curse of the Imperial Loo-chim. Isn't that so, my brother, my chim?"

Lord Puc stared death at Kirtn and said nothing. Jal swore softly as he gave Dapsl the signal to begin. "Start with Saffar's entrance," he said in Universal. "And move quickly, for the love of the Twin Gods. I don't know how much longer I can keep them from killing something!"

Rheba forced herself to look away from the deadly blue lady. She tried to see beyond Ilfn, where the Senyas boy stood, but he was hidden behind his Bre'n, nothing showing but a thin, tawny arm and fingers clinging to hers.

"—four!"

Dapsl's hiss brought her mind back to the exigencies of the Act. She sent energy to bloom around clepts and J/taals. The Act began. Beneath her robe, her skin itched suddenly, miserably. In a gesture of defiance, she tore off her slave robe and threw it aside. If her Bre'n had to go naked, so would she.

But she was not naked, not quite. Lines of power made incandescent traceries over her body, veins and whorls of gold that were so dense on her fingers that little other color was left. Her lower arms were laced with intricate patterns, pulses of gold like an endlessly breaking wave. Tendrils curled up her arms, across her shoulders, around her neck like filigree. A single line swept down her torso, then divided to touch each taut hip.

She felt the cool air of the room like a benediction. It was far more comfortable to control fire without cloth stifling her. Her own sigh of relief hid from her the sound of Ilfn's gasp, and Kirtn's; both Bre'ns knew the danger of so many new lines on so young a dancer. And they both knew what the fire lines touching her hips meant. She was too young to be developing the curling lines of passion. For an instant the two Bre'n akhenets looked at each other, silently protesting what they could not change. Then they looked away, faces expressionless beneath fine fur masks.

Like currents of energy, Rheba sensed the silent exchange between the two Bre'n. It disturbed her, so she put it aside. The most difficult part of the Act lay ahead and she was already tired.

Dapsl cued her entrance.

Fssa crooned, a sound both soft and penetrating. The call ended on a questioning note, but no one answered. Rheba/Saffar came onto the stage, seeking her lost chim. She had built no fires around her body to illuminate it—nor did she need to. Akhenet lines rippled and blazed as she shaped energies to the peculiar demands of the Act. Fssa spoke for her again, as he spoke for everyone in the Act.

Kirtn/Hmel, striving to reach the crown in the midst of demons, seemed not to hear. Saffar came closer, drawn to him by the subtle bonds that connected all chims. Hmel leaned toward the crown again. Violet fire cascaded, drawing gasps from the Imperial Loo-chim. Against the dark fire Hmel's outline blazed wildly.

With a musical cry, Saffar turned toward her chim. She touched him. Fssa screamed. Black fire leaped as the demon still in Hmel tried to kill the innocence in Saffar. Against Fssa's background of screams, demon shrieks and the harmonics of pain, Saffar fought to free Hmel of the demon curse.

The battle consumed the stage, fire and screams, darkness and light, hope and despair, demon and human. Just as it seemed certain that Saffar would be crushed by the demon strength of the chim she loved, she surrendered. Her sudden stillness shocked Hmel. His grip on her loosened. She could have slipped away, but did not. Instead, she sang.

And it was Rheba, not Fssa, who shaped those notes.

The first pure phrases of a Bre'n love song rose like silver bubbles out of the black lake of hell. The notes came faster and clearer, surrounding Hmel with a net of beauty. He screamed in raw agony, for demons cannot stand against beauty. Saffar wept, yet still she sang, each pure phrase like a knife driven into the body of her lover, seeking the demon at his core.

Fssa joined the singing, an echo that haunted violet demon fires. He screamed for Hmel, wept for Saffar; but he let Bre'n and Senyas sing for themselves and shivered with delight at such perfect sounds.

A glittering black demon shape fought over the incandescent surface of Hmel's body. Saffar clung to him, using desire as a weapon against the demon. He writhed and screamed as the demon was driven out of him. Song and Hmel's natural desire for his chim tore at the demon, separating it from Hmel until it stood revealed for what it was—an embodiment of unnatural lust, a demon both male and female at once, animal and human and all possibilities in between. Black, shivering, it gave an awful shriek and flew up into the darkness above the Act.

Gently, Hmel pulled away from his chim. He walked between the fire demons to the place where Saffar's crown glowed, waiting. The demons made no flames to stop him;

they were themselves frozen by the departure of their animating force. Unmoving, impaled on invisible talons, the demons waited in their grotesque positions for another chim who could be seduced into forgetting its other self.

The crown blazed when Hmel put it on Saffar's head. All other light faded, leaving a gold nimbus surrounding Hmel and Saffar's long embrace.

The silence that followed the end of the Act was even longer. Finally the Loo-chim stirred, still transfixed, shattered blue eyes unbelieving. As one, the chim sighed. Lord Jal made a few discreet noises, recalling the Loo-chim to the question at hand. The room brightened at Dapsl's command, breaking the spell woven by a fire dancer and a Bre'n.

"The Act pleased you . . . ?" Jal smiled as he asked, knowing that the Act had done just that. There were many aesthetically superior Acts in the Concatenation compound, but not one of them spoke so completely to the obsessions of the Imperial Loo-chim.

Lord Puc blinked several times as though demon fire still troubled his sight. He looked at Kirtn, but saw mostly Hmel. Lady Kurs looked at Rheba, but saw only Saffar's grief over her lost chim. The Imperial Loo-chim looked at itself. During a long, silent exchange, lines of tension were reborn on the chim's face. But there could be no disagreement about the disposition of the Act.

The male polarity turned toward Lord Jal. "An Act worthy of the Concatenation, Jal. I congratulate you."

Lord Jal bowed and turned toward the female polarity.

"I agree, of course," she said, her voice brittle. "They will be the last, and best, Act of Last Year Night. But I don't congratulate you, half-man. You've set our own furred demons among us. There will be grief now, as there was in Saffar's time." She paused, then looked toward Kirtn. "But before grief, there will be pleasure such as only demons know."

She took her chim's arm and guided him toward the door. When they reached Ilfn, Lord Puc stopped. Before he could speak, Lady Kurs intervened.

"She and her pet will stay here until after the Concatenation." The female polarity's voice was calm and very certain. When Lord Puc would have objected, she said, "Only a few days, sweet chim. Until the old year ends we'll have each other. Afterward, we'll have . . . them."

# XIX

Rheba shivered and moved closer to Kirtn. As always, she was cold. She felt the steady rhythm of his heart against her cheek, the warmth of his fine fur, and the resillience of muscles relaxed in sleep. She smoothed his sleek hair beneath her palm. He murmured sleepily and shifted, bringing her closer. She settled against him and tried to sleep, but could not. Her feet itched, her legs itched, her shoulders and breasts itched. It seemed that even the inside of her backbone itched.

Gently, trying not to wake him, she rolled away and shed her robe, preferring to be cold rather than to have her lines irritated by the rough cloth. She stood up, went to the fountain along one wall for a drink, then returned to Kirtn's side. Behind her, J/taals and clepts slept in a tidy sprawl. Fssa lay curled around Rainbow, but he was not in his speaking mode.

On the other side of Kirtn lay Ilfn and Lheket. The boy was long, thin . . . and as blind as a stone. She felt pity tighten her lips; Ilfn had told her that the boy's blindness was a flight from what he had seen in Deva's last moments.

Reluctantly, as though drawn against her will, Rheba walked around Kirtn until she could see Lheket more clearly. She looked at the boy for a long time before her itching skin distracted her. She stood, scratching absently, staring down at Lheket and trying to see the father of her future children in the thin shape of the sleeping child. At last she made a gesture of bafflement and negation and turned back to Kirtn.

"Is it his blindness you dislike?"

Ilfn's soft question startled Rheba; she had thought the Bre'n asleep. She heard Ilfn's love and protectiveness of her Senyas in her voice, and saw it in the hand smoothing the sleeping dancer's hair.

"I don't dislike him," Rheba said. "I simply can't see him as my mate. He's such a sweet child. So . . . weak."

Ilfn looked from the soft gold lines coursing over Rheba's body to the pale, barely marked hands of her sleeping rain dancer. "He's young. Too young. I've had to keep him from—"

The Bre'n's voice stopped. Rheba waited, then finished the sentence. "You've kept him from using his power?" She did not mean for her voice to sound accusing, but it did.

"Yes!" whispered Ilfn fiercely. "If Lord Puc even suspected what Lheket could become—" Her voice broke, then resumed in the calm tones of an akhenet instructing a child. "The Loo like their slaves powerless. I've done what I had to. Lheket is still alive. Before you judge me, fire dancer, remember that." There was a space of silence. Then, "In the days since he has felt the Act's energies pouring through this room he's been hard to hold. I'll have to choose, soon."

"Choose?"

"To kill him or to shape his gift. It's a choice all Bre'n akhenets make." She looked up, sensing Rheba's horror. "Didn't you know that, fire dancer? Didn't your Senyas parents tell you what your Bre'n was?"

"I—" Rheba swallowed and tried again. "I didn't know."

"What of your Bre'n parents?"

"They died in one of the early firefalls. After that, it was all we could do to hold our chields against the sun. The years I should have spent learning Bre'n and Senyas history, I spent learning now to deflect fire."

"But at your age—ah, yes," sighed Ilfn. "Your age. I keep forgetting that you are at least ten years younger than your akhenet lines indicate. So much power." Ilfn shifted, moving away from Kirtn without disturbing her sleeping boy. "Sit down, fire dancer. You resent me, but I know things you should know."

"I don't resent you," Rheba said quickly.

Ilfn laughed, a gentle rather than a mocking sound. "You have many and powerful lines, but you lie as badly as a child half your age." Her hand closed around Rheba's, gently pulling her down. "On Deva you never would have had to confront your emotions about your Bre'n before you were wise enough to understand them."

"Deva is dead."

"Yes." The word was long, a sigh. "Listen to me, akhenet," said Ilfn, her tone changing to that of a mentor. "You shift between woman and child with each breath. The child in you resents my pregnancy, Lheket's future claim on your body, and everything else that would separate you from your

143

Bre'n. There's no point in denying it. The Senyas instinct to bind Bre'n is as great as the Bre'n instinct to bind Senyas. There is a reason for that instinct. Without Kirtn you would die, victim of your own powers. Without you Kirtn would die, victim of a Bre'n's special needs. I would no more stand between you and your Bre'n than I would gladly lie down with Lord Puc. But slaves have few choices, and none of them easy."

Rheba looked away from the Bre'n woman's too-dark eyes. Compared to Ilfn, she had suffered very little at the hands of the Loo. "I hope," she whispered, "I hope Kirtn pleased you." She looked away, embarrassed, not knowing what to say, feeling more a child than she had in years. "I'll try not to be afraid or jealous. I know that it's wrong. You're my sister. Your children are also mine."

The last words were sure, all that remained to her of the akhenet rituals of her childhood. For the first time she understood the need of ceremony to mark times of great change in akhenet lives, change such as had happened when Kirtn went to Ilfn and they conceived children. A ritual would have told her what to say, what to feel, reassured her that the world was not turning inside out. There were no rituals left, though, and she was afraid that she had made an enemy of her Bre'n's mate.

Ilfn's hands came up and stroked Rheba's seething hair. "Thank you for naming me sister, even though you had no part in choosing me. I never thought I would be called that again."

Rheba stared at Ilfn, realizing anew that the Bre'n was a person with her own history on Deva, her own families and lovers and losses to mourn. And now, only memories.

"I'll have fine children," continued Ilfn, her gaze turned inward. "My Senyas father was a gene dancer; he gave me the ability to choose my children. I wonder if he knew just how much the race of Bre'n would need that." Her smile was thin, more sorrow than pleasure in her memories. "He gave Lheket that gift, too. Your children will be powerful, fire dancer, and they will come by twos and threes as mine will."

Rheba looked away, unable to bear either the past or the future that was reflected in the older woman's eyes. The past was ashes; the future nothing that Rheba could or wanted to touch. All that was real to her was now, this instant—Kirtn. But the Bre'n woman and her akhenet boy were also real.

Silently, Rheba struggled with her childish desire to shut out everything but Kirtn. When she had dreamed of finding other Bre'ns and Senyasi, of building a new future for both races, she had not dreamed that it would be this painful.

"But your children," said Ilfn, looking down at Lheket, "are years in the future, and you're too young to know how short years really are." Tenderly, Ilfn put her soft-furred cheek against Rheba's smooth cheek, where lines of power lay cool and gold, quiet, waiting to burn into life. "You're braver than you know," whispered the Bre'n, "and more powerful. Take care of your Bre'n. He needs you, child and woman, *he needs you.*"

Rheba pulled back, disturbed by Ilfn's words and her intensity. "What do you mean?"

Ilfn moved her head in the Bre'n negative.

"Tell me," whispered Rheba. "I haven't had any real training, no quiet years of learning with my Bre'n and Senyas families. If there's something Kirtn needs, tell me!"

"I can't. It's forbidden."

"But why?"

"Each akhenet makes the choice you will make." Ilfn spoke reluctantly, using words as though they had edges sharp enough to cut her tongue. "The choice comes from your very core. To describe it is to violate its purity. It would be better to kill you both than to do that."

"I don't understand," said Rheba, her voice rising. "First you tell me that I'm doing something wrong, or not doing something right, then you tell me that you can't say any more."

Ilfn turned away from Rheba's anger and watched her sleeping Lheket. The Bre'n profile was cold and distant as a moon. It was one of the faces Rheba had seen in Lheket's earring, a face both beautiful and terrible, utterly serene.

Rheba turned away and looked at Kirtn, seeing him as though he were a stranger, powerful and obscure. *Child and woman, he needs you.*

The sleeping Bre'n stirred, dream shadows changing his face. Rheba felt something twisting inside her as she realized for the first time that Kirtn was inhumanly beautiful, as perfectly formed as a god. His gold mask glowed like two enormous eyes, and she ached to touch the copper hair that was so different from the copper plush of his fur. His powerful body moved again, graceful even in sleep. Muscles coiled and slid easily beneath the thin sheen of fur. She shivered, wanting to go to him, to lie down next to him, to pull his warmth and power around her like a robe, to build a cage of fire around them both, together.

145

Akhenet lines pulsed achingly throughout her body, traceries of fire in the darkened room. She bent over Kirtn until her hair drifted across his shoulders like a cloud of fire. Her hands moved as though drawn against her will, seeking the textures of muscle and fur. But when she was a breath away from touching him she drew back, frightened by the heat of her own body.

She sat without moving until dawn, shivering with cold and unnamed emotions, practicing the akhenet discipline of thinking about nothing at all.

# XX

"This," said Dapsl, using a drawing stick across a piece of plastic, "is the ampitheater. The Imperial Loo-chim has the seats of honor right there"—the stick went to a point just beyond the center curve of the stage—"and the rest of the chims are arrayed on either side according to rules of precedence no slave could understand."

Rheba leaned against the wall, trying to keep her eyes open. The Act had rehearsed all morning, making the lost night's sleep like a sandy weight on her eyelids. Besides her, Lheket stirred restlessly. His beautiful, blind green eyes turned toward her, but no recognition moved in their depths. She took his hand and murmured soothingly. He had been disturbed ever since Ilfn had left, ostensibly to find salve for Rheba, but actually to contact the rebel slaves.

In response to Rheba's touch, Lheket reached up toward her, seeking her hair. Her hair, however, was bound in a knot beyond his reach. Seeing his disappointment, she shook her head, sending her hair cascading down her back. The silky strands brushed across his face. He giggled.

"Tickles," he whispered in Senyas.

She smiled before she remembered that he could not see. She touched his cheek gently. "Quiet, rain dancer, or Dapsl will get angry."

Lheket subsided, but he kept a strand of her hair in his hands. She frowned and tugged gently. His fingers tightened. She sighed and leaned closer to him, taking the strain off her hair. With Ilfn gone, he seemed to need constant tactile reassurance. Not that she blamed him—being a blind slave among aliens would unnerve even an adult.

She wondered if Ilfn had been successful in contacting the rebels who were planning the Last Year's Night uprising. They would not be pleased to add new lines to their rebellion

147

script at this late date; but they would have no choice. Either Rheba's Act was included in the rebellion, or Ilfn would not give the door codes.

She sensed Dapsl's glare and returned her wandering mind to his lecture. Her attention was not really required. Kirtn was memorizing every word, for it was the Bre'n who would choose their escape route out of an amphitheater full of Loo aristocrats and their guards. The J/taals, too, were very attentive. Their military experience was the pivot point of any plans Kirtn would make.

"—ramp leads to the area behind the stage. You'll wait in the tunnel until you're cued, then come to the quadruple blue mark on the left wing of the stage."

Kirtn watched the crude drawing of the amphitheater that was growing beneath Dapsl's stick. "What about curtains, lights, energy barriers, props—"

"Nothing," said Dapsl firmly. "Acts that can't provide their own light perform during the day. The amphitheater is pre-Equality. It was built by people who either didn't want or didn't know how to use a mechanized stage. There will be absolutely nothing on the stage of use to you except your own skills."

*And thus, no energy source for Rheba to draw on.*

Though neither she nor Kirtn said anything, the thought was foremost in their minds. Their performance would be given at night, along with the other bioluminescent Acts. She would have no exterior source of energy but the Act itself, unless she set fire to the stage and then wove more complex energies from the simple flames.

But the stage, like the ampitheater, was made of stone. She did not believe she could set it ablaze, especially in the time given to her during the Act. To take heat out of the night air, condense it, shape it, and then use it to ignite even highly combustible organic material required a long, concentrated effort on her part. She would have enough difficulty simply maintaining the cold light required for their Act.

"But the amphitheater isn't protected," said Kirtn. "Did the Loo-chim—or whoever built it—plan on sitting in the rain and watching slaves drown?"

Dapsl grimaced and pulled on his longest braid. "This is the dry season. It almost never rains on the Last Year Night."

Rheba looked at the boy beside her, smiling faintly as he played with her lively hair. Rain dancer.

"Never?" shot back Kirtn. "Do they use weather control?"

Dapsl made an oblique gesture. "If the weather is bad, there's an energy shield over the amphitheater that can be activated. It's been used in the past. That won't affect the Act, will it?"

Rheba made a dismissing gesture. "Shield, no shield. It doesn't matter," she said casually, hoping Dapsl believed her.

He chewed thoughtfully on a braid end, then spat it out and returned to the business of familiarizing the Act with the stage they would use for the most important performance of their lives.

"Since we have been given the honor—the *great* honor—of being the last Act of the Last Year Night, we won't be called out of the tunnel until there is just enough time left to perform and finish on the absolute stroke of midnight. The timing is crucial; too soon or too late will spoil the ritual and displease the Loo-chim. That wouldn't be wise."

Rheba's smile was both grim and predatory. She hoped to do more than displease the Loo-chim before the Last Year Night was over. The thought made her hair stir, strands lifting and seeking blindly for her Bre'n.

Lheket smiled dreamily, instinctively drawing on her energies. His eyes changed, darker now yet somehow more alive. The tips of his fingers began to pulse a pale, metallic blue, first hint of latent akhenet lines. When she looked down she saw the blush of blue on his fingertips. Realizing what had happened, she damped her own power. He made an involuntary noise of protest.

"Keep that cub quiet or I'll send him back to his room," snapped Dapsl. "It's bad enough that I have to put up with a furry whore unsettling the Act, but to put up with her belly warmer is—"

Whatever Dapsl had meant to say died on his tongue when Kirtn and Rheba stared at him, their predatory thoughts naked on their faces. A clept snarled. Like the J/taals, they took their signals from Rheba, the J/taaleri. Fssa, hidden in her hair, made a sound that was between a snarl and a growl. The clept subsided. Rheba wondered what the snake had said to the clept, but did not further infuriate Dapsl by opening a dialogue with Fssa.

"Continue," she said, her eyes like cinnamon jewels with darker flecks of rage turning in their depths. "And remember, small man, whose Act you belong to."

"Two days," snapped Dapsl.

"Two days," she agreed. In two days the Act would be performed, and they would be rid of Dapsl until the next time they were required to perform. The Loo could not divide a Concatenation Act, but the Act could choose to live apart.

"The only thing," continued Dapsl in a tight voice, "in the ampitheater besides the softstone seats and the stone stage is the silver gong in front of the Imperial Loo-chim. It is struck twice to bring on an Act. It is struck four times at the end of an Act." He smiled unpleasantly. "Often the Loo-chim doesn't wait for the end if the Act displeases it. Then the gong is struck three times, and the slaves are taken to the Pit. That won't be a problem in our Act, though. The Loo-chim has made it obvious that it can't wait for the obscene tongues of their furry—"

Kirtn moved in a supple twist of power that brought him to his feet. Dapsl changed the subject hurriedly.

"After the gong sounds twice, you have a hundred count to take your place. The gong will sound twice again. The Act will begin. After the Act is over, the gong will sound four times. You have a hundred count to clear the stage, descend the ramp, and return to the tunnel. Questions?"

Rheba had many questions, none of which Dapsl could answer. Apparently Kirtn felt the same way, for he kept his silence. Dapsl looked around, diappointed. After a moment he tossed his braids over his shoulder and turned away, rolling up the plastic sheet.

"I'll take that," said Kirtn, reaching for the diagram of the ampitheater.

The sheet slid out of Dapsl's grasp before he had a chance to object. "What—?"

"The J/taals," Kirtn said. "I'll explain the layout to them. Fssa didn't translate while you were talking because we know it annoys you. Rheba told them we'd explain later."

Dapsl stood, trying to think of a reason to object. "It's the first time you've ever shut up that flatulent beast on my account."

Kirtn gave the Bre'n version of a shrug, a movement of his torso that revealed each powerful muscle. "Just trying to keep everyone calm. We're all touchy, the closer the performance comes."

"Grmmm," said Dapsl, his pale eyes narrowed. But he could think of no reason to object. "Be careful with it. Lord Jal bent the rules just to give us a writing stick and plasheet. If you ruin it, I can't get another."

Kirtn started to reply, but saw Ilfn. He watched her come soundlessly into the room. Even so, Lheket sensed her return. His thin face turned toward the door, his expression radiant.

150

Kirtn wished that Rheba would show her feelings for him so clearly; but she would not. She had schooled herself to show as little of her feelings as possible since Deva died. Or perhaps it was simply that she had no such depth of emotion for him.

He turned away from his thoughts and went to Ilfn. "I have the amphitheater plans," he said in Senyas, his voice harsher than he meant it to be, residue of his thoughts. "Did you—"

She held up a small pot made of swirls of blue-green glass. "I found everything we need." She looked at Dapsl.

"He doesn't understand Senyas or Bre'n," said Kirtn.

"Good. I managed to speak with my contact for a few minutes while I got Rheba's salve."

Rheba brought Lheket to his Bre'n. The boy's smile was as brilliant as his sightless emerald eyes. Ilfn's hand went out, stroking the boy's face reassuringly. He turned and brushed his lips against the velvet of her palm.

The gesture was so natural that it took a moment for its impact to register with Rheba. Her eyes widened. She studied the woman and the boy, using her fire dancer sensitivity. She found nothing but mutual love expressed in touches that were sensual without being explicitly sexual. Yet the potential for passion obviously existed. The thought disturbed her. Was sexual intimacy normal for a Bre'n/Senyas akhenet pair?

Her memories gave her no immediate answer. She tried to recall her Senyas mother and her Bre'n father. Had they been lovers as well as akhenet pair? The memories refused to form. All that came was the incandescent moment of her parents' death. She had deliberately not thought of her parents since Deva died. She found she could not do so now. It was too painful.

"Rheba?"

Kirtn's questioning whistle brought her out of the past. "I'm fine," she lied, shivering. Her eyes were dark, inward-looking, reflecting a time and a place that seared her mind. "I'm fine." Without thinking, she took his hand and rubbed her cheek against it, savoring the velvet texture of his skin. Her lips touched his palm. Then she realized that her actions were very like Lheket's with Ilfn. She dropped Kirtn's hand.

"Rheba?"

The whistle was soft, worried, as pure as the gold of his eyes watching her. "It's nothing," she lied, rubbing her cheek where it had touched his hand. "Nothing." The last word was a whisper.

Kirtn began to touch her, then retreated. He sensed that his touch was disturbing to her now. There was no reason for her to react that way—except that akhenets who were worked too hard became irrational. She must rest. Yet she could not. Concatenation Night was only two days away. "Why don't you lie down, Rheba? Ilfn and I can explain the amphitheater to the J/taals."

"No." Rheba's voice was curt. She looked at Ilfn. "Did you get anything more useful than a smelly pot of goo?"

The Bre'n woman hesitated at Rheba's tone. She looked from the girl to Kirtn and back again. "The unguent will help you, fire dancer. Your akhenet lines are new. They must itch terribly."

Rheba, who was at that moment scratching her shoulder, said only, "We've more important things to worry about than my skin."

Kirtn took the pot from Ilfn and began rubbing the unguent into Rheba despite her protests. "Nothing is more important than your well-being. Without you, fire dancer, we would die slaves."

Rheba looked around as though seeing Dapsl and the J/taals and stone walls for the first time. Her voice was as brittle as autumn ice. She gestured to the plasheet. "Unroll it. Explain to Ilfn and the J/taals how we're going to die trying not to be slaves."

# XXI

Kirtn started to say something, then did not. Rheba's hair was shimmering, the ends twisting like ultrafine gold wires held over a fire. If she had any control left, she was not exercising it. Anyone who touched her would receive a jolt of energy that could range from painful to debilitating. But then, that was why Bre'n akhenets learned to control pain.

Deliberately, he buried his right hand deeply in her hair. The air around her head crackled. A shockwave of energy expanded up his arm. His left hand clenched, the only outward sign of the agony that came when he drained off some of her seething energy.

When Rheba realized what she had inadvertently done to him, she cried out an apology and jerked her hair from his fingers. Her eyes were huge and dark, pinwheels of uneasy fire stirring their depths. Without hesitation he put his hand into her hair again. This time the long golden strands curled around his arm like a molten sleeve. He smiled and smoothed her cheekbone with his thumb.

"It's all right," he murmured. "I knew what would happen if I touched your hair then."

"Why did you do it if you knew?"

"Unstructured energy is dangerous, fire dancer. You could have killed one of the J/taals just by brushing against them." He smiled, then turned and left her side before she could say anything. As he walked over to the J/taals, clepts gave way before him. He stopped and spoke to M/dere.

From his hiding place in Rheba's hair, Fssa began to translate Kirtn's words into the J/taal language. Startled, Rheba reached up into her hair. She had forgotten the snake was there. He felt very warm, hot, but seemed not to have suffered any damage in the outburst of energy Kirtn had triggered from her. Apparently the Fssireeme could deal with

153

forms of energy other than sound waves. Nonetheless, she made a silent promise to remember the inconspicuous snake before she let her emotions get the better of her control.

She walked over and stood next to Kirtn as he described the amphitheater to the J/taals. Fssa's translation was simultaneous, unobtrusive, and an exact tonal reproduction of the person speaking. Ilfn stood on the other side of Kirtn, listening carefully. Next to her stood Lheket, a silent, shoulder-high presence who never stood more than an arm's length from his Bre'n.

After Kirtn finished, M/dere looked at the diagram for a moment, sheathing and unsheathing her claws as she thought. "The spaceport," she said finally. "Where is it on this sheet?"

"Over here and to the left," said Ilfn, pointing to an area behind the amphitheater. "If we use the Bay Road, it's more than five *mie* from here. But there's an estate over . . . here." Her hand switched to the left side of the amphitheater. "It's a Loo-chim park, closed to all but the Imperial Loo-chim and a few favorites."

"Then how do we get in?" asked M/dere.

"From here. The park was part of the state complex once. Most of the buildings there are ruins now. Only the amphitheater is kept up. The tunnel system goes underneath all of it. I was told there's a way from the amphitheater tunnel into the park. From there, it's less than two *mie* to the spaceport."

M/dere looked at the map again. Ilfn's moving finger had left no trace of its passage on the resistant plasheet. The J/taal leader stared, then called her clept. She bent over the waist-high animal, murmuring commands that Fssa did not translate. The clept opened its mouth, revealing serrated rows of teeth. On its fangs bright-blue drops formed. M/dere dipped an extended claw into the fluid and began drawing on the map. Clept venom smoked faintly, leaving behind vague, dark stains as it corroded the durable plasheet.

"The tunnel exit . . . here?" asked M/dere.

Ilfn gestured agreement, which Fssa translated as a J/taal affirmative.

"The park . . . here?"

Again the affirmative.

"The spaceport . . . here?"

"A little farther to the right."

"Here?"

"Yes."

"How big is the spaceport?"

"I don't know. Many *mie*."

"The J/taaleri's ship . . . where?"

Ilfn looked at Kirtn. "J/taaleri?"

"Their employer," he said. "Rheba."

Ilfn's eyes widened. She glanced quickly at Rheba, then back to the map. "The ship is here, on the edge of the spaceport by the park. It's a derelict yard, from what I was told." She looked up at Kirtn, silently questioning.

"The *Devalon* wasn't derelict when we landed," said Kirtn. "They probably put the ship in the derelict yard when they found out that the *Devalon* only responds to us."

"I'd hoped that was it," breathed Ilfn. "Our ship is the same."

"Is it here?" demanded Kirtn.

"No. If it were, Lheket and I would have left as soon as we got out of the Fold!"

"Then where is your ship?" asked Rheba.

"I don't know." Ilfn's dark eyes became hooded, looking back on pain. "We answered a call for help as we came out of *replacement*. It was a trap. The *Autumn Moon* was left in orbit around a dead planet called Sorriaaix. They abandoned the *Moon* when they couldn't learn its secrets."

M/dere's movement brought Ilfn's attention back to the present. The J/taal's claws were tracing random marks around the amphitheater, disguising the meaningful marks of tunnel, park, spaceport and ship.

"That animal is ruining the diagram!" cried Dapsl, pushing through the people crowded around the map. He tried to snatch away the plasheet, but Kirtn's hand held him back. Rheba felt a moment of panic as she tried to remember what languages they had been using. Had it been only Senyas and J/taal? Or had they forgotten and slipped into Universal, which Dapsl understood? How long had Dapsl been watching—long enough to see the map before M/dere disguised the additions to it?

"Careful," said Kirtn. "Don't you know that J/taal claws are poisonous?"

It was not true, but Dapsl shrank back anyway. The clept venom was real enough; it still shone bluely on M/dere's claw tip.

"What's she doing?" demanded Dapsl. Then, when M/dere resumed making random marks, "Stop her!"

Kirtn shrugged. "Why? We don't need the diagram anymore, and scribbling on it seems to amuse her."

Dapsl fell silent. His shrewd eyes swept the diagram as he

struggled against the hand holding back his wrist. Then he stopped moving, studying the plasheet as though he had never seen it before. His braid ends bounced as he turned on Kirtn.

"Let go of me." His voice was cool and hard, a voice they had never heard him use. "I've done everything I could for this Act, more than any other Whip could have. But you wouldn't know about that," he said, sweeping the group with a single contemptuous look. "None of you is civilized enough to appreciate a Loo Whip. You're no more than animals."

Dapsl pulled free of Kirtn and stalked out of the room.

Kirtn looked at Rheba, who shrugged in lithe imitation of the Bre'n gesture and turned back to the map. "What about the guards? When do we leave the stage, and by which exit? Will anyone be able to help us fight our way to the spaceport?"

Ilfn hesitated. To the rest of the people, she appeared uncertain. But Rheba and Kirtn knew Bre'ns; it was obvious to them that reluctance rather than uncertainty held her tongue. Kirtn whistled coaxingly. The sound was so unexpected and yet so beautiful that Lheket's head came up and turned in Kirtn's direction. The boy answered the whistle in a lower key, a pure ripple of sound that brought an approving look from Kirtn. The boy repeated the whistle in yet another key. Ilfn gave in and began to speak.

"The end of your Act will be the signal for the beginning of the rebellion. The instant the Hour Between Years is struck, slaves will pour into the streets. Most will only be celebrating, I think. Others will be fighting their way to the spaceport. Almost everyone in the city will be half-phased by then—Imperiapolis' drugs are varied and strong. By midnight, everyone is dancing in the streets, firing off smelly rockets. The commoners and slaves wear elaborate costumes patterned after Loo myths. From what I was told, the streets are chaotic. Only foot traffic is allowed. That's why we won't be conspicuous. Slaves are expected to dance and get phased out. Maybe it's the Loo way of testing slaves' Adjustment. I don't know. But during the Hour Between Years, there is no law."

"Weapons," said M/dere impatiently.

Ilfn closed her eyes. "None. Sirgi—my contact—doesn't have any. Or if he does, he isn't sharing them with Lord Puc's whore."

Kirtn's lips flattened. The sound he made brought the clepts snarling to their feet. "Who is this man that he believes he's better than you?"

"A red furry from a heavy planet so far away he can't

156

even point to its direction in the sky." She shrugged and smiled. "He's short, strong, and half-bright. He's also very determined to get home. He was a priest there, or some such thing. He has a very small opinion of women, slaves or not."

"Does he know about our J/taals?"

Ilfn's smile changed indefinably, dangerously. M/dere examined her suddenly, plainly reassessing the Bre'n woman's usefulness in the coming fight; the J/taal smiled, pleased. The smile was very like Ilfn's.

"I failed to mention our J/taals," murmured Ilfn. "Not that it really matters."

"Why?"

"Your fire dancer is the most deadly weapon on Loo."

Kirtn began to object, then did not. What Ilfn said was true. Of all the Senyas akhenets, fire dancers had the most potential for destruction. Silently he promised himself that he would not let it come to that for Rheba. She had seen and suffered too much already; turning her into a killer would destroy her.

"Can we trust the other slaves?" asked Rheba quietly.

Ilfn hesitated, saying much through her silence. "So long as they need us, yes. Sirgi is very interested in the *Devalon*. I explained several times that even if he could get inside the ship, it wouldn't respond to anyone but the akhenet team it was built for. I don't know if Sirgi believed me. In any case, I had to promise to take as many slaves with us as we could hold."

"I'd do that whether he asked or not," said Rheba.

"I told him that. I don't think he believed it, either."

Rheba whistled a sour note. "What else?"

"Nothing. They'll wait by the first outside arch. When we come, I give the code. Then we'll be in the park. After that, getting to the spaceport is a matter of luck."

"We know all about luck," Rheba said. "We learned on Deva."

Ilfn's eyes reflected that bitter knowledge. She said nothing.

"I'd feel better if there were a source of energy in the amphitheater for me to draw on—even moonlight," said Rheba.

"No moons," said Ilfn. "They don't rise until after the Hour Between Years."

"When you were outside today, how did the sky look?"

"Dry."

"Then they won't have the weather shield activated," said Rheba. She shifted her attention to Lheket, a rain dancer innocent of akhenet lines. "Can he at least call clouds?"

157

"No," said Ilfn quickly.

"Why not?" asked Rheba, her voice cold. "He's akhenet, isn't he?"

"Untrained."

"Whose fault is that?" she snapped.

Ilfn spoke softly, though her expression was forbidding. "He's only a child."

"He's old enough for simple rain dancing. On Deva, he would have been apprenticed to an akhenet farm years ago."

"This isn't Deva. There aren't any other dancers to help him."

Kirtn interrupted before Rheba could answer. His whistle was low, penetrating. "What are you afraid of, Ilfn?"

"I—" Her whistle fragmented. She spoke Senyas, then, each word clipped. "I've never allowed him to dance. I don't know if he can, without training. And where is the Bre'n family, the Senyas family, the akhenets paired to help him in the first dangerous attempts? *He's very strong.* If I can't control him, I'll have to kill him."

Rheba remembered the ease with which Lheket had drawn power out of her, his reflexive thirst for the rich currents of force that were an akhenet's birthright. There was no doubt about his strength. And no one knew better than she what would happen if a strong, untrained akhenet blew up in their hands. She had seen it happen more than once on Deva, toward the end, when everyone was desperate for akhenets to help hold the deflectors. The result had been almost as terrible as the sun itself. Unless death was the only other choice, it would be better to leave Lheket's power dormant until they could devote themselves to easing him into his potent birthright.

"Ilfn is right," sighed Rheba, then repeated the words in a Bre'n whistle that was rich with resonances of acceptance and regret. "I can sustain the Act using only our akhenet energy. Once we're out of the amphitheater and tunnel complex, there will be other sources of energy for me to draw on. But I don't like it. Inside that amphitheater, I'll be about as much use as an empty gun."

She looked longingly at Lheket. The blind green eyes looked back at her, unfocused. Yet he always knew where she was—like a flower following the sun, he sensed her turbulent energy. As she sensed his—a silent pool, potential dormant, seen only in a slow welling of power from its depths. It was tempting to tap that power, but she would not. Awakened, Lheket was as dangerous to them as an unstable sun.

Rheba sensed someone behind her, standing in the archway that led to the rest of the compound. She turned suddenly. Dapsl was there, and with him Lord Jal. Next to the lord was a pale, dark-haired woman of medium height. Her face was devoid of expression.

Lord Jal made a small gesture with his hand. Dapsl and the woman remained standing while the Loo lord approached Rheba. The woman's eyes never left Rheba, as though it were important to memorize every nuance of her. Casually, Jal's hand brushed Kirtn, then Rheba.

There was an instant of sleeting pain, then Rheba froze. All voluntary control of her body was gone. She could only stand and stare in the direction her head had been turned before Jal touched her. She could not speak. She had to struggle to do such semiautomatic things as swallow or blink. Though she could not see Kirtn directly, she sensed that he, too, was held in the grip of whatever drug Lord Jal had used on them.

Before anyone realized what had happened, the lord moved among the J/taals. Because their J/taaleri was silent, apparently unconcerned by Jal's presence, the mercenaries made no move to protect themselves even after M/dere had passed on a silent mental warning as her body froze.

Jal brushed against Ilfn with his hand, rendering her helpless. He ignored the blind child as he took a dart gun from his robes. He held the muzzle of the gun against Rheba's throat where her pulse beat slowly under her tawny skin.

"Whip, tell M/dere that if her clepts move, I'll kill Rheba."

Dapsl relayed the commands in broken J/taal. It became obvious that he understood the language much better than he spoke it.

"Now," said Jal. "Release her voice."

Dapsl nervously walked up to M/dere, touched her neck with an invisibly fine needle, and backed away hurriedly.

"Tell her to make her animals lie down," said Jal, the gun held unwaveringly at Rheba's throat.

Desperately, Rheba tried to gather fire, but her akhenet lines lighted only sluggishly. The drug had taken her mind as certainly as it had her body.

M/dere grunted harsh commands. The clepts dropped to the floor as though struck. They watched Jal out of hungry silver eyes, but did not move.

"If you speak without my invitation, I'll kill your J/taaleri. Say yes if you understand. One word only."

Dapsl barely finished his stumbling translation before M/dere spoke.

"Yes."

Jal looked at Dapsl. "You were right, Whip. Rheba is their J/taaleri, though how that came about—" He made a dismissing gesture. "It doesn't matter, now." He turned back to M/dere. "I haven't harmed your J/taaleri, so there's no reason to be rash," he said, ignoring Dapsl's halting translation of Universal into J/taal. "In fact, you should thank me. I'm doing your job—saving her life." He turned with surprising quickness and touched Rheba again. He supported her as she sank soundlessly to the floor.

The clepts made chilling noises, but did not move. Nor did M/dere speak, for Lord Jal's gun was never far enough from Rheba's throat to ensure that a clept could kill him before he killed her.

"She's perfectly safe," said Dapsl from the doorway. "The drug is harmless. And so is she, now. Lord Jal wouldn't be so stupid as to ruin a valuable slave."

M/dere remained silent. The clepts looked at her, then put down their heads and stopped making any sound at all.

Lord Jal bowed slightly. "I counted on the J/taals' famed pragmatism. I abhor wasting slaves." He looked at the two slaves waiting in the doorway, Dapsl and the strange woman. "Did you see enough, i'sNara?"

"Yes, lord." The woman's voice was colorless, as devoid of feeling as her white face. She came and bent over Rheba, studying her face, her long hair, the vague golden lines that ran over her hands and feet. She pulled up Rheba's robe, revealing more lines on legs, arms, torso. "Does she work naked?"

"Sometimes," said Dapsl. "But that would be difficult to duplicate. Her skin designs are very complicated. And they pulse obscenely."

"A robe, then," said Lord Jal.

"Yes," said i'sNara absently.

Kirtn watched the stranger hover over Rheba, but he could do no more than make tearing attempts to move a single finger. His efforts did little more than darken his copper fur with sweat. From time to time Jal looked over at him, making sure that the drug was still working. The woman straightened suddenly. The air around her seemed to go slightly opaque, as though something were condensing around her body. She blurred, reformed, and the air was clear again.

But it was Rheba who stood there.

Lord Jal walked around her without saying anything. After

the second circuit, he stopped. "More eyelashes, i'sNara. And the hair—can you make it seem to move by itself?"

Kirtn watched with nausea coiling in his stomach while i'sNara duplicated Rheba's long, dense eyelashes and gently dancing hair.

"Good. Mmmm . . ." Lord Jal walked around her again. "Straighter posture. She's a proud bitch. Yes, like that. Now walk." Lord Jal watched. "No. She's stronger than she looks. I wish I'd been able to bring you to see the Act, but after what my Whip told me, I didn't want to risk wasting any time."

"You did well to immobilize them without having to waste a single clept," said Dapsl.

Lord Jal grunted. He looked at M/dere. "Tell her to have that clept on the far side of the room walk up and down—but not close to us!"

Dapsl said a few words in the J/taals' grating language. M/dere spoke. A clept rose and prowled the length of the room, never getting close enough to Jal for a killing leap. I'sNara/Rheba watched silently.

"That's enough," said Jal. As soon as the clept lay down, he walked over to M/dere, touched her neck and froze her speech organs again. He turned back to i'sNara. "Rheba walks like that clept. Graceful, but not delicate. Her strength shows in her balance." He smiled absently. "Now that I think about it, she's a handsome wench. Just more trouble than any sane man would want."

I'sNara/Rheba walked. Kirtn could not control the sickness that swept through him when he saw Rheba's lithe movements duplicated by a soulless slave.

"Good." Lord Jal turned and looked at Kirtn. "Listen to me, furry, and pray that you aren't as stupid as you are strong. Your rebellion hasn't the chance of a raindrop on the sun."

Kirtn went cold, but his stance did not change, could not change. He was prisoner to a slaver's drug. All he could do was listen while his hopes of freedom were destroyed one word at a time.

Beyond Jal, Dapsl's broken J/taal words came like a grating echo as the Loo beat flat their hopes with steel words.

"Slaves who are unAdjusted enough to even *plan* rebellion are executed. But in less than two days, you'll be the Imperial Loo-chim's problem. They'll reward me very well for this Act, enough that I'll never have to hear Lady Kurs call me

161

half-man again. I'm not going to let a slave's foolish dreams come between me and *my* freedom!"

Lord Jal looked at the Act, frozen in anguished tableau, and Rheba unconscious at his feet. "As you've probably noticed," he continued dryly, "i'sNara is a Yhelle illusionist of the Tenth Degree. She is also mine. And now she is Rheba to the last eyelash. She'll be Rheba on Last Year Night, a fire dancer down to the least flickering flame on the clepts. No one but you will know that an illusionist rather than a fire dancer is performing in the Act. No one in the audience will separate illusion from Act.

"Nor will you rebel at the stroke of midnight. If you do, Rheba will die. If you don't perform well, Rheba will die. If anything happens in the Act or during the Hour Between Years that displeases me or the Imperial Loo-chim, Rheba will die. Do you understand me, furry?"

Jal's hand snaked out at eye level. For the first time Kirtn noticed the transparent gloves the Loo wore, and the needles impaled at each fingertip. The hand touched his neck, and muscles quivered, responsive again, but only enough for speech.

"Answer me, furry."

"I understand."

"Do you also understand that if word of this little deception get out, the Act will be executed?" asked Lord Jal, his tone casual but his eyes hard as glass.

"Yes," said Kirtn. It was all he said, but the barely suppressed violence in his voice made Lord Jal step back involuntarily.

"Remember that," said the Loo lord, "or before you die I'll separate you from your furry hide one thin strip at a time." He turned his back and pressed a stud at his belt. "Be yourself," he snapped at the illusionist.

I'sNara's appearance wavered, then became Yhelle again. In a moment, a guard appeared at the archway, called by the signal on Jal's belt.

"Lord?" said the guard.

"Pick up this slave," said Jal, nudging Rheba with his foot. "Follow me."

"Yes, lord."

Kirtn raged silently, helplessly, as he watched Rheba vanish down the hallway, carried off like a sack of grain at the command of a Loo lord.

# XXII

⊷─◆─◆─◆─⊷

The stone floor was cold. The chains around Rheba's ankles, wrists and neck were made of a metal alloy that drained heat out of her everywhere it touched. The clammy stone walls and floor were a little better, but she did not appreciate that fact. She was unconscious, curled in a fetal position on the floor, instinctively trying to preserve body warmth.

Tangled in her cold hair, Fssa made a sound halfway between a whimper and her name. "Rheba . . . Rheba, *wake up.* It's been so long since you were awake. Fire dancer, *wake up*," he said, using Kirtn's voice, desperately trying to reach her. "It's cold here. Wake up and make us a fire!"

The snake's voice was like water rippling over stone at the far edge of her awareness, an endless susurration that impinged little on her emotions. The words continued, first in Senyas and then in Universal, and finally, as Fssa lost energy, in Bre'n. His whistle retained its purity, even though the snake was compacted densely in upon himself, thinner than Rheba's smallest finger and shorter than her lower arm. It was the Fssireeme way to conserve body heat.

After a very long time, she moaned. A convulsion shook her body, a deep shuddering that went on and on as she tried to throw off the debilitating effects of drugs and cold. Chains scraped over the floor spasmodically. The grating sounds woke Fssa, who had succumbed to a state that was not far from sleep. But for the Fssireeme, to sleep was to die.

*"Fire dancer . . ."*

Fssa's whistle was ragged, despairing. It reached through the fog climbing in Rheba's mind as no sweet notes could have. She shivered convulsively, bringing her knees even closer to her body and wrapping her arms around her legs.

163

She was all but numb with cold, yet moving brought such agony as to make her sweat and moan aloud.

"Fire dancer . . ." The whistle sounded very distant, very weak.

"Kirtn . . . ? Is that you? Where are you? Are you hurt?"

As he heard her speak, Fssa permitted himself to draw off just a bit of her body heat, believing that since she had awakened she would be able to start a fire to warm them both. With the heat he took from her came renewed energy, and fluency. His whistle became sure again.

"Not Kirtn. Fssa."

Rheba did not hear. She had opened her eyes—and seen nothing. "I'm blind," she said. "Oh my bright gods, Jal has blinded me!"

It took Fssa a moment to realize what had happened. He tried to tell her that the dungeon was lacking the form of energy she called light, but she was calling Kirtn's name again and again and could not hear anything but her own screams. Fssa drew off a bit more of her heat/energy, just enough to permit him to make an unbelievably shrill whistle.

The sound was like a slap in the face. Rheba's screams subsided into dry sobs.

"Rheba, it's Fssa. Can you hear me?"

The rhythmic shuddering of her body paused. "Fssa?"

"Yes. I'm—"

"What happened?" she interrupted. "Where's Kirtn? How did we get here? Is Kirtn all right?"

Questions came out of her like sparks leaping up from a fire. Another whistle split the dungeon's stony silences. She subsided.

"Do you remember Lord Jal coming into the Act's room?" whistled Fssa, the tone low and soothing now that he had her attention.

"I—" Her body shook continuously, but it was with cold now rather than fear. "Y-yes."

"After he knocked you out, he told the rest of us what a clever fellow his Whip was."

"W-whip?"

"Dapsl." Fssa swore with the poetic violence of a Bre'n. "When Lord Jal gave that purple wart a nerve wrangler, I should have guessed that Dapsl was truly a lord's Whip!"

"W-what's t-that?"

"A master slave, one who controls the others so that the lord won't have to bother." Fssa's whistle took on the tones of despair. While Rheba was unconscious he had had a lot of

164

time to consider what had happened. None of his conclusions were comforting. "Even worse, the slanted cherf speaks J/taal. Not well," he continued disdainfully. "He understands much better than he speaks, like most amateurs."

"D-did he understand about the reb-b-bellion?"

The snake's sigh was answer enough, but he enlarged on it. "He overheard and understood too much. But the rebellion will go on without us. In order for Lord Jal to avoid killing us, he had to avoid telling the other Loo lords about our plans. The other slaves, at least, will get their chance."

"B-but the Act. I have to p-perform. They can't d-do it without you and m-me."

"Jal thought of that," whistled Fssa in the minor keys of despair. "A Yhelle illusionist is doing your part. She duplicated you down to the last eyelash. As for the Bre'n song," again the sigh, "it will be a solo, not a duet."

"B-but the fire."

"The fire will be illusory, but the audience won't know the difference."

"At l-least the Act w-will have a chance at freedom."

Fssa's whistle slid down minor octaves in the Bre'n negative. "Lord Jal will kill you if the Act rebels."

"Unless Jal t-takes me out of this icy b-box," she said, trying and failing to control the convulsive shivering of her body, "I'll be d-dead before the new year. The L-Loo must be able to tolerate much lower temperatures than I can. N-normally it wouldn't matter, I'd j-just make fire, b-but now I'll just shiver until I c-can't move anymore."

"Make a fire!"

Her laugh sounded more like a sob. "Out of what, snake?"

Silence answered her question. For the first time since his birth, the Fssireeme was speechless. Then, very softly, "You can't use stone to make heat?"

"Not all b-by itself. I n-need something, some energy source outside the stone and myself. If I had that, I c-could eventually fire the stone. But I don't. And I c-can't."

The shivers were less now, but that did not mean that she was warmer; rather the opposite. Cold was stealing from her muscles even the ability to contract violently and send sugars into the bloodstream to be converted into heat.

"Fssa?" Her voice was suddenly thick, her words slow. "Am I blind?"

"No, fire dancer," whistled the snake gently. "The form of energy you call light just isn't to be found down here."

165

"That's what I was afraid you'd say. It would have been b-better if I were blind."

She could make light, but it would cost energy she could not spare. Nor did she particularly want to see the dimensions of her tomb. Chains clinked and chimed faintly as she shifted position, trying to ease a muscle that had not yet gone numb. After she moved, another round of convulsive shivering claimed her. When she was finally still again, it was very quiet. She listened, but there was nothing to be heard except her own breathing and the occasional small clatter of her chains rubbing over stone.

"Fssa?"

There was no answer.

"Fssa? Are you c-cold too?"

Silence. Then chains scraped and clinked as she ran numb fingers through her hair, trying to find the Fssireeme. He had sounded so strong that she had not thought that he might be in as much danger from the cold as she. More, with his smaller body mass. She did not know enough about his physiology to be certain, but thought that he took on the temperature of his environment—until it became too hot or too cold and he died.

"Fssa! Answer me! Where are you?"

There was only the sound of her cries echoing off stone walls. Despite the cost to her own reservoir of energy, she made a tiny ball of cold light. It was something even the smallest fire dancer child could do, a minor trick. But her strength was so depleted by cold that she felt every erg of energy it took to keep the light alive.

The cell was not large, no more than two body lengths in any direction. Even so, it was a moment before she spotted Fssa. The snake was curled in upon himself in a neat spiral that left the minimum of body heat escape into the clammy cell. His skin was very dark, darker than she had ever seen it.

"Fssa," she called.

The snake did not answer.

Worried, she called more loudly. The fourth time she called it was a scream that echoed off the black stone walls. Desperately, she sent the light to hover over him. When it was in place, she gradually changed the light's structure until it gave off heat as well as illumination. The drain to her was greater that way, but she was afraid that Fssa was dying. She would not permit herself to believe that he was already dead.

She watched the bright orange flame jealously, letting none of its heat slide off onto stone. Orange fire licked just above

166

Fssa's closed spiral. At first she was afraid that she would burn him; then she remembered that he had taken much worse heat when Kirtn had released her chaotic energy in a single pulse.

It was a long time before the snake changed. A random quiver of color passed down his dense ebony length. Gradually the color brightened, blue to orange, then yellow, and finally brilliant streaks of silver.

"Fssa?" she called.

The snake's head lifted out of the spiral. His opalescent sensors reflected the light she had made. He expanded into the warmth hovering around him. His delighted whistle soared above the flickering hot light. "You found a way to burn stone!"

"No," she sighed.

"Then where did this fire come from?"

"Me."

*"You're using your energy to keep me warm?"* The whistle was shrill, utterly horrified. He threw himself away from the light, but it followed him, shedding precious life over him. Her life. "Noooo."

The snake's anguished whistle was like a whip across her nerves. "Be still, you silly snake! The more you move, the harder it is for me to keep you warm!"

There was a long silence. Fssa did not move. His head was tucked underneath a coil, as though he would hide even from himself. A plaintive whistled issued from beneath the hovering flame. "Don't use up yourself, fire dancer. I'm not worth it."

She was too speechless to reply. She let the continued fire speak for her.

"You don't understand," continued Fssa desperately. "I'm not what you think I am."

"I think you're beautiful."

Fssa's answer was a complex Bre'n whistle that resonated with pleasure and despair. "No, fire dancer. I'm not beautiful. I—I'm a parasite."

The last was a whistle so rushed that it took her a moment to realize what the Fssireeme had said. "A parasite? You don't take blood or bone or flesh from a living host. You don't take anything that isn't freely given. The cold has curdled your mind."

"Not blood or bone. Heat."

Only the Bre'n language could have conveyed the levels of shame and self-disgust that the Fssireeme felt. Only the Bre'n

167

language could answer him. Rheba forced her chill lips to shape Bre'n speech. "You don't take anything that isn't freely given," she repeated, but the whistle was rich with overtones of sharing and mutual pleasure that mere words lacked.

"But you didn't know about me before. *I was stealing from you.*" The whistle slid down and down.

"Fssa—"

"No," interrupted the snake. "Listen to me. After I tell you you'll stop wasting yourself on a useless, ugly parasite." The snake's whistle overrode her objections. "On my home planet, before men came and changed the Fssireeme, we lived in two seasons. There was Fire, and there was Night. During Fire, there was enough energy for everyone to eat. Then Night came, as much Night as there had been Fire. Months without Fire. But we needed Fire or we died. So we . . . stole . . . from other animals.

"We would project an aural illusion. Our prey would think it was another of its kind. We would come in close, very close, tangling ourselves in the prey, stealing its warmth. There we stayed, draining it until it died or until the time of Fire came again. Then we slid away, swimming again through the molten sky-seas of Ssimmi." The whistle changed into a poignant fall of pure sound. "It was long, long ago, but my guardian told me. He didn't lie. I'm a parasite . . . and your hair was like an endless time of Fire."

Rheba tried to answer, but had no words. She did not think less of Fssa because his body lacked the means to warm itself. Yet obviously the Fssireeme's early evolution was a source of much shame to him and his kind. She did not think he would listen to her. She yanked suddenly at her chains, trying to reach the snake. She could not. She forced herself to be still and tried to think logically. It was futile. Between the chill and having to maintain a separate fire over Fssa, she lacked the energy for coherent thought.

"You're beautiful, Fssa," she whistled.

The snake keened softly, a sound that made her weep.

"Take back your fire. Let me die."

"No."

There was a long time when there was no sound but her breathing. At last she sighed and shifted position. She reached for Fssa but the chains defeated her again. The snake's sensors glittered, then turned away as he moved farther across the cell. The fire followed.

"It's easier for me to warm us with my body," she said. "No matter what you tell me, I'm not going to call back my fire. You might as well be sensible and come back here."

Fssa slithered farther away.

Rheba wanted to cry with frustration and growing fear. She hated the dark; and the fire she had created only made the dungeon seem darker. "I'm lonely, Fssa. Come braid yourself into my hair and we'll sing Bre'n duets. Please, beautiful snake. I need you."

"Do you mean that?"

"You're beautiful."

"That's four times today. You only have to say it twice."

Rheba laughed helplessly. The flame over Fssa guttered and blinked out, but it did not matter. He was coiling around her arm on his way up to his accustomed place in her hair. He rubbed his head over her cheek in silent thanks, then began whistling sweetly. She tried to whistle harmony to his song, but her lips were trembling too much. She tried to tell him in words how much his company meant to her. He tickled her ear and whistled, gently turning away her thanks. He made another mouth to carry her part of the duet.

After a time, she was able to hold up her half of the harmony. The sounds of a Bre'n love song echoed down the black corridors of the Loo dungeon.

# XXIII

———◆———

Lord Jal came, just as Kirtn knew he must. The Bre'n stood on the far side of the room watching the doorway. Dapsl, the Loo lord's Whip, preceded Jal into the Act's room. A long nerve wrangler writhed in the small man's grasp. Violet fire ran like water over the final third of the whip. The wrangler licked out toward Kirtn, but stopped short of actually touching him.

"See?" said Dapsl, turning toward Lord Jal. "It's just as I told you. He won't perform, and that damned snake has disappeared. The Act is a shambles. We're ruined!"

At a curt gesture from Lord Jal, the complaints ended. He approached the Act warily, his long robe hissing in quiet counterpart to his walk. The robe was silk, very sheer, with subtle, brilliant designs woven into its surface. Despite the room's chill, Jal wore neither cloak nor underclothing.

"So you've decided to die, furry?" asked Jal, his voice indifferent.

"I've decided that my fire dancer is already dead."

"Ridiculous!"

"No enzymes have been transferred."

Jal hesitated, uncertainty flickering to his dark eyes. "It's been less than two days. Surely the bitch can survive that long."

Kirtn turned his back, refusing further acknowledgment of the slave lord's presence.

"Listen to me, slave," snarled Jal, reaching out to grab Kirtn's arm.

The natural heat of Lord Jal's hand was like a Senyas dancer's; yet unlike Rheba, the Loo did not seem susceptible to the cold. Kirtn froze, held by a devastating thought. Then he turned on Jal with a speed that made the Loo leap back out of reach.

170

"Is she warm enough?" Kirtn asked urgently. "Is the place where you're keeping her heated?"

Jal looked first puzzled, then irritated. "That won't work, furry. From what Dapsl told me—and what I saw on Onan—I knew better than to put her within reach of any kind of energy. There's nothing where she is but stone. Not even clothes. Nothing at all that can burn. But she'll survive. Loo slaves have survived the dungeon in a lot colder weather than this."

"They weren't Senyasi," said Kirtn flatly. He closed his eyes, trying to control the sweet hot rage uncurling in his gut, trying not to think how good Jal's neck would feel between Bre'n thumbs, trying not to smile at the thought of Jal's blood washing over Bre'n hands—trying not to succumb to *rez*. "Senyasi can't tolerate cold," he said, eyes still closed. Each word was very distinct, as though by forming each word carefully he could guarantee that the arrogant lord would comprehend the truth in the words. "Temperatures that are merely cold for you would be fatal for her." He opened his eyes, ovals of hammered gold. "Do you hear me?"

Jal's eyes were narrowed, black, suspicious. "You're trying to trick me into moving some kind of heat into her cell. Only the Twin Gods know what would happen then."

Kirtn whistled a curt command. Lheket left Ilfn's side and came to stand by the big Bre'n. "His clothes," snapped Kirtn to Jal. "Compare them to your own."

After a moment of hesitation, Lord Jal's blue hand closed around the boy's outer robe. Jal's frown deepened. He fingered the thick cloth, realizing that the boy was actually wearing two thick robes as well as several layers underneath. Such an outfit would have had Jal sweating before the last layer was in place, but the boy's skin was actually puckered with cold.

Abruptly, Jal released the boy's hand. He turned on Dapsl and began berating him in the lowest form of the Loo language. Kirtn watched, wishing that Fssa were there to translate.

Jal's head snapped around to stare at Kirtn. In the silence, the writhings of Dapsl's restless violet whip sounded unnaturally loud.

"I'll see that she is warm enough," spat Jal.

Kirtn's gold eyes watched the Loo for a long moment. Then the Bre'n turned away again, deliberately ignoring the slave master. Jal swore and yanked the nerve wrangler out of Dapsl's hand. Purple fire coursed from Kirtn's fingertips to

171

his shoulder. He did not respond. Fire bloomed again, then again. Smiling, Kirtn stood motionless. He had taken much worse pain from his fire dancer; he could take much more.

Jal looked from the whip to the slave who could ignore pain. With a sound of disgust he jammed the wrangler back into Dapsl's grasp and cursed the day he had found the incorrigible races of Senyas and Bre'n. "What do you want from me?"

"Rheba."

"Impossible!"

Kirtn smiled again as he turned around. He had not expected to win her freedom. All he wanted was to get himself and one other person into her cell. Corpses burned quite nicely, as every fire dancer knew.

Jal waited, but the Bre'n only smiled his chilling smile. "If you could see that she was all right, would you perform tonight at the Concatenation?"

Kirtn appeared to consider the proposal, but there was really no need to do so; seeing her was exactly what he wanted. "Take me to her now."

Jal pressed a stud on the belt that gathered his robe around his hips. He studied the figures in a small crystal window next to the stud. "Hardly more than an hour until you have to go into the tunnel . . ." He glanced up at the predatory golden eyes watching him, then glanced down quickly. "All right. A few minutes."

"No. As much time as there is before the Act goes onstage."

"Ridiculous!"

"Every minute there is," repeated Kirtn, "or there won't be any Act."

"You'd kill all of them," asked Jal, waving a long-nailed hand at the J/taals and clepts, Ilfn and Lheket, "just for a few minutes with your kaza-flatch?"

"Yes."

Jal's hand dropped. He looked at Dapsl, who looked away. He looked at i'sNara, all but invisible in the corner. When the Act was not being rehearsed, she appeared as herself; Kirtn would not tolerate the imitation Rheba for one second longer than necessary.

"Could you do both of them?" asked Jal of i'sNara.

She hesitated, then made a small gesture with her left hand, the Yhelle negative. "One or the other with fire, lord. Not both. Perhaps f'lTiri?"

Jal looked thoughtful, then angry. "F'lTiri's only Ninth

172

Degree. The Act has to look right or the Imperial Loo-chim will have my eggs for breakfast." He glared at Kirtn again. "All right, furry. But if you don't perform well tonight, I'll kill you myself!"

Kirtn laughed. The savage sound brought Ilfn to her feet and made Lheket move blindly toward the comfort of her touch. Her anguished whistle finally stilled Kirtn's terrible laughter, but even Jal could not bear to meet the Bre'n's slanting golden eyes. Jal shuddered beneath his silk robe.

"I'll take you there myself," he said finally. "I wouldn't trust a guard with you—or you with it! You'll walk in front of me with head bowed, like a slave being sent to the dungeon for discipline."

Kirtn bowed his head, a model of obedience, but the echos of his feral laughter still vibrated in the air. Jal palmed a small weapon from his belt and followed Kirtn out of the room. The Bre'n saw little of the hallways he walked, for his head was bowed in slave imitation. What he did see was enough. He would be able to lead Rheba out of the dungeon.

The air became perceptibly cooler as they walked down a winding spiral staircase made of stone. The steps were concave in the middle, worn down by the passage of time and slaves. Moisture appeared on the walls, beading up and sliding over the chiseled stone passageway. By the time they reached the bottom of the stairs, Kirtn's fur had roughened, a reflex that trapped an insulating layer of air between tiny hairs and skin.

Even so, he felt the relentless chill of darkness and stone. And if he felt it, how much worse must it be for his unfurred fire dancer? Head bowed, he reviewed the many ways there were to kill a man, and the many refinements of pain possible before death. The Loo lord who had left a fire dancer to die in this hell of icy rock would pray for his own death . . . but it would be long before that prayer was answered.

As though sensing Kirtn's thoughts, Jal looked up nervously. In the dim light thrown by his belt studs, he could see little but a huge shadow stalking ahead of him, head bowed, to all outward appearances just one more Loo slave. Jal wished that he could believe that appearance. He dropped back farther, his hand tight around the deadly white weapon he had taken from his belt.

Kirtn glanced back casually at the Loo lord, but he was out of reach. The Bre'n had not really expected anything else. Lord Jal was not a careless man.

"Keep walking," said Jal. "Turn right at the next branching of the tunnel, left at the third opening after that, then left at the second arch. She's in the right-hand cell in the middle of the long hall. Use this for light."

He tossed a small button toward Kirtn, who caught it reflexively. It gave off little light, but Bre'n eyes did not require brightness to see well. Kirtn whistled, shrill and penetrating, a call that demanded an answer. There was none, though the whistle echoed deafeningly down stone halls and turnings. Fear squeezed his throat, but he whistled again, urgently. All that came back were more echos . . . and then silence.

He turned and began running down the hall with the sure strides of a predator. The button he had been given glowed just enough to warn of dead ends and passageways. As an energy source for Rheba to draw on, the light would be all but worthless. As he ran he counted doors and arches, turned right and left and raced down a long hall.

It was cold, colder than it had been before he turned at the arch. Icy cold, slick walls of stone gleaming sullenly. He tried to keep down his fear, but like *rez* it kept uncurling, testing the edges of his control. Piercing Bre'n whistles shattered against stone. No answer came back. He held the button high in his right hand, looking for any break in the wall that could be her cell.

Finally, stone gave way to a cold shine of metal. He lunged at the door. It was locked. With a soundless snarl he attacked the chains holding down the massive sliding bolt. Metal twisted and snapped. The bolt slammed open with a metallic scream. The thick metal door swing inward.

Rheba lay inside, huddled on the cold stone floor. She did not move.

He leaped into the cell, whistling her name repeatedly, getting no answer. Her flesh was clammy, almost as cold as the bitter walls. He buried his hand in her hair, seeking the energy that was a fire dancer's life. Fssa slipped to the floor and lay without moving.

*Rez* turned inside the Bre'n, seething seductively, promising incandescent oblivion to his very core. But not yet. Not yet. First he must be very sure she was dead.

He lifted her off the cold floor, held her against his warmth, held her as he had ached to do, woman not child. He poured his energy into her, willing his own heat to warm the chill pathways of her body, forcing out cold as he breathed hot life into her.

Reluctantly, slowly, Rheba's mind acknowledged the fierce power battering it. Lines of power flickered vaguely, then blazed beneath his demands. Feeling returned to cold flesh. With a scream of agony, she was wrenched out of the blessed numbness that was a near twin to death. A lesser akhenet would have died of the Bre'n power pouring through mind and body, but she had proved her strength when she survived Deva's end. With a final ragged scream she accepted life again.

Then he held her gently, appalled by the pain he had given to her. He whistled keen regret, apologies as beautiful as the lines burning over her. She shuddered a final time and clung to him, making a song of his name. She kissed him with more than forgiveness, child-woman blazing between his hands.

Behind them the door groaned shut and the massive bolt slammed back into its hole. Laughter bounced off metal and stone—Jal's laughter. The button in Kirtn's hand changed, showing a likeness of the Loo lord's face. Lips moved. Thin sound vibrated in the air around the button.

"That was a very thick chain on the door, furry. You're even more dangerous than I'd thought. As dangerous as you are valuable. F'lTiri will imitate you well enough for the Act. Imperial lusts will overlook a rough performance, so long as you and the other furry survive to slide on Loo-chim *nuga*. Enjoy the next few hours with your kaza-flatch, furry. The female polarity won't let you out of her sight until she's tired of riding you."

Kirtn ground the button between heel and stone. Jal's voice stopped, but the sound of his laughter still seeped through the door. It was absolutely dark until Rheba made a tiny ball of light. As it hovered over his shoulder, Kirtn put his strong hands against the door, testing the hinges, then hammering with all the force of his huge body. Metal groaned but did not give.

A howl of Bre'n fury exploded in the dungeon. He threw himself at the door in an attack as calculated as his howl had been wild. Metal groaned again, but did not shift. If he kept after the door, he might eventually loosen its hinges—but there was not enough time left before the Act.

A sound from Rheba drew him away from his futile attack on the door. She stood with Fssa coiled in her hand, but the coils kept coming apart. She coiled him again. He came undone. Other than a flickering of the small light she had created when Kirtn crushed the button, she did not show her emotions. Patiently, she coiled Fssa into a semblance of life for the third time.

"That won't help," said Kirtn, his voice soft.

"He's not dead." Her voice was brittle, desperately controlled. "He felt almost this cold the first time I touched him in the Fold, when he was so scared."

The coils loosened and spilled out of her hands like black water. The light guttered, then flared into a single burning point where Fssa's body hung from her hand. There was no response, though the light she created was hot enough to burn flesh.

Kirtn lifted the snake from her fingers and draped the cold body around his neck. Fssa's flesh was very dense; he would burn more brightly than even a Bre'n.

"You haven't much time." His voice was kind, yet implacable. When she refused to look at him, he turned her face toward his. "Are you ready, fire dancer?"

"For what?"

"For fire."

"There's nothing to burn."

"There's me."

Silence, then a hoarse cry of refusal. He waited, but the lines of power on his dancer remained quiescent.

"You have to melt out the hinges, the bolt, or the door itself," said the Bre'n in Senyas. "The door is nearly as thick through as I am. I think the hinges would be a mistake; you're more likely to fuse them than unhinge the door. The door may be easier to melt through than stone. That's your decision, fire dancer. Either way, stone or metal, you'll need something to burn before you can weave enough energy to melt your way out of here."

"No."

"You'll have to have a base," continued the Bre'n as though she had never refused, "from which to weave more complex energies. You'll have to burn me."

"No!"

"It's your akhenet duty to survive and bear children." His voice was still calm, but he was whistling in Bre'n now, and the sounds contained possibilities that made her flesh move and tighten. "Ilfn is pregnant. In time, you will be too. Bre'ns and Senyasi will not be extinct. But first you have to escape, fire dancer, and to escape you have to burn me."

"Never." The word was Senyas, unambiguous, containing neither regret nor apology nor defiance, simply refusal, absolute. "I will never kill you."

"It doesn't matter, my dancer. I'm dead already." His whistle was sweet, pure, a knife turning in her. "I was dead the first time I mated with Ilfn."

176

"What are you talking about?"

"*Rez.*"

"But why?"

His only answer was a whistle that slid down all the octaves of regret. For a moment she did not recognize the opening notes of the Bre'n death song. When she did, she could not control the tears that fell over the golden lines on her face. She wanted desperately to contradict him, to tell him he must be wrong, that he could not go into *rez*, turning on himself, his mind literally consuming his body cell by cell to feed Bre'n rage. She wanted to argue and scream and plead, but was afraid that any one of those actions might simply precipitate the very *rez* she so desperately wanted to avoid. She needed time to think, time to plan, time to outwit *rez*.

"What do you want me to do?" she asked in a trembling voice, using Senyas, for her inner refusal would have shown in Bre'n.

It was all Kirtn could do not to gather her in his arms and hold her for the last time in his life. Yet if he did, neither of them would have the strength to do what they must. "After you escape from here, hide in the tunnel until just before the Act goes on stage. Then, take over the Act. One of the illusionists can imitate me. If they refuse, kill them and use just my outline. Let M/dere handle the fighting. She'll get you and the other akhenets to the ship. Take the slaves who can keep up with you, but don't wait for anyone."

She said nothing, not trusting her voice. The only other time she had seen Kirtn so violently controlled was when she told him that Deva would die before first moonrise.

"I'll give you my energy," he said, speaking Senyas because neither one of them could bear the poetry of Bre'n. "Use it to create fire to melt rock or metal. When I've given you all my energy, use my body as you did the J/taal bodies back in the Fold. Only this time, take the energy that is released, compress it, and let it explode inside stone or metal. The shock waves will destroy solids and generate more heat. At that point, you'll be able to burn your way out of this cell."

His voice was so reasonable that she could almost believe he was talking about a length of wood rather than his own flesh. She began to refuse, but was stopped by the shadow of *rez* at the center of his yellow eyes. Time. She needed more time.

She walked past him and ran her hands over the door, releasing distinct currents of energy. Her akhenet training let

177

her read the currents as they moved through the metal. The bolt on the far side was thicker than her own body. The hinges were equally massive. It might be easier to use heat to crack the cold rocks than to melt through the door—yet the thought of sending molten rivulets down the high-density alloy made her lines blaze hotly with pleasure.

She turned back to him, holding knowledge and argument inside her, pretending to agree. There was a way, a small fire dancer trick that she had used against childhood playmates. She would take what he gave her, draining off his power until he lacked the energy to flash into deadly *rez*. Then they would talk rationally about ways and means of escaping from the dungeon.

"Ready," she said.

She backed away from the door until she came up against the cell wall. She stepped forward just enough to allow him to stand behind her. When he touched her, energy raced through her body, setting akhenet lines to pulsing with the joined beat of two hearts.

A thin stream of barely visible energy stitched around the door like a questing fingertip. She controlled it precisely, using the minimum amount of her own and his energy. That was nothing new, certainly not dangerous to either of them, merely an akhenet pair at work.

Kirtn felt his energy flowing into her and wished for many nameless things in the time before he died. But he was akhenet, disciplined. The energy pouring into her did not waver with his unvoiced regrets. He sensed heat building in the door. His golden eyes reflected the uncanny gleam of Senyas fire. He poured more energy into his fire dancer, wanting to feel the searing core of her power while he still could.

She refused. Her lines surged, channeling his power back to him in a reflex that was born of her refusal to let him die. He realized that he was not as spent as he should have been by this time. She had been taking his energy—and then returning some of it to him so subtly that he had not sensed the exchange. At this rate he would be drained gradually, unconscious before he found the death that he must have to set her free. And then he realized that was exactly what she had planned.

With a terrible cry, he flashed into *rez*.

# XXIV

The first instants of *rez* were deceptively safe, like the rumble of an earthquake presaging the violence to come. Images shattered in her mind, images of herself as seen through Kirtn's eyes.

*She was a toddler, absently striking fire from straw. She was seven, lighting candles with her fingertips in her first dancer ritual. She was seventeen, awash with triple moonlight, laughing with a boy lover in Deva's scented autumn.*

*She was a searing core of radiance taking the Devalon and flinging it into space instants before the sun licked out, devouring Deva in pure light. She was a woman dressed in lightning, calling down fire on a gambling hell. She was a dancer wearing only her lines of power, mouth soft and bittersweet as she gave him a woman's kiss in a Loo room where enslaved stones wept.*

*She was lying on an icy stone floor. A dead Fssireeme slid out of her cold hair.*

And then *rez* raged through her with the force of an exploding star. She was being torn apart by the life force pouring into her like a cataract of molten glass.

Screaming, writhing, she deflected *rez* as she had been trained to deflect other destructive energies. But she was only one, and young. He was Bre'n, and in *rez*.

*Burn me! Burn me to ash and gone!*

Energy shaped itself into wild lightnings, visible and invisible, impossible colored shadows smoking over stone walls. She gave back to him what she could, a feedback loop that quivered and shook with violence barely channeled. There was a stink of scorched stone, but not flesh burning, not yet, she would not.

*I won't!*

She screamed again and again, her hair a corona of wildfire, driven to her knees by the force of Bre'n demand. The cell shrank smaller and smaller, too hot, far too small to hold the clash of lightnings. There was no air. Stone turned soft beneath her hands. Rivulets of orange and gold and white ran down the walls.

She could not breathe.

*Burn me!*

*Never!*

Her shriek was lost in the sound of *rez* doubled and redoubled by stone that smoked and spat ghostly flames. The energy she deflected came back to her from all sides, reflected by walls. Her skin split and blazed, forming new lines of power each instant as she tried to cope with impossible energies, tried not to breathe, tried not to die, tried not to—

*Burn me!*

She did not answer him, could not, the cell was too small to hold more words, they had to get out, get out, *get out*. There must be a way out, a place where the air was cool enough to breathe and did not stink of burning stone, Bre'n rage, fire dancer fear.

An orange rectangle smoked and sputtered in front of her, a metal alloy door as thick as a Bre'n body. Behind her was only *rez*, killing what she loved, killing her and him.

They must escape.

The door must burn.

There was no other way.

*Burn!*

She no longer deflected his energy. She took. Random lightnings fused into a beam of coherent light that would have blinded any but fire dancer eyes. She pointed. Incandescence ravaged the door. She had neither time nor skill for finesse; *rez* battered at her, both feeding and demanding her dance.

Reflected fire washed back at her, heat like a hammer blow. She retreated from the seething door, pushing the body of *rez* behind her, trying to save Kirtn and herself from the backlash of the fire she must use. Akhenet lines raced like lightning over her, sucking up heat, returning it to her as energy to feed the deadly beam of light gnawing at the door.

Too hot. Too little air. Akhenet lines overwhelmed by unbridled energies. She would cook before the door melted, she and her Bre'n burned to ash by *rez*, ash and gone.

Her eyes were closed now, but she did not need them open to see. The image of the door was seared on her retinas, a rectangle that was orange at the edges and vapor at the center and white in between, but most of all hot, by the Inmost Fire it was hot, the core of light shriveling her flesh, she was burning alive, burning and dying. . . .

Behind her closed eyelids brilliance flared, followed by a cool shadow like a wall between her and the melting door. There was only one gap in the coolness, a hole through which poured her deadly coherent light, light eating the door, an incandescent hell that somehow did not reach her any more. The door collapsed in upon itself in a deadly molten shower that somehow did not touch her.

Perhaps she was dead already.

Fire died, leaving only the seething metal on the far side of the cell, streams of molten alloy that she could only see through the single hole in the shallow wall that had appeared in front of her. She touched the wall. It gave slightly. The hole closed, leaving her in darkness.

Weakness poured through her like another color of night. She fell to the floor, but it was Kirtn, not stone, that broke her fall. He did not move. She remembered the instant when she had taken his energy with a violence to equal his *rez*. For a moment she was frozen, afraid to see if he was still alive, afraid that she had killed him.

She spoke his name in a voice that was raw from screams and fire. She tried to speak again, but could not. Frantically her hands moved over him, seeking the least quiver of life. Her fingers told her that he was whole, burned in places but not maimed by the fire he had compelled from her. She reached out to stroke his face.

Her hands were solid gold, smoldering with the residue of power. She stared at them, unbelieving.

After a long time, Kirtn's eyes opened, reflecting the akhenet fire of her hands. He looked around blankly. When his eyes focused on her he shook his head as though unable to accept that he was alive.

"What—?" His questioning whistle ended with a cough.

"You went into *rez*," she answered hoarsely. "I danced. I don't know why we didn't die."

Wonderingly, he touched her face. Beneath his fingers akhenet lines pulsed in traceries of gold so dense it was almost a mask. "You controlled *rez?*" he whistled, half question, half impossibility.

When Rheba tried to answer, her throat closed around its own dryness. With a small sound she threw her arms around him. She wanted to tell him how afraid she had been, how *rez* had begun with images from his mind, how the terrible core of *rez* was a power so deep that she had died swallowing it and then had been reborn as a sword edge of light slicing through metal.

"Coherent light?" He whistled as he stroked her crackling hair. "What a dangerous fire dancer I chose."

His whistle was light, but it contained all the ambiguous harmonics of truth. Before she could sort out his many meanings, she realized that he had taken images out of her thoughts when she could not speak, as though *rez* had somehow forged a connection between Bre'n and Senyas minds.

"*Rez?*" she said hoarsely. "Did *rez* do that?"

"No." He pulled her closer to his body. In the light shed by her smoldering akhenet lines, he saw her lips, cracked by dryness and bleeding. He licked them gently, giving them a healing moisture that her own mouth lacked. "Many akhenet pairs are minor mind dancers, but only within their own pairs, only when they are mature, and touching each other."

Suddenly, blackness shriveled, collapsing in upon itself. Heat washed over them, but it was a bearable heat. Behind it came the suggestion of coolness from the burned-out door to the dungeon hall. Speechlessly, Kirtn and Rheba watched as the "wall" folded and refolded, getting lighter and smaller as it did so until it had become a mirror-bright creature slithering over the hot floor toward them.

"Fssa!" Kirtn's hand went to his neck where he had draped the corpse of the Fssireeme. Nothing was there now but his own fur, scorched even closer to the skin than was normal.

Rheba reached toward Fssa, then jerked back her fingers with a cry. He was far too hot to touch. With an apologetic whistle, the snake backed out of reach of his friends. He stretched and flexed his body, leaving black marks on the gray stone floor.

"Are you really all right?" asked Rheba, disbelief in her raw voice.

"Oh, yesssss," whistled Fssa dreamily, a shiver of pleasure running down his mirrored hide. "No Fssireeme has lived like that except in a guardian's memories . . . to be a glittering sail only a few molecules thick. *It felt so good!* It's been so cold. It's always been cold since Ssimmi."

Bre'n and Senyas looked at one another, trying to absorb Fssa's words. In response to heat that would have killed them, the Fssireeme had transformed himself into a sail that soaked up energy so efficiently its shadow had saved their lives.

"Ahhhhh," whistled the snake, "it was lovely to really s-tr-e-t-c-h." As though sensing their bemusement, Fssa added, "Unless it's really hot, Fssireeme freeze to death in their thinnest shapes." He whistled a trill of pure pleasure. His sensors, darker now than the rest of him, turned toward Rheba. "That was a wonderful fire you made," he said earnestly, "but you must be careful where you do it. You're too fragile to survive fire like that in closed places unless there's a Fssireeme around."

She laughed despite the dryness of her throat. The snake's whistle was an irresistible blend of complacence and concern. "Cool off, snake. I won't carry you when you're that hot. Or do you want to crawl all the way to the Concatenation stage?"

Fssa gave out a dismayed whistle. Reluctantly he expanded, releasing heat into the cell. He was careful to direct the heat away from them, however. The fragility of his new friends had come as a surprise to the Fssireeme. When he was within the temperature range they considered "normal," he wound over to Rheba. She touched him hesitantly, then lifted him into her hair. Halfway there, her strength gave out. Her hands dropped to her sides.

Kirtn put the snake into her hair, then searched over her body with careful hands, looking for wounds. He found none.

"Just thirsty . . . tired," she said, responding to his unasked questions. She tried not to groan as exhaustion swept over her in a tidal wave of weakness. "Tired."

Kirtn tried to give her energy, but could not. *Rez* had drained him as surely as it had exhausted her. Yet they could not stay here.

"The Act," rasped Rheba, echoing his thoughts. "How long have we been here?"

He did not answer. *Rez* was timeless. It could have lasted an instant or an eon. He had no way of knowing. Nor did she. The rebellion could have started while they fought to burn out the stubborn heart of a Loo dungeon door. The rebellion could be over, won or lost, slaves dead or free or enslaved yet again. Loo guards could be coming down the stone hallways right now, guns in hand, to find a bright snake and an exhausted akhenet pair. Easy prey.

Rheba and Kirtn dragged themselves to their feet. They walked raggedly across the cell, staggered between lines of cooling metal and into the hallway. Neither of them spoke. They both knew that she was too tired to make small fires for the Act, much less set the Loo city ablaze in a bid for freedom.

"The amphitheater," she said, her breath hurting in her raw throat. "Energy."

"The weather shield," agreed Kirtn.

Her breath stopped for an instant, then she accepted what must be done. If they were to escape Loo, she must risk losing the only person who could give her children.

Lheket would have to dance.

# XXV

The Act's room was deserted. The only thing moving was the finger-length fountain that delivered water to the slaves. Rheba drank gratefully. Kirtn found her robe in a corner. She pulled it on, put up the hood, and looked at him expectantly. He shrugged.

"It'll have to do," said the Bre'n. "It doesn't hide your new lines, though. Keep your hands in the folds and your head down until we find i'sNara."

A low sound passed through the room. She did not hear it, but he did. He cocked his head, trying to pinpoint the source of the sound. Finally he decided it had been conducted by the rock itself. The sound came again, slightly louder. Her head came up. The new lines curling around her eyes flared gold.

"What's that?" she asked, turning her head in unconscious imitation of him.

"We're close to the ampitheater. It could just be the Loo making approving noises after an Act."

"Or it could be a mob of rebellious slaves."

"It sounds," said Fssa softly, "like the memories of Ssimmi, heat and thunder."

"Thunder? It's the dry season," said Rheba.

Kirtn did not say anything. He was already halfway out of the room, striding down the hall toward the tunnels that converged on the amphitheater. She followed, nearly running to keep up with the long-legged Bre'n.

His worst fear was disproved within minutes. The rebellion had not yet begun. The tunnel network surrounding the amphitheater was lined with Acts. The slaves were either too tired or too fearful to care who was pushing past them. Their Acts were over; now they had to stand and wait in cold halls until the last Act left the stage and the Hour Between Years began. Unlike old slaves, these were not free to roam Imperiapolis for that hour. They could not leave the tunnel until their new owners arrived and took them away.

Rheba could not help glancing quickly to the faces as she followed in Kirtn's wake. Most people wore a look of barely controlled desperation. It was the hallmark of new slaves. Old slaves, like i'sNara, showed no emotion at all. Rheba wondered how many of the silent people knew about the rebellion, how many would help, how many would simply get in the way.

Ilfn's whistle slid through the thick silence in the hall. The sound came from one of the many culs-de-sac that appeared at random along the length of the tunnel. The room was so small that Kirtn and Rheba had to crowd against Ilfn in order to get out of the hall. Pressed between wall and his Bre'n, Lheket stared sightlessly through them.

"You haven't much time," said Ilfn in urgent Senyas. "Your Act is next. They're lined up just off the ramp, waiting for their signal."

Impatiently, Rheba pushed in closer. Something about Lheket's face, his stance, compelled her attention. With half her attention she listened while Kirtn told Ilfn what had happened—and what must happen.

"Lheket will have to dance," finished Kirtn. "Rheba has to have an energy source to work with, and the weather shield is the only possibility within the amphitheater. Calling rain shouldn't be hard, even for a first-time dancer. The ocean is so close, there's moisture everywhere, all he'll have to do is gather it."

Ilfn laughed wildly, stopping Kirtn's flow of words. "Are you as blind as Lheket? *Look at him.*"

They stared. A low rumble muttered through the rock again, just below the threshold of Rheba's hearing. The Bre'ns heard it clearly enough, though. Kirtn looked more closely at the boy, peering through the very dim light given off by the fluorescent strips that divided all walls into two horizontal blocks. Vague blue-silver lines glowed across Lheket's hands and chin.

Rheba gasped. When she touched Lheket, her hand flared gold. Sound trembled in the air. She looked up at Kirtn and then back at Lheket. Currents of shared power coursed between the two Senyas dancers. The boy's eyes lit from within, green as river pools. Her hair lifted, rippling with invisible energy. "He's dancing!"

"Of course he is," said Ilfn, her voice low and ragged. "I

tried to stop him but this time I couldn't." Her whistle was shrill with emotion, her dark eyes wild. "About an hour ago he changed. *He woke up.* All that had been sleeping in him came alive, as though he had been called by a ring of master dancers. I couldn't hold him back."

"*Rez,*" breathed Rheba.

"What?"

"*Rez.* He must have felt me channel Kirtn's *rez.*"

Ilfn's whistle stopped as though she had been struck. She stared from Rheba to Kirtn, then back to Rheba. "Impossible," said Ilfn in Senyas. "No one, Bre'n or Senyas, can control *rez.*"

"Not control," said Rheba. "Channel. I merely—" No easy explanation came to her. She made an impatient sound. "It doesn't matter. Do you think that Lheket has called enough clouds to make the Loo activate the weather shield?"

Another rumble trembled through the underground tunnel. Ilfn laughed again, a sound that made Rheba shift uncomfortably.

"What do you think that is?" said Ilfn. "He has the clouds raging like Bre'ns in *rez.*"

"Thunder?" said Kirtn, looking at Lheket with new interest.

"Yes." Ilfn's whistle was both proud and harried. "He's called a storm. It's all I can do to keep it from being a hellbringer!"

Kirtn made a Bre'n sound of satisfaction. The shield would definitely be up. Rheba would have all the energy she needed to work with. "Do you need help handling him?" he asked.

Ilfn hesitated. "On Deva, I'd need help. But here . . ." She smiled suddenly, a cruel Bre'n smile. "Here I don't care if he drowns the whole city and every Loo in it."

"We're in it too," pointed out Kirtn.

"I know." Ilfn's tone was curt. "I'm draining off enough of his energy to keep him under a semblance of control. It's that or kill him."

Rheba felt an impulse to stand protectively between Lheket and his Bre'n, then realized how foolish that was. The first thing anyone learned on Deva was *never* to stand between Senyas and Bre'n. Yet she could not help a whispered plea. "Don't hurt him."

Ilfn glanced up. The Bre'n's expression softened as she realized that Rheba had some affection for the blind rain dancer. "I'll hold him as long as I can," she said simply.

The air vibrated with sound Rheba could not hear. Kirtn

bent over Ilfn, whistled softly, and was answered by a smile so sensual it made Rheba catch her breath. Then Ilfn changed before their eyes, smile fading, mind turned inward as her hands settled on Lheket's shoulders. Only her eyes seemed alive, and his, lit from within by akhenet power.

Kirtn turned and pushed back out into the crowded hall, breaking a path for Rheba. He looked back, saw that her hood had dropped and pulled it up with a quick jerk. "Jal might be around."

"You're not exactly inconspicuous yourself," muttered Rheba.

Kirtn shrugged. There were other large, furred races gathered in the hall. However, there were none whose hair lifted and danced on invisible currents of force. Even among smooth slaves, Rheba was as distinctive as a shout.

He stopped so suddenly that she stepped on his heels. The tunnel had branched into two smaller halls and several culs-de-sac. M/dere stood at the point where the tunnel divided, as though waiting for someone. She saw Kirtn immediately. She found her way through the crowd to them with astonishing speed.

Rheba shook her head slightly. "Fssa?" she murmured. "You awake?"

A satisfied hiss answered her. Fssa was in his element when her hair pulsed with energy. If he had his way, she would dance all the time. He stretched slightly, creating a flexible whistling orifice. As M/dere spoke, a Bre'n whistle floated up from beneath Rheba's hood.

"J/taaleri," said M/dere, bowing her head. "I'm ashamed. I let you be taken without lifting my hand."

"There's nothing you could have done and no need to apologize."

Fssa shifted behind her ear, making a different orifice with which to speak J/taal. She suspected that whatever he said was not quite what she had said. The speech went on long enough to make her restless, but M/dere listened with utter attention. At the end, she bowed again, but there was pride on her face.

"Thank you, J/taaleri. Do you want us to kill the illusionists now?"

Rheba looked quickly to Kirtn. He shrugged. "Whatever you want, fire dancer. Just make sure that they don't get in our way."

"Tell your people to be sure that the illusionists can't escape or give warning," said Rheba slowly, "but don't hurt

188

them. They may know something useful about the city. They've been slaves a lot longer than we have."

M/dere concentrated for a moment. "It's done. Come quickly."

They followed M/dere into a small room just off the ramp that led up to the amphitheater stage. The illusionists were standing very still, J/taal hands over their throats and J/taal clepts snarling at their feet. At Rheba's command the illusionists changed into themselves.

The male illusionist was slightly broader than the female, slightly more muscular, and had hair that was chestnut rather than black. Like her, he showed no expression. He looked at Kirtn with interest, as though comparing the Bre'n to the illusion that had recently been projected.

"Before you kill us," said f'lTiri, "remember that we are slaves like you. Like you, we had to obey men we hate."

"I'm not planning on killing you," said Rheba. "M/dere will just knock you out. By the time you wake up, the rebellion will be too far along for you to warn anyone."

I'sNara moved slightly, drawing a rich snarl from a clept. She stared at Rheba with clear, colorless eyes, but when she spoke there was emotion in her voice. "Let us go! We have a right to try for freedom too!"

"Slaves don't have rights," said f'lTiri, his voice flat. "Don't ask anything, tura i'sNara."

Emotion drained out of i'sNara, leaving only emptiness. She did not move again. F'lTiri's body twitched as though he would go to her, but a clept's bared teeth made movement certain death.

Rheba hesitated, wanting to trust the Yhelle illusionists, yet not wanting to jeopardize whatever chance the Act might have. "Can you appear to be J/taals?" she asked suddenly.

The illusionists wavered, then reformed. There was a murmur of surprise as the J/taals found themselves holding what appeared to be two other J/taals. The clepts rose to their feet, sniffed, then snarled again. The illusion was visual only—touch, smell and hearing were not affected.

Rheba looked at Kirtn. He whistled a puzzled affirmative. Whatever she had in mind was agreeable to him. Like her, he had seen enough death on Deva to last him ten lifetimes.

"You both know the Act," said Rheba in a clipped voice. "You'll be demons. If you say or do anything to call attention to yourselves, the clepts will kill you before any Loo lord can stop them."

189

The captive "J/taals" murmured agreement. They had no doubt of the clepts' speed and ferocity.

"I don't think anyone will notice two extra demons," she said. "Except Dapsl. Where is he?"

"The Whip is with Lord Jal. Your mercenaries made him uncomfortable." F'lTiri smiled, revealing the small, hard teeth of a J/taal. "When the gong sounds for us, he'll be back."

Rheba swore in Senyas. Fssa translated it into Universal and then into J/taal, embroidering her epithets with a Fssireeme's creative glee. "Shut up, snake," she snapped, "unless you know how we can get Dapsl to see two less J/taals.

Fssa was silent.

The captive J/taals shifted. The air shivered, then re-formed around . . . nothing. The Yhelle illusionists had vanished.

"What—?" gasped Rheba.

A strained voice came from the place where i'sNara had stood. "This is our most difficult illusion. We can't"—J/taals reformed and the voice became less harsh—"hold it for long, but it should get us onstage. Once there, Dapsl would not dare to stop the Act. The Loo-chim kills Whips that displease it."

A gong sounded four times. The penultimate Act had ended.

This time Rheba did not hesitate. "You've just joined our Act. At the end of it, when Saffar kisses Hmel, the fires won't dim out. I'll send fire across the whole weather shield. That's the signal for the rebellion to begin. In the confusion it will be easy for everyone to get offstage and into the tunnel. Ilfn and Lheket will be there. Follow them. If you're still with us when we reach the spaceport, I'll give you a ride home."

F'lTiri laughed softly, a surprising sound from a J/taal face. "No wonder the mercenaries worship you. You're as mad as they are. A ride home . . ." His voice broke on the last word and something close to fire burned behind his colorless eyes. He bowed his head. "We'll follow you, J/taaleri."

Dapsl's strident voice came from the direction of the stage ramp as he shoved through the crowd, nerve wrangler dripping violet fire. At the first sound of his voice, both illusionists vanished. Other than the clepts' great interest in two empty places in the room, it was as though the illusionists had never been in the room at all.

"You—i'sNara," said Dapsl, pointing his whip at Rheba.

"Hurry it up." The whip flicked over her hood, pulling it down. "Get that hair moving, damn you!"

Rheba had an instant of fear that Fssa would reveal himself. She felt the snake slide down and wind securely around her neck below the hood. Warmth flared on her skin as Fssa shifted his color to match the myriad golds of her hair and skin. She shook her head, freeing her hair. It lifted around her head in a silky, whispering cloud. The gesture cost her energy she could not spare, but satisfied Dapsl.

He turned his attention on Kirtn, looking at the Bre'n critically. "The scorched fur is a good touch, but you've still made the damned beast too handsome."

Kirtn almost smiled.

"Well, it's too late to adjust the illusion now. Go on, get on stage. If the female polarity is disappointed by the looks of the real furry, I'll send you to her instead!" He glared at the rest of the Act. "Move!" he said in guttural J/taal. "The twin gong will sound and we'd better be ready! M/dur, where's that damned crown?"

Rheba froze. She had forgotten about Rainbow.

M/dur reached inside his robe and pulled out what looked like a heavy, pitted necklace. It shifted in his hands, becoming thicker, more dense.

Dapsl glanced. "Why the bitch ever wanted that ugly thing in the first place—" He began making restive motions with his whip. "Onstage," he said harshly. "Onstage!"

Rheba led the Act out of the room and up the ramp, hoping that no one would stumble over the two invisible illusionists in the rush. At every second she expected a cry of outraged discovery from the Whip. She was so intent on gaining the sanctuary of the stage before the illusionists lost their invisibility that she shoved roughly past a lord who was standing on the ramp. Too late she realized that the man was Lord Jal. She looked back over her shoulder. He was staring at her oddly, as though he suspected that reality rather than illusion had jostled him. Before he could protest, the Act gained the stage in a silent rush.

The gong rang twice. The Act began.

# XXVI

Onstage the air was cool, smelling of rare perfumes and a whiff of lightning. Overhead, an invisible dome quivered silently, shielding the audience from random drops of rain. Thunder sounded suddenly in response to unseen lightning. The shield thickened, then relaxed; it was designed to supply only enough energy to meet the needs of the instant.

Rheba reached for the shield with immaterial hands. Her hair whipped and sparkled. Instantly she withdrew, leaving only the most meager tendril connecting her to the shield. She let energy trickle down, then shaped it to the requirements of the Act.

As the Act unfolded, the shield surged again, deflecting the building storm. Rheba's fires leaped with the unexpected increase in power, drawing a gasp from the Loo audience. Silently she fought to damp out the unnecessary power. After several moments the shield—and the Act—returned to acceptable energy levels.

A part of her kept listening for Jal or Dapsl to give away the game, but no words were spoken except by Fssa. Dapsl stood just offstage, his whip lashing restlessly in his hands. If he suspected anything he kept it to himself. Nor did Jal reappear, although as a slave Act owner, he had a seat in the third row. The seat was empty.

Power surged as thunder rumbled overhead. Instantly she damped down. Even so, Kirtn's outline flared in great tongues of gold. She put Jal and Dapsl from her mind, concentrating only on controlling the unruly, unpredictable energy source. After a struggle, she managed to capture enough energy to keep going until the end of the Act, when she would be forced to tap the shield once again.

She stepped into the center of the stage, going through the motions of Saffar struggling with and then seducing Hmel.

Thunder hammered the stage an instant after lightning slid over the protective shield. The audience did not notice; the saga of Saffar and Hmel was more compelling than mere lightning.

Purple and orange flames leaped around the J/taals, drawing a gasp from the watching Loos. If Dapsl noticed the two extra J/taals, he said nothing. Kirtn/Hmel reached between the writhing demons and brought out the crown. When he set it on Rheba/Saffar's head, the crown blazed with all of Rainbow's pure colors. The crowd sighed with pleasure.

Rheba whistled the last notes of Bre'n harmony, then turned her face up to Kirtn's. As his lips closed over hers, she allowed the demon fires to die. The crowd murmured in wonder as a lacework of burning gold light grew around the couple on stage. The light was not called for in the Act, nor did she realize that she had created the brilliant net of fire. All she knew was that she burned when Kirtn touched her, and he seemed to touch her everywhere.

Kirtn lifted his mouth and looked at her with eyes as gold as her akhenet lines, eyes ablaze like the fire dancer burning in his arms. With a wrench, discipline returned. Her eyes watched him, seething with nascent fire, urging a consummation that she could not name.

*Dance.*

The silent Bre'n command swept through her mind. The stage trembled with repeated thunder. Beneath the Loo-chim's hands, the gong rang four times, signaling the end of the Act and the beginning of the Hour Between Years. Rheba laughed and reached for the rippling weather shield, drunk with fire dancer passion.

As she turned to face the astonished Loo, there was a soundless explosion of fire around her. Streamers of flame leaped from her hands. Her robe shriveled to ash and fell away, leaving her naked but for the akhenet lines blazing over her body. She laughed again, sheer delight at the energy coursing through her; and flames surged, limning her and the Bre'n in frighting tongues of fire.

Fssa spoke from her lashing hair, his voice as deafening as thunder and more terrible. The Act did not understand the words that scourged the Loo, castigating them for carnal sins. The Loo moaned and swayed in terror until the Imperial Loo-chim stood, surrounded by guards. Energy weapons glittered in the unnatural light.

*Dance.*

More emotion than command, Kirtn's presence inflamed

193

her. Fssa laughed maniacally, reveling in her incandescent hair. As lightning skidded on forked heels across the dome, she reached for more power—and brought down the end of the world.

The shield had surged to meet the demands of the storm; what she touched was raw force too powerful to channel, much less control. Reflexively she threw away the energy, deflecting it out across the amphitheater in gigantic dragon tongues of destruction. The screams that came where fire touched were drowned out by the awful roar of untrammeled energy blazing out from her hands.

Vaguely she heard Kirtn's voice yelling at the Act to *get out! off the stage! into the tunnel! run!* and she felt Fssa ripped from her hair by a Bre'n hand; but it was all at a distance, a dream from another life. The only real thing was the shield raving over her head and the raw hot death deflected by her hands.

Energy weapons added their blue blaze to the hellish fires. She felt the coherent beams of light being born, growing in tight lines toward her, world slowing until she stood aside from herself and watched the individual atoms of deadly light form lines lengthening toward her. They were so ordered, so perfect, lethal in their exact resonance.

She curled the light back upon itself, atoms marching in a different rhythm, perfection destroyed. The beams went from blue to yellow-white, energy scatterred, harmless. Then she touched the core of light and the weapons fused, useless. It was more efficient than merely deflecting the energy, and not too much more difficult.

Bre'n laughter curled around her, savage and infinitely sweet, wrapped in lightning. As though in answer, the storm broke with awesome ferocity. Shield power doubled, tripled, quadrupled, became a solid ceiling overhead. *Too much power.* She screamed and writhed like a snake on a spit but there was no relief, only energy molten in her, burning her. She deflected all but the smallest part of it, and even that part was agony. There was nothing but the primal roar of unleashed hell. The amphitheater was a white inferno capped by a shield seething at maximum output.

Like a wounded animal, she struck back at the source of her pain. She turned energy from the shield back on itself as she had done with the weapons, creating countercurrents of force the shield was not built to withstand. Like her, the shield could deflect or use most of the energies battering it;

194

but, like her, the shield always retained a part of the energies that touched it.

Assaulted from without by lightning and from within by a fire dancer, the shield exploded. Instantly rain slashed across the unprotected amphitheater, vaporizing where molten rock pooled sullenly. In the blue-white glare of lightning, Rheba looked out across the audience. The seats were empty of all but rain hissing over hot stone. She stared along the empty rows in disbelief. She had burned the slave lords of Loo to ash, and now a rain dancer's storm was taking even that bitter remainder away. There was nothing left. Like Deva.

Ash and gone.

And the rain was tipped with ice that numbed to the bone. Dazed, unbelieving, she let Kirtn lead her from the steam-wreathed stage. She looked over her shoulder once, as though expecting the amphitheater to be filled again with the aristocracy of Loo, expected again to smell expensive perfumes and see Dapsl standing aside with his whip overflowing violent pain. She had hated them, all of them, but she had not intended to destroy them so completely.

She stumbled on the slick rock. Kirtn caught her. Silently she clung to him, needing his strength more now than she had a few minutes before. He carried her away from the stage.

The ramp into the tunnel was slippery with sleet. Rheba had deflected heat back out over the audience, protecting the slaves behind her at the expense of the slave masters in front. That was all that had saved the tunnel complex from becoming a crematorium.

The tunnel was deserted but for the people who had been injured in the first panicked flight from whatever had happened onstage. The injured screamed or moaned or were silent. Kirtn did not stop to help the casualties; there was nothing he could do for them. He accepted the fact grimly, knowing that the tunnel, like Deva, would haunt his nightmares for the rest of his long life.

The archway into the park was open, unguarded. Icy rain swept in on each gust of wind. Thunder belled in the enclosed hallway. Kirtn hesitated for an instant, then plunged into a night stalked by lightning. Rheba struggled in his grasp, silently demanding.

*Put me down.*

He set her on her feet, waited to be sure she was in control of herself, then led the way through the park at a hard run. Thunder came like battering fists. They were blinded by light-

**195**

ning that was too hot, too bright, too often, a violence that shattered buildings.

"Lheket's out of control!" shouted Rheba, then realized that was why Kirtn was running her mercilessly through the night. Ilfn needed them.

Beyond the park, the streets were a chaos of storm and rebellion. In the black-and-white brilliance of Lheket's hellbringer, slaves paid off debts with a brutality that made Rheba grateful for the darkness between sheets of lightning. Destroying the weather shield over the amphitheater had caused an energy surge that had slagged the city's power source. Imperiapolis was a city of darkness and death, powerless.

A group of men leaped out in front of Kirtn and Rheba. Lightning revealed their number and their savage intent, but not whether they were Loo or slaves. Without breaking stride, Kirtn hit the group. Lightning reflected in his demon eyes, and his hands were a deadly thunder. Rain washed away the attackers' screams.

Fire dancer and Bre'n ran on, untouched. Lightning lanced down so close that they smelled the stink of scorched stone and heard the hiss of vaporizing rain. Thunder was instantaneous, a hammer blow that drove them to their knees. Lightning slashed again and again, stirring the sky to a frenzy. Thunder became a living destruction tolling endlessly across the city. They could not stand and there was no place to hide. They held each other and waited to die.

Suddenly, silence and darkness closed over them. The wind moaned in long withdrawal, pulling the storm in its wake. Rain fell steadily, unmixed with ice.

Lheket's dance had ended.

Rheba pushed herself to her feet, wondering if the storm had been controlled at the cost of Lheket's life. She refused to think about it, but tears blinded her just the same. Kirtn's hand caught up hers, guiding her. Overhead, clouds reflected the ruddy light of fires burning out of control. That was all the light Bre'n eyes needed. She ran beside him, blindly trusting his sight.

The spaceport seemed to retreat in front of them, carried off by clouds of steam writhing up from gutted buildings. Distant explosions sounded. The city smoked and seethed and devoured itself, fed by the hatred of slaves.

The spaceport was a shambles. It was impossible to tell the derelict yard from the main berth area. Ruined ships lay like toys, scattered by relentless lightning. Fires burned. In their sullen light, ships were black and scarlet. Kirtn ran between the ships without hesitation, his eyes fixed on the *Devalon* rising out of the crimson light ahead. Protected by the larger hulks surrounding it, the *Devalon* had survived the storm. Kirtn and Rheba ran toward the haven promised by their ship.

Three shapes appeared out of nowhere, barring their way. Before Kirtn could react, the shapes melted back. Clepts leaped up, making odd sounds of pleasure. The J/taals reappeared again, so close to Rheba that she gasped. She had forgotten how quick the J/taals could be—and how deadly.

M/dere bowed and handed Rheba a glittering shape. Fssa. With a cry of delight, she snatched up the snake and braided him into her hair. M/dur bowed and gave Rainbow to Kirtn. Rainbow pulsed with color, alive with the power it had absorbed before Kirtn flung it to the safety of J/taal's hand.

"The rest of the Act?" demanded Kirtn.

"At the ship," whistled Fssa.

"Ilfn? Lheket?"

A Bre'n whistled answered, but the whistle was not Fssa's. Ilfn stepped slowly out of the dense shadows in front of the *Devalon*. In her arms was Lheket, unmoving.

"Alive," whistled Ilfn proudly.

Kirtn's answering whistle was a mixture of relief and rue. "Next time, don't let him dance if we're out in his storm."

Ilfn smiled fondly and rubbed her cheek over the boy's forehead.

"Is he all right?" asked Rheba, looking at the limp boy supported by Ilfn's strong arms. His hands wore braids of blue-silver light.

"He's a dancer," whistled Ilfn, referring to Lheket for the first time in the tones of an adolescent rather than a child.

Rheba glanced uncertainly at Kirtn, but there was no tinge of apprehension for Lheket in the Bre'n's smile. With a sigh, she allowed fear and adrenaline to ooze out of her. The time of violence was over; she could let go and find the healing oblivion that Lheket had instinctively sought. Her hair whispered, releasing energy until she was blessedly empty. She whistled the complex Bre'n trill that activated the ship. The ramp tongued out invitingly. She moved toward it, grateful as she had not been since Deva simply to be alive.

"Not so fast, kaza-flatch."

She froze. It was a voice she had thought never to hear again, except perhaps in nightmares.

# XXVII

———◦◦━━━◆━━━◦◦———

Slowly, Rheba turned around to face Lord Jal. He followed her every motion with a weapon that looked like a small crossbow. The distance was not great; he would have no difficulty killing her with the squat arrow that was already in place, waiting to be released. Nor would she be able to use the weapon against him, for its operation depended on stored mechanical energy rather than chemical or atomic energy.

"I see you understand my choice of weapons," said Jal.

Rheba, caught in the flood of light from the *Devalon*'s portal, said nothing. Without seeming to, her eyes checked the position of the J/taals. Close, but not close enough. They could reach Lord Jal and kill him, but she would be dead first. The same was true of Kirtn: he could kill, but not before she was killed. Ilfn, with Lheket in her arms, was as helpless as Rheba. Rheba bit back a sound of despair and silently began collecting energy she did not expect to live long enough to use.

"Over there," said Jal, gesturing to a clear space between abandoned ships. "All of you get over there. Slowly. If I don't like what I see, the bitch dies where she stands."

Snarling silently, clepts and J/taals retreated. Kirtn flexed his hands longingly, but had no choice except to follow. Ilfn carried Lheket away from the *Devalon*'s shadow, hatred in every line of her body.

"Whip," said Jal in a loud voice. "Bring the rest of the slaves."

Dapsl appeared from behind the ship. A whip hung from his small hand, but dripped no violet fire. Lord Jal had been very careful to use no weapons that Rheba could turn against them. Dapsl stood aside and gestured abruptly. A line of slaves bent around him, heading for the place where Kirtn

198

and the others stood beneath the canting wreck of a spaceship.

Three chims of guards brought up the rear of the procession. All six men and women were armed with rapid-fire dart guns. The energy they used would be minimal, the darts poisoned. Nothing there for a fire dancer to steal.

As the guards took up positions all around the slaves, the J/taals and clepts shifted position, marking out one guard apiece. At the least inattention on Jal's part, J/taals would strike. So long as their J/taaleri was under a Loo gun, though, they would do nothing to endanger her. Rheba watched, and understood the J/taals' movements. She also understood that she would have to call for an attack. When she did, the Loo would die. And so would she.

Fssa stirred in her hot, rain-wet hair. "You were beautiful, fire dancer."

The Fssireeme's goodbye was so soft that its emotion registered with her before the meaning did. She felt Fssa slide out of her hair, hang for a moment, then drop to the ramp. In the rain he was nearly invisible. She sighed goodbye to the Fssireeme, knowing his sensitive receptors would pick up sounds Jal would never hear. There was no answer. She had not expected one. She hoped that he got away; he had earned whatever small haven the slave planet could give him.

"The most dangerous slaves on Loo," said Jal, a certain grim irony in his tone as he watched the silent file of people walk to the opening between ruined ships. "Odd how they all ended up here, isn't it?"

Rheba said nothing. Jal laughed.

"But maybe it isn't so odd after all," continued the Loo. "The male polarity's furry was one of their leaders. Imagine my delight when I found them huddled behind your ship. A few of them still are. They didn't believe that primitive weapons killed just as efficiently as the modern variety."

Jal's face changed. Rheba's breath stopped in her throat. She had thought only Bre'ns could contain that kind of rage.

"But I underestimated you, kaza-flatch. You were the most dangerous one of all. What happened to the city, bitch? What happened to the amphitheater and the Imperial Loo-chim?"

She said nothing.

Lord Jal's fist struck his now-useless master's belt. "The city power is dead! Slaves run wild! Where are the voices of Imperial rage? *Where is the Loo-chim?*"

"Dead."

"Dead?" said Jal, voice thin with disbelief.

"All of them. Dead. Like your belt. Like your city. Like you should be. *Dead*."

She almost died then, Jal's hand tightening on the trigger. But he was a survivor. He needed her for a bit longer. He controlled himself with a coldness that was more frightening than his rage had been.

"As you might have noticed, the spaceport is burning," Jal smiled, and she took an involuntary step backward. "You've destroyed a city and a culture that is greater than your animal mind can comprehend. What you haven't burned, that demon storm washed away." He stopped, struck by a thought. "Was the storm yours, too?"

"No," she said, but she could not help looking toward Lheket.

Jal followed her glance, saw the boy unconscious in the Bre'n woman's arms. Then Jal stared back at Rheba with eyes that knew only hatred. "You've destroyed my people, my city, and even my ship. You're going to take me back to Onan. Now."

She did not bother to agree or disagree. She was not going to take Jal anywhere, because as soon as his safety was assured he would kill her. She knew it. He knew it. There was nothing left to say. She stared past him.

A small movement caught her attention. Fssa was sliding from shadow into the firelight reflected by a shallow puddle at Jal's feet. Water divided cleanly about the snake. He vanished beneath the hem of the Loo's sheer robe.

She looked away, not understanding, but not wanting to call attention to Fssa. Her glance caught Kirtn's. He, too, had seen Fssa vanish.

Jal shivered, drawing his wet robe more closely around him. "Up the ramp, bitch. It's cold out here." With both hands he steadied the crossbow. He was shivering violently, as Rheba had shivered in the dungeon. "C-cold . . . !" His body convulsed, jerking aside the crossbow.

Rheba threw herself off the ramp the instant Jal's crossbow veered from her body. Before she hit the ground, six guards died in a J/taal onslaught. Dapsl disappeared into a melee of former slaves. When they parted moments later, he lay dead, his whip tight around his broken neck.

Kirtn and Rheba rached Jal in the same instant. The trader was dead, already cold to the touch. No, not cold, *freezing*. As they watched, raindrops congealed on his flesh, encasing him in a shroud of ice.

Fssa slid out from a fold of clinging robe. Rheba expected

him to be cold, black, but he was not. He glowed metallically with the heat he had stolen from Jal, not only the heat of life but some of the very energy that had kept his atoms alive. As cold as a stone orbiting a dead star, Lord Jal lay on the spaceport pavement, staring up at the sky with eyes blinded by ice.

"I told you," whispered Fssa, all sadness and shame. "I'm a parasite. That's how Fssireeme live during the long Night."

His whistle was bleak and terribly lonely as he moved sinuously toward the darkness, away from his friends. Rheba realized then why he had said goodbye; he thought that they would not accept him once the proof of his true nature lay dead before their eyes.

"You're not a parasite," said Kirtn quickly. "You're a predator. Like us." He bent down and scooped up the retreating Fssireeme. He held the snake at eye level. Fssa glittered like a necklace spun from every precious metal in the universe. "You're very beautiful, snake. And if you try to run away from us again, I'll tie you in knots."

"I'll help," Rheba said quickly. "My knots are tighter."

Fssa's sensors scanned from Bre'n to fire dancer. Then there was a shimmer of incandescence as he dove from Kirtn's hands into Rheba's hair. He vanished but for the sound of soft laughter just behind her ear.

M/dere and the other J/taals approached, hands full of the weapons and transparent pouches they had stripped from the Loo. Silently she offered the spoils of battle to her J/taaleri. Rheba was on the point of refusing when she saw a bone-white gleam from one transparent purse. With a cry, she snatched the pouch and spilled its contents into her hand.

Two Bre'n carvings stared back up at her, lying on a pool of loose gemstones that quivered and winked. Ignoring all but her own earring, she stared, transfixed by its infinite mystery. The Face turned slowly between her fingers, revealing tantalizing curves, profiles endlessly changing, a murmur rising in her mind as of voices singing sunset songs, whispered harmonies hinting at the central enigma of Bre'n and Senyas, man and woman, hushed voices telling her . . .

"Rheba." Kirtn shook her gently. "We've got to get off planet before any other Loo finds us."

She blinked, not knowing where she was for a moment, held in thrall by the Face that was like her Bre'n, always familiar yet never fully known. Colors flashed at the corner of her sight as M/dere gathered gems and put them back into

201

the pouch. The other earring was gone, fastened to Lheket's ear by the gentle fingers of his own Bre'n.

"Yes, of course," said Rheba, putting on her own earring. "Fssa. Translate." She turned toward the waiting people who had once been slaves. "We'll take anyone who wants to go. If you know the way to your planet, we'll take you home. If you don't, we'll do what we can to find your planet. Or . . ." She hesitated. "You can stay here. The slave masters are dead."

No one moved to leave.

"All right." She stepped aside, giving free access to the *Devalon*'s ramp. "Get aboard."

The J/taals and clepts spread out, distributing themselves among the people who mounted the ramp. Until M/dere had taken the measure of her J/taaleri's new shipmates, they would be kept under the mercenaries' unblinking eyes. Rheba saw, and started to object. After a glance at the people climbing up the ramp, she changed her mind—it was as bizarre a collection of beings as she had ever encountered.

The first person up the ramp wore a robe that was more blood than cloth. On her shoulder rode a sleek animal as black as a hole in space. They were talking to each other in a rapid series of clicks. Rheba watched, but could not be certain whether the animal was pet, symbiont, partner or superior.

The next two were men. At least, they looked rather like men. Their eyes, however, shone like Fssa's sensors, and their nails dripped opalescent poisons. Their bodies were covered by a tawny fur that was matted with blood. She doubted that it was their own blood. She looked up at Kirtn. He was watching the same two people with an intensity that equaled M/dere's.

The illusionists boarded, too exhausted to do more than wear their own colorless exteriors.

A trio of men and women came next. They were obviously of different races, and just as obviously a team. They looked absolutely harmless. Rheba and Kirtn knew that Jal's assessment of the slaves was probably much closer to the truth. Very dangerous. Nothing harmless could have survived Adjustment and the Hour Between Years.

Standing close together, Rheba and Kirtn watched former slaves board the *Devalon*. Each person seemed more striking than the last. The Bre'n sighed as a quartet went up the ramp, their bodies black and silver and hard, their eyes quite white, laughing and talking among themselves as though at a festival; and in their hands black daggers, shards of glass, and two babies teething on pieces of a dead Loo's bloody power belt.

Wordlessly, Rheba and Kirtn looked at one another.

"I wonder," fluted Kirtn, tones of rue and amusement resonating in each note, "what the trip will be like."

Rheba's hand traced the outlines of her Bre'n earring. Faces murmured to her, telling her about Bre'n and Senyas and another kind of fire. Her akhenet lines smoldered. From them flared a glowing net that surrounded Kirtn with hot possibilities.

She smiled, touching him with hands that burned. "I guarantee, my Bre'n, that it won't be boring."

ANN MAXWELL lives in Laguna Niguel, California, with her husband, Evan, and their two children. She is the author of a number of excellent science fiction novels and has co-authored many books with her husband on subjects ranging from historical fiction to thrillers to nonfiction. Some of her earlier works have been recommended for the Nebula Award and nominated for the TABA Award. Also available in Signet editions are Ann's fine science fiction novels, *The Jaws of Menx* and *Dancer's Luck*.